Three-Legged Horse

MODERN CHINESE LITERATURE FROM TAIWAN

Three-Legged Horse

CHENG CH'ING-WEN

Edited by Pang-yuan Chi

COLUMBIA UNIVERSITY PRESS

NEW YORK

*Columbia University Press wishes to express its appreciation
for assitance given by the Chiang Ching-kuo Foundation for
International Scholarly Exchange and the Council for Cultural Affairs
in the preparation of the
translation and in the publication of this series.*

▲

COLUMBIA UNIVERSITY PRESS
Publishers Since 1893
New York   Chichester, West Sussex

Library of Congress Cataloging-in-Publication Data
Cheng, Ch'ing-wen, 1932–
[Short stories. English. Selections]
Three-legged horse / Cheng, Ching-wen ; [translated by Carlos
G. Tee ... et al.].
p.   cm. — (Modern Chinese literature from Taiwan)
ISBN 0–231–11386–2
I. Cheng, Ch'ing-wen, 1932– —Translations into English.   I.
Tee, Carlos G.   II. Title.   III. Series.
PL2841.C53A27   1999
895.1'352—DC21   98–22603

∞

Casebound editions of Columbia University Press books
are printed on permanent and durable acid-free paper.
Printed in the United States of America
Designed by Linda Secondari

c 10 9 8 7 6 5 4 3 2 1

CONTENTS

CONTENTS

FOREWORD

PANG-YUAN CHI

Very few of Taiwan's writers have so quietly and steadily perse-
vered in their creative work for forty years the way Cheng
Ch'ing-wen has. He has never made big waves in Taiwan's literary circles, but his name is one that commands and receives respect. Cheng has succeeded in maintaining a high level of qual-
ity in all of his almost two hundred short stories. Each story has
a central character through whom Cheng, with his light-hand-
ed application of ink and occasional splashes of color, paints his
pictures of specific times, places, and circumstances. His collected stories cover in considerable detail numerous aspects of
Taiwan's past and present. Critics Peng Jui-chin and Hsu Su-lan
have both compared Cheng's approach to writing to a towering
royal palm that does not tempt passersby with showy flowers or
fruit or intentionally try to attract notice.[1] So many things in
contemporary society that use flashiness and glitz to compete

---

1. Peng Jui-chin, "A Royal Palm: Cheng Ch'ing-wen as a Writer for Twenty Years," *Taiwan Literature* (Oct. 1977): 176–90.

for the public's attention end up leading to emptiness and loneliness. Yet Cheng describes his own stories very positively: "I
look at their stick-straight backbones; they are never cringing,
nor arrogant. They quietly, stubbornly point in a direction, little bit by little bit, and slowly grow and develop."[2] "Everyone
has to find his own path in this life. As a writer, I wanted to find
something of a resting place for the soul in a country without a
set orthodox religion; in the process I unexpectedly discovered
some truths that look rather simplistic on the outside, but that
have far-reaching significance."[3]

Cheng Ch'ing-wen, a native speaker of the Southern
Fukienese or "Taiwanese" dialect, had just graduated from elementary school when Japan surrendered to China in 1945 following the fifty-year Japanese occupation of the island. After
struggling with the Japanese language in school for six years,
Cheng began to learn how to write in Chinese. The abrupt
switchover to a new written medium brought him an even
greater feeling of alienation than had the major political and
social changes Taiwan was undergoing. But fortunately, Cheng
Ch'ing-wen was just at the age when he began to be able to
remember, observe, incorporate, and mentally file things away.
He turned his six years of Japanese schooling into an asset.
Cheng moved from his tiny riverside village to Taipei, where he
received a full Chinese-language high school and college education. He worked at the government-run Hua Nan Bank for
forty years, married and had children, prospered professionally
and received promotions, and eventually retired. Cheng was a
quiet and steady kind of person to begin with; and through his
relatively smooth and even routine life, he developed himself

---

2. Hsu Su-lan, "The Lonely Royal Palm—Discovering Cheng Ch'ing-
wen's Stories of Taiwan," *Taiwan Daily News* (Dec. 31, 1997–Jan. 1, 1998).
3. Cheng Ch'ing-wen, preface to *The Last of the Gentlemen*, Literary
Publishing Co., 1984.

into a detached observer. Cheng found inexhaustible sources of material in the delicate situation of his home country of Taiwan during an age of kaleidoscopic change, and in the many different kinds of people who found themselves helpless in the face of impossible situations.

Since Taiwan's earliest period of Han immigrations, this 3,600-square-kilometer island has never been noted for tropical scenery and delights of the kind depicted by Rudyard Kipling in his *Road to Mandalay*. Neither has it ever been a place of exile for criminals. The people of Fukien province who wended their way across the Taiwan Straits to this island were small-time merchants seeking opportunities for trade, and farmers who relied on the cooperation of the elements for their livelihood. They were frugal and conservative by upbringing; most were very ordinary, unassuming, solid types. Compared to some of the authors of Taiwan who are better known in the West, such as Huang Chun-ming, Chen Ying-chen, and Wang Chen-ho, Cheng Ch'ing-wen avoids highly dramatic portrayals of the intricate machinations of his characters' love lives, their aspirations, disappointments, regrets, and compromises. As authors go, Cheng Ch'ing-wen could be described as laid back, straightforward, with few expressions of wild ecstasy or violent fury. He seldom recites litanies of woes. While many of the characters in his stories lead lives filled with torment, seldom is this suffering detailed in more than a few summary lines. This kind of highly restrained and disciplined style is rare in contemporary Taiwan writing, and is for this reason to be prized. Through these variegated life stories, Cheng adopts his own unique angle in examining the changes the Taiwan countryside has seen over the past half century, especially the areas around Cheng's hometown and the river that passed through it; what he refers to as "The Great River" is in fact the Tamsui (Ta Sui) River, which stretches from the Taiwan Straits at the northern tip of Taiwan to embrace the Taipei basin. Cheng's works recall

Anton Chekov's and Ernest Hemingway's short stories, James Joyce's *The Dubliners*, and Sherwood Anderson's *Winesburg, Ohio*, all of which exercised a considerable influence on Cheng's writing.

Although the works chosen for this anthology cannot cover Cheng's full range of subjects and artistic styles, they do capture some of the highlights. *The Three-Legged Horse*, the story of a man who has spent half of his life carving lame horses, is set against the backdrop of Taiwan's period of Japanese colonial rule, which lasted from 1895 to 1945. In this unusually deep-digging vignette, a man is cursed by a double misfortune: an ugly birthmark, and a job with the colonial police force that forces him to betray his own people. There seems to be no redemption in sight for him, not even in art. The horses are all carved with broken legs and expressions of despair. This work echoes a painful period in which humble human lives are crushed by overwhelming political changes.

The old man in *The Last of the Gentlemen* is much more fortunate. Blessed with a peaceful conscience, he can watch with a bit of melancholia the rapid degeneration of his small hometown into a crowded suburb of Taipei. The author wrote *God of Thunder's Gonna Getcha* in the more tender yet bemused tone of an old woman who is obsessed with memories of the days of war and hunger, and who compulsively snatches leftovers from the plates at her son's restaurant.

Cheng Ch'ing-wen tells the story of social change in Taiwan through a whole spectrum of characters—a story of going from poor to rich, from a society bound by all sorts of political and moral taboos to a newly democratic and open society fraught with its own particular tragedies and comedies. His pursuit of a poignant simplicity comes through in his early *A Fisherman's Family*, as well as in *Betel Nut Town*, *The Mosquito*, and *Secrets*, which date from his middle period. In his *Autumn Night*, written in 1990, a self-denying mother-in-law and a daughter-in-law who challenges her authority might strike readers as rather incredible characters. But the ultraconservative Taiwan of just a few decades ago was characterized by numerous sexual taboos. The author convincingly builds up the frightening atmosphere of a lone walk on an autumn night, which sharply points up the courage of the young woman. The bit of rather dry, pithy dialogue when husband and wife are reunited is a vivid expression of carnal desire marked with typical Taiwanese subtlety.

Some Taiwan critics feel that Cheng Ch'ing-wen is a lonely voice in Taiwanese fiction writing, perhaps because his pieces lack the sensational appeal that liberal helpings of sex and violence might have endowed them with. Even in the tense atmosphere that Cheng creates in his story *Hair*, through the reactions of onlookers to the impending decapitation of a woman who has stolen a chicken, Cheng exercises considerable restraint in his treatment of the climax, in which the woman's braids are chopped off. The author succeeds in carrying through with compassion—while avoiding melodrama—the central theme he wishes to develop, namely, the love of a poor, miserable man for his troublesome, pitiable wife.

Yet Cheng Ch'ing-wen's language can be auspicious and buoyant when treating cherished subjects like the young ferryman in *The River Suite*, a lyrical short story he penned in 1964, when he was still writing poetry. The old town on the Great River, his childhood home, has in both its peaceful and violent modes consistently provided him with inspiration. Here the young ferryman, who staunchly guards the main entrance of an old house, fair weather or foul, stares obsessively at the lithe washer girl, basket in one hand and wooden clogs in the other, as she walks down to the riverbank. He watches her for five years without exchanging a single sentence with her, though longings well up inside him and his feelings of love and infatuation slowly grow, bit by bit, as in a four-part suite. The entire piece is a song without words. Through his description of the surging waves and raging current of the river during a typhoon, Cheng reveals the ferryman's inner struggle for self-realization. This is a subject close to the author's heart, because his old hometown with its clear-flowing river had by this time already disappeared.

As if dissatisfied with his sparse portrayal of the man married to the wife's family in his 1977 story, *Mosquito*, Cheng returns with an even more exuberant style to the subject of such humiliation in his 1990 *Spring Rain*, which chronicles one man's victory over a deprived beginning and loneliness. In this recent work, the main character, who grew up in an orphanage, comes to realize that the continuity of life should not be limited to one's own family—and he ends up himself adopting orphans. The theme and language of this piece transcend failure and pathos. As the main character of the story trudges on through torrential rains to his wife's grave to announce to her his adoption of a son, the trees and flowers that surround him bud and thrive in the life-giving downpour. The sky and earth symbolize the hope introduced by a newly born life.

This image calls to mind the Chinese tradition of humanism, which reaches back to the Confucian *Book of Odes* and earlier, and which is the source of the Chinese ideal of a tolerant and accommodating character. This lyrical yet realistic tradition contributed to the molding of Cheng Ch'ing-wen's literary style, distinguished for its simplicity of language and genuineness of emotion. The struggles of the "little people" featured in Cheng's works may not offer indulgent romantic excursions into a mystic world, but the realistic details of actual daily life he provides may well become treasured records for posterity. As the twentieth century draws to a close, we may find these stories the valuable witnesses of a writer who shares with us the laughter and tears of some people he personally met along the twists and turns of Taiwan's recent history.

ACKNOWLEDGMENTS

Thanks and recognition are due to the following translators of stories included in this volume as they originally appeared in various issues of the *Chinese PEN* (Taiwan) *Quarterly* from 1974 to 1996:

Lien-ren Hsiao (*The River Suite*)
Jane Parish Yang (*A Fisherman's Family*)
Karen Steffen Chung (*Hair and Spring Rain*)
Michelle Min-chia Wu (*Autumn Night*)
Chen I-djen (*The Last of the Gentlemen*)
Nicholas Koss (*God of Thunder's Gonna Getcha*)
Carlos G. Tee (*The Three-Legged Horse*)
Anne Behne (*The Mosquito*)
Jeffrey Toy Eng (*Secrets*)
James R. Landers (*Betel Nut Town*)
Fred Steiner (*The Coconut Palms on Campus*)

We also thank Jody Gladding for reading and editing the stories to unify their style for this collection.

Three-Legged Horse

The River Suite

I

He stood at the stern of his boat, punting hard with a bamboo pole. The boat skimmed over the glassy surface of the water. He was the best boatman in Old Town. Across the river was a beach where he had built a ferry slip of sorts with the beach sand. A man was now standing on that slip. He poled hard again, his shoulder muscles rippling. Of all the townsfolk of Old Town, only he could get his boat across this broad expanse of water with just ten strokes. Already, the boat was midstream.

Relying on his ability as coxswain, the dragonboat team of Old Town had won three championships in a row in the past few years and now permanently claimed the silver cup.

As he drew up the half-immersed pole, beads of water dripped down its length. Still coated with black sand, the end of the pole dragged along the water surface, leaving a black trail. All the muscles between his shoulder blades and along his arms moved in rhythm. He himself could feel them ripple.

The day was just dawning as the boat skimmed the still water. Opposite the boatman was the beach and to his back was a levee.

Old Town was an ancient city. Because it stretched out for some distance along the river, it had been compared to those strips of cloth formerly used by Chinese women to bind their feet: long and foul-smelling things. Nobody could deny that Old Town was long, but it was far from foul-smelling. It was simply old, like a huge moss-covered rock. Here, even two-story houses were rare; old temples could be found everywhere, however, and those old temples were the most imposing, the most stately structures in the whole town.

The river Old Town sprawled along was called the Ta Sui. Even in ancient times, people said, the town had had a street, but it had long ago collapsed during a flood. Floods were still eroding the streets of the town; you could almost feel them being eaten away bit by bit.

Many, many years before, the junks from Foochow, Swatow, and Amoy could dock easily right below Old Town's temple of Matsu, the goddess of the sailors. Full of odd cargo, those huge junks could come directly into Old Town to load and unload. Consequently, the town became a marketplace. It was also reputed to be one of Taiwan's few commercial ports at the time.

Most of the old main street had now been broken up by floods and had sunk into the river waters. What was left hardly mattered, a remnant so old and worn, no more change was possible.

The boatman stroked forcefully again. Shrouded by a thin, watery haze, the whole river surface shivered. The water was not deep, but the river bottom was uneven. Careening slightly, its bow a bit raised, the boat skimmed toward the sand slip and pulled up alongside it with a slight jolt. The man came aboard. The boatman poled, backing the boat away, and then turning it around.

From habit he looked toward the flight of stone steps leading from the water's edge to the top of the levee. Half an hour earlier, smoke had risen from that chimney, that old and slightly crooked chimney. He did not wear a wristwatch, yet he knew smoke had risen from that chimney half an hour ago. For more than five years now, it had been his habit to watch that chimney from the river. Half an hour before; he couldn't be wrong about the time.

He gazed at those stone steps, those old, cut-granite steps, several of which had been replaced with cement ones after floods. Rank weeds lined them all.

What would she wear today? The same dress as yesterday? Or the same as the day before yesterday? He still remembered very clearly that she was dressed in white two days ago and yesterday wore pale blue. Perhaps she would still be wearing the same clothes.

He guessed right; she had on that pale blue cotton shirt and white skirt. It was she, he was certain. By just glancing at her out of the corner of his eye he could tell. He liked to glance at her out of the corner of his eye.

He stroked hard, and the boat shot toward the river bank, the momentum almost throwing the passenger off balance as he rose to go ashore. Had the distance been greater, he could have really exerted himself. He felt a little dissatisfied. He was the best boatman in Old Town.

As he stooped to pick up the money, he became aware of her walking down the stone steps, a basket in one hand and a pair of wooden sandals in the other. Yes, she always took off her wooden sandals and held them in her hand when she came down those stone steps. He imagined her skirt was gently swaying now. He wouldn't be wrong. He knew, as he always knew, that she would not look up when he stole a glance at her. Yet when his back was turned, he always felt her looking his way.

Now she was at the water's edge. Carefully gathering up her

skirt, she settled into a squat. The water rippled and lapped, making suds. Then she raised the wooden bat she used for washing and started to beat the clothes she'd brought with her. The beating sound echoed and reechoed across the water. Then there was only the gentle lapping of the water again.

He still remembered the time an article of clothing she was washing had got caught up by the current. With a startled cry, she had risen to her feet. She'd been standing at the same place she was standing now, and he had been where his boat now rested. He still remembered how he'd used his bamboo pole to recover the article and give it back to her. Blushing, her head lowered, she'd smiled, but only faintly, and, without a word of thanks, had held out her hand to take it. This he also remembered.

Another time, she herself waded into the water to catch a garment that was washing away. He was also on hand at the same place; she did not cry out, but she blushed all the same. When she got ashore, her skirt was half soaked. Ever since then, she had been very careful.

Did she dislike his bringing his boat to rest precisely at this spot along the river?

"Ferryboat!"

Someone on the opposite bank was calling him again. He pressed his toes hard against the floor of the boat and poled briskly with a backward thrust; then he stepped backward and half squatted. The boat shot like an arrow toward the middle of the river. His muscles rippled, the muscles of his broad shoulders and sturdy legs.

The watery haze was thinning out, the east tinged a faint yellow-orange. She would be leaving soon, he thought. Already she would be almost finished with her laundry! How many times had she quietly slipped away in the space of time his back was turned to her?

But as he brought the boat around, her small figure came into view. She was squatting at the edge of the water, her hands moving quickly up and down. The water, with her as the center, made concentric circles that kept opening toward him. The boat gently slid into place. He stole a glance at her, poling hard as he half squatted and stood, squatted and stood. He shifted his gaze over her head and up along the flight of stone steps to the old house. One day he'd seen a streamer of red cloth draping the doorframe of that house; the next day, she had again appeared on the stone steps. He still remembered this, remembered it always, as if it had happened only yesterday.

II

The auditorium of Old Town's government-financed elementary school was jammed with students, teachers, and parents. On the stage, seated in order of importance, were the town dignitaries: provincial councilmen, the police chief, the mayor, and several prominent, wealthy citizens. They were always present at any of the town's public gatherings.

The boatman was given a seat of honor among these officials. He wore what he considered his Sunday best and had, for this particular occasion, bought himself a pair of white rubber boots. Nevertheless, when he compared himself with the others, he cringed a bit at how shabbily dressed he was.

Ever since he'd become a boatman, he was rarely seen in town. Once in a while he attended a play, but on such occasions he always sat in the rear. Yet today he was the focus of attention, wearing a round, red name tag with a ribbon that someone had pinned on his shirt.

The pupils sat below the stage, craning their necks to get a better view of him. Teachers stood close by, gesturing, ready to intervene at any moment if a pupil blocked someone else's view.

He thought back to that torrid afternoon he'd sat at the stern of his boat dozing. Several elementary-school children were wading in the shallow water.

"Don't go into the water!" he had warned them.

The river had recently been dredged for sand, making the river bed uneven and treacherous.

"Don't go any deeper!"

But the children had simply ignored him. He had shaken the bamboo pole to disperse them, and they'd fled. It was a hot day. His broad, tan shoulders gleamed in the scorching sun. The river flowed lazily. He pulled his bamboo rainhat over his eyes and, hands behind his head, began to doze.

How much time passed he didn't know, but he woke to someone crying from somewhere, "Help! Ferryman!"

He strained his eyes to look across the river. Heat waves rose from the dry beach. There was no one on that beach or by the river either. Were his ears playing tricks on him? No. His occupation had taught him how to get forty winks and how to wake up at any time he liked. His ears would not deceive him, he was sure.

"Help, hurry!" Only then did he realize the voice was coming from his side of the river. He looked upstream and saw someone on the levee waving at him.

"Quick, someone's drowning. Quick!"

Jumping from his boat, he ran upstream. The water was not deep, and he could see two children struggling not far from the shore. He waded over and dragged them in, one after the other.

"There's one more!"

A child standing beside a tree was yelling to him; the others had run away, it seemed, and only this child was left.

"Where?"

"Over there, right over there."

He plunged into the river again and swam in the direction the child pointed.

"Here?"

"No. You're out too far."

He stopped and was just about to turn around, when

suddenly something grabbed him and wound its arms tightly around his legs. He tried to move his legs, but they were held fast, and he could not get them free. A sudden panic seized him as whatever it was pulled him under.

"What is this?" he asked himself, regaining his composure. He held his breath; the thing was still dragging him down. The water was not deep, and his feet struck the loose, sandy river bed. He made a few strokes with his hands and tried to kick his legs, but the moment he started working them free, the thing's hold on him grew even tighter. He drew in a breath of air, as well as a mouthful of water, which he spat out. Still the thing clung to him, dragging him downward, and again he felt his feet strike the riverbed. He slowly opened his arms, making one more attempt to propel himself forward. This time, he succeeded. He surfaced, tilted back his head, and breathed in. Something was still pulling at him, drawing him back into the water with all its strength. The blood in his legs was hardly moving now, as that something seemed to go into convulsions. Then the hold weakened a bit, only a bit. He lost no time in kicking his legs free of the child.

He looked at the three schoolchildren seated opposite him. He could no longer tell which of them had grabbed hold of his legs. No matter how he tried, he could never believe that any of these three skinny, sickly-looking kids could have been strong enough to grip his legs like that, almost defeating his effort to free himself.

Now, as he looked back, it scared him a bit. If the water had been deeper, if the grip had not been on his legs but on his neck, if . . . Well, there wasn't any point in thinking about it.

The mayor rose and assumed his position as master of ceremonies. The presentation began.

The mayor handed him a written commendation and shook his hand to the loud applause of the students seated below them.

The police chief and provincial councilmen all shook hands

7

with him. The principal thanked him on behalf of his students and said he was the bravest man in Old Town. The chairman of the PTA presented him with gifts and also shook his hand.

This was a new experience for him, all this hand shaking. He did not know these men, even when they were shaking hands with him. Nor did he know the three students. All these people seemed like strangers.

Everyone came over to shake his hand; the long series of hand-shakes made him uncomfortable. Below the stage, the students kept on applauding. Never before in his life had he been on a stage. He looked over the crowd below and saw thousands of small eyes focused on him. He was a bit scared, yet his eyes kept scanning the crowd below, seeking something he could hardly define. Then a human figure came to mind.

Glory, bravery . . . these were the words they kept repeating, words that, they said, described him alone. Yet they meant nothing to him. He could not imagine how these words applied to him.

III

The wind was blowing hard, carrying with it a fine, slanting drizzle.

He sat in the stern of his boat, rocking as it swayed. It was already dark, and a typhoon was approaching; the boat was swaying, and the trees on the opposite bank were swaying, too. He lit his kerosene lamp and hung it on a dead tree branch stuck in the sand of the beach. The lamp was swinging and bumping against the branch; he had wrapped rags around the branch for fear that the lamp might break.

On the opposite bank was a back street of the town and halfway down this street was a small public park. Streetlights set at equal distances lined this street. Also on the opposite bank was the road leading to the temple of Matsu, and he could even see how the eaves of the temple turned up at the corners.

To the left of the road, on this back street, was that old house. And that door, that old door! Once, over the doorframe, he saw a streamer of red cloth hanging; yet the very next day she appeared again at the riverside. Seeing her, he felt relieved. But what could he have said to her?

He looked toward that weathered door; the trees on the opposite bank were swaying, sometimes blotting out that door and sometimes revealing it, like a game of peekaboo.

Evenings—and he could not say how many evenings—he would look toward that door, the door that remained tightly shut day and night. Then he recalled the day he went to the school to accept that award, and those words of praise—glory, bravery, paragon—that did not seem to apply to him at all.

He also remembered those huge, sweaty palms and that strange feeling he had had when those palms made contact with his own. He'd hoped then to see a face that was, comparatively speaking, familiar to him; yet, as his eyes swept the crowd, he saw only a myriad of faces, and they were all a blur to him.

In his thoughts, he could not connect this occasion with any other in his life. Only on this side of the river, only when his eyes were directed toward that door, or only when he knew his back was to that door—that mythic door—did he feel the warmth of a friendly world and peace in his heart.

The wind was still blowing, gradually rising to a furious level. The rain fell in big strips, like coarse shreds of tobacco. Most likely no passengers would take his ferryboat today, yet he would wait a little longer. If, after braving the storm, someone should come, only to discover the ferryman gone, would he have the courage to turn back?

Once, many, many years ago, on a stormy night, when the war was dragging to its end, a Japanese soldier carrying a secret order arrived at Old Town. The river had risen, and the ferryboat had stopped carrying passengers. The orderly tied his clothes to his head so that he could swim across the river.

9

Eventually he lost his clothes and bayonet and had to turn back, for which he was severely punished, and a group of thirty or forty Japanese soldiers were sent to drag the river for that lost bayonet.

At the time, the boatman was still small, and his grandfather was still alive. "How could a Japanese soldier manage to swim the Tan Sui Ho during a storm?" his grandfather would often ask him. Of all the townsfolk of Old Town, only he had once swum halfway across the river during a flood to drag back a live pig being carried away by the current. But that had happened a long, long time ago. Grandfather had had that adventure when he was still young, before his son—the boatman's father—was even born. As far as Grandfather could remember, as far as he had ever heard, no one had ever dared to go into the water during a raging storm. That Japanese soldier could have been called brave, although he was not brave enough, because he was forced to turn back and lost everything in the bargain.

Once again, he looked at the door. The streetlights glowed in the distance, but half of the door stood in total darkness, because of the shadow cast by the doorframe. In spite of this, he could still make it out. Even with his eyes closed, he could discern its lines and shape. It seemed that for the past five years he had existed only for the purpose of recognizing it.

Again he thought of his grandfather who had been a boatman and, in his day, also the best boatman in Old Town. But that was not why he was now a boatman and the best in Old Town. His parents had died long ago. Though he often told stories about boatmen, his grandfather did not necessarily intend to make him into a boatman.

The kerosene lamp was still swaying against the branch. Now it was clear no passenger would come, so he kept his eyes fixed on the door that was partly obscured by the swaying trees. Why not wait a little longer? he thought to himself.

The sky was pitch-black, but the streetlights on the opposite bank let him watch the moving fog, patchy and dark yellow. Grandfather was a good man. He jumped into the river to rescue a pig from drowning. All his neighbors got a share of the butchered pig, but he was not given a commendation. If Grandfather had been alive, he would have said, "You saved three boys. Well, so what? The water was so shallow." It was hardly worth mentioning, really. He'd just been lucky. He was seized by that child, right at the moment he stopped swimming to turn around, and it nearly did him in. He had saved some grown-ups, but those experiences were nothing like this one.

The door, the door behind the trees, still held his attention. He longed for the day when he could go behind that door and take a look. He had wished for this for so long, but the opportunity had never presented itself. Was there an old well inside that house, too? There was an old well inside his own house, though he had never used it.

Then, suddenly, all the lights went out. The typhoon had not arrived yet; why were all the lights out? Instantly, darkness enveloped him, yet his eyes were still directed toward that point. Now everything was wrapped in darkness; nevertheless, he could still feel the swaying of the trees and the lurching of the boat. He never shifted his eyes from that point in empty space.

IV

For a long time now he had not been able to sleep in his own house. Once he returned home at night, he just couldn't sleep. The night before, the winds had steadily increased, and a driving rain had begun. He had asked someone to help him pull his boat up on the shore.

The whole town was engulfed in darkness, lying still as the storm raged. Grandfather had once told him that he'd seen half a street wash away in a flood.

He'd boiled some water and bathed in it; it had been quite a long time since he had had the luxury of a hot bath. He lay in bed wanting only a good sleep, yet sleep would not come. First that chaotic school gathering and then that old door lost in murky darkness would appear over and over in his mind. And that red streamer hanging over the doorframe. What did it mean? A birthday? No, not likely. A wedding? No, not likely, either. An engagement? That was possible, though so far he'd seen no more evidence of it. If someone was engaged behind that door, could she be the one?

He tossed about in bed thinking but could find no satisfactory solution to any of the questions in his mind. Why not let the matter rest? But how could he? Each day he either faced that door or turned his back to it. Was there any difference between the two? Always he was seized by the desire to look her full in the face, yet he could not. Only one time had he seen her face-to-face, and she had blushed. Whether his own face flushed he could no longer remember.

No sooner had he opened his eyes in the morning than he saw it was already dawn. Electric wires whistled in the wind, and a driving rain beat with increasing intensity on the roof. The sky wore such a lusterless, yellow face that you couldn't tell what time it was. He did not feel hungry, so why not stay in bed a little longer?

"Come on, let's go see the flood!" People were scurrying through the lane outside his window.

"Let's go see the flood! What a sight!"

The night before he'd had help pushing his boat ashore and tying it to a big banyan tree beside the river. Was it still secure? Had the floodwater risen under it? That boat was his life, so he had better go out and take a look.

He put on his bamboo hat and thatched raincoat, kicked aside his wooden sandals, pulled open the door, and went out. The rain lashed at his body; he tied his bamboo rainhat tight and trotted along the lane.

The place his boat was tied has already flooded, and the boat was swaying in the water. He examined the rope and saw that it was still holding strong and probably would for some time.

He walked upstream along the river. Gray clouds hung low over the grayish yellow water. The wind was high, the rain driving, now in a slanting sweep, now hammering straight down, now, as if through a big sieve, falling in graceful lines all the way down to the river. The river surface was blanketed in thick fog; when a gust of wind blew, you could see the indistinct outline of a half-immersed bamboo grove in the hollow of the opposite beach.

The wind was howling, roaring like a huge wild beast let free. It twisted and turned like an angry dragon.

He stopped at the small park. The red brick levee intended as flood control was all but submerged. Never in the past ten years had he seen such a flood.

The river water kept pounding the levee, giving those red bricks a meticulously washed look. As one muddy wave rushed over them and receded, another and another crested behind it.

The water, the muddy water, tumbled and swirled, dissolving clods of earth into one gushing stream. The flood had crumbled a whole earthen hill, churned with all its strength, and then rushed back down from high ground, taking everything that lay even close to its path with it. Its force was so terribly strong, so irresistible.

Plants were uprooted. Flowers, twigs, and bamboo stems floated in a tangled mass. Stalks stripped clean rode the waves, rolling like torpedoes in a charging navy fleet.

Was this how it was when his grandfather had gone into the water and brought back a squealing pig? If Grandfather had been alive, he would have asked him.

He walked on and stopped again at the wall encircling the small park; beyond the wall was the road running past the entrance of the temple of Matsu. Many people gathered below the wall, and he noticed the mayor, wearing a raincoat, was among them. He nodded slightly to the mayor but got no response. Perhaps the mayor did not see him standing there or did not recognize him in his broad-brimmed bamboo rainhat.

The water level was still rising slowly and was now almost as high as the top of the levee. Undaunted, Old Town still stood secure, while rushing waters licked the levee.

"What a flood! It's the biggest I have ever seen, bigger than the one ten years ago," said a thirtyish-looking man, full of excitement.

"No," an older man in his fifties or sixties put in a word of his own. "The biggest? Pshaw! About fifty years ago, probably before you were born, there was a much bigger flood, and the water rose this high." Talking, he walked over to a big, gnarled banyan tree and drew a line across the trunk. "At that time this tree was only half as tall as it is now. Forty years ago! That's a long time." Rain kept dripping from the tree and hitting his bald head.

Grandfather had mentioned that big flood, too, and there might have been a still bigger one before that, only Grandfather was no longer alive to confirm it. The story Grandfather liked to tell was how he had once rowed a boat on a submerged street.

He walked on, following the park wall until he came to a point where he had to leave it. There, a crowd had gathered. The stone steps down to the road were underwater. His impulse was to keep walking along the river, but suddenly he hesitated.

The river was still blanketed in fog; the wind blew against the current, whipping up giant billows of foam that kept rising almost to the crest of the waves and falling back again.

Ignoring his misgivings, he walked on.

Once again he gazed at that old door. The strips of red paper bearing the inscriptions of spring greetings, which someone had pasted around the door at New Year, were all faded and falling apart.

He walked farther on along the river and came to the section of the bank called "The Big Turn." There he looked out and caught a glimpse of that wide expanse of whiteness; choppy, muddy water rushed in his direction, rounded the bend in a powerful curve, and then rushed again toward the middle of the river with so much force that the entire surface of the river seemed to careen in torrents.

He rounded the turn and stopped before a stretch of vegetable garden plots, most of which had been flooded. He stood there for a while and then turned back. The wind was now blowing in the opposite direction, bringing with it rain that kept lashing him. Rain dripped from his raincoat; holding his bamboo rainhat on with one hand, he bent defiantly into the head wind.

When he passed that familiar door again, he saw it was open. He looked in, just a quick glance, to see a woman, stooped under the eaves, scrubbing the ground. She was barefoot, her sleeves tucked back, and a tin pail beside her. He could not see her face, but he was somewhat surprised at how fair her skin was, especially where it hadn't been exposed to the sun. He had not seen her this close up since the day he had rescued her laundry for her.

Suddenly she picked up the pail and splashed water over the ground. She saw him, too. The corners of her mouth twitched slightly, an expression as much a smile as not, but then she turned her face away. Only then did he become conscious of his own behavior: standing transfixed at her door, after five years. He saw nothing inside that house except for her.

As he stepped onto the road again, a boy suddenly cried. "A water buffalo! A water buffalo!"

He looked over his shoulder to where the boy pointed and saw a water buffalo—or rather, a pair of horns—surfacing between swells and being carried by the rushing current toward the levee. Was that a water buffalo? Or only a pair of horns? The pair of horns emerged sporadically in the rushing waters and looked so small.

The water buffalo floated past the Big Turn, carried by the current toward midstream. The animal, it seemed, was still struggling for life, yet, after spinning it around like a top, the water carried it out into the fog where it was soon lost to view.

Then he saw her again. She was out on the levee drawing water, the tin pail in her hand. He saw her dip one foot gingerly into the water to gauge its depth and then immerse the other foot when she believed that she was on firm ground. Just as she was bending to fill the pail, the thought occurred to him: What if she slipped? He could not say whether or not he really wanted to see her fall into the water. Yet after those three students had fallen into the river, he did have a dream in which she fell into the river, too.

An uprooted bamboo floated past her, spinning in the water like a waterwheel.

"Help! Help!"

Two faint cries came from somewhere beyond the Big Turn.

He looked up and saw a man half squatting in the river, waving desperately. The river waters were moving him swiftly along and would soon be passing the Big Turn.

"Help!" His voice was already hoarse. The current was so swift that it rounded the Big Turn in a flash. Now he could see the man was squatting on a bamboo raft, holding on with one hand, waving with the other.

"Help!" The man seemed to be shouting to him. Suddenly he was aware of someone patting him on the shoulder. He turned around to see the mayor standing right behind him, smiling. This was the same expression he'd worn when he was presenting that award to him at the elementary school. The mayor's eyes bore into him, and he smiled and smiled. Then he became aware of the girl standing on the levee, also looking at him, the tin pail still in her hand. That first time, when her laundry had washed away, he remembered, she had also stood looking at him in this way.

Any moment now, the man would be carried past him by the swiftly flowing current. Allowing himself no time for second thoughts, he took off his bamboo rainhat and raincoat. The water was so cold, yet in he went. The man and his raft had now rounded the Big Turn and were pitching about some ten yards away from him, as the current pulled them out toward midstream. The water was so cold. He had gone into the river in winter, yet even in winter the river water was not as cold as this. He swam with all his strength; towering waves kept crashing overhead. You have to grab hold of that raft, he thought. Suddenly a torrent of water rushed toward him and into his nostrils; he shook his head to clear his nose, for what irritated his nostrils was not water but sand or earth. His nose seemed to be stuffed with something, and he felt like he was suffocating. He must swim and reach that raft, which was now heaving and rolling in front of him. He was being pulled back and forth, up and down, by a power unlike anything he'd ever experienced before. A ruthless power that, though neither definite nor sharp, was nevertheless engulfing him. With a number of strokes, he moved forward once again, as waves kept crashing down on him and lifting him up. The raft was only about ten yards away, yet the distance seemed infinite. As he crested a wave, he caught sight of the man on the raft and saw that he had one arm outstretched toward him, the swimmer, as if he were the one who needed to be saved. A giant wave crashed over his head, pulling him down and filling his nostrils again with spray. He felt himself being dragged all the way down. No, I will not let myself sink like this, he thought, well aware that beyond a certain depth, he would never be able to surface again. He propelled himself as best he could, trying only to keep himself afloat.

The bamboo raft was made up of three sections connected

like three railroad cars; it must have been lying somewhere waiting for high water to wash it into the river, which now waved it
about like something for sale. The wind kept tossing it, and so
did the swells. A bamboo raft is expected to drift lengthwise;
turned crosswise, it can easily be capsized by a windstorm. His
throat still burned. The man sat on his haunches at the other
end of the raft; they looked at each other in silence. The wind
roared and the river water raced. When a gust of wind dispelled
the thick haze for a moment, he could see the banks receding
rapidly. The levee had been left behind, and with more gently
sloping terrain, the river gradually became broader. The current
slackened somewhat and tended to rise toward the riverside.
This he had not foreseen.

He gestured to the man, hoping that he would move over, but
the man just stared at him without stirring. Half crouching and
half creeping, the boatman boarded and shifted himself to the
front section of the raft. The wind was still blowing violently. He
loosened a piece of bamboo and used it to probe the water's
depth. The raft kept tossing. The bamboo sank as far down as it
could, without touching river bottom. He had to separate the
other two sections of the raft, so he jerked loose their wires.
Waves whipped up by the wind kept lashing at him. They looked
as high as a house, though from the levee they might not look
high at all. He used a long piece of bamboo to work the two
other sections free from the one he stood on. He worked hard at
this; he must find a way to get the raft closer—even a bit
closer—to shore. The two sections finally broke loose and swung
into the current, gradually drifting downstream. He propelled
the remaining section with several strokes of the bamboo; the
raft seemed to be moving, though he couldn't be sure. The flow
was still swift, but apparently not as swift as before.

I can't let us drift all the way down the river, he thought.
With great effort, he guided the raft with the stick. One piece
of bamboo was not strong enough to move the raft, so he pulled

off another one and used them both as oars. Waves kept tossing the raft, making it impossible for him to get to his feet. He rowed hard, trying to keep the bowlike part of the raft parallel with the current to minimize the risk of being overturned.

He rowed and rowed, yet the raft still moved too slowly. Setting down one piece of bamboo, he used the other to probe the depth. This time it struck bottom, yet just as it did the raft jerked violently and all but hurled him into the water. He lost hold of the bamboo, which was washed under the raft, scraped against it, and then bobbed up to the surface before a wave carried it out of sight.

He took up the other stick and shoved it into the water again. This time it didn't touch the bottom. The riverbed was as uneven as its surface. He tried to row and then tried again to touch bottom. The stick jerked, and he poled hard. His palm felt numb, so he loosened his grip and studied the stick for a while with his eyes. The raft had moved a bit closer to shore.

He loosened a third bamboo stick. The current was still swift. Each time he poled, the raft turned crosswise. Waves kept crashing down, making the raft swing violently. He punted with his body leaning backward, trying to make the raft move lengthwise. Now his arms felt numb, too, but he had to keep trying to get the raft out of midstream.

He poled and poled, using not only his hands but also his feet. He had to pole with whatever strength he had left.

"Give me a hand, will you!" he shouted at the top of his voice because the wind was howling. But the other man just looked at him, as if he heard nothing at all.

"Give me a hand!" he yelled again, pointing to the bamboo stick. The man moved, trying to get to his feet, but after staggering a moment as the raft lurched suddenly, he sank to a squat again, clinging to the rope that was wound around another part of the raft.

The boatman began poling once more, alone. Now he had

only one thought: he must propel the raft as best he could. His arms ached dully and seemed to be convulsing, yet he was not a bit afraid, did not even seem to know what fear was. He knew he must continue poling and must do it as best he could. The river waters kept rising. Now he could see things on the bank clearly, could see the eucalyptus along the road. All the trees were bent to one side by the force of the wind; leaves were flying everywhere, along with broken twigs.

Now the raft was in shallow water, and the current had slackened. On the bank was the vegetable garden where the sweet-potato vines had been all but submerged, leaving only some clusters of leaves above water. He was still on his feet, stroking hard, and the raft glided forward with a gentle swing and finally skimmed toward the bank. The man still squatted on the raft, tightly clutching it with his hands. They had meant to grab hold of the land, yet when the raft finally came to rest beside the bank, neither of them moved. They just stayed where they were, one crouching and one standing, looking at the land in silence, not wanting to speak or to go ashore.

Then they both got into a boat. The strong wind had not yet died, and the boat inched along the edge of the water. Under the boat lay the submerged vegetable garden. He wiped his face with the back of his hand, rubbing off a layer of dirty mud. The rain fell on his head, washing dirty water down his face and coating it again. As he looked back, the whole thing seemed to have taken about five minutes, maybe a little longer; yet the return trip took them more than an hour, and still the levee protecting the town was not in sight.

Cold: that was how he felt. Now two more men, both friends, joined him and were poling the boat, standing at the bow and stern. The boat slowly moved on against the current. He was the best boatman in town, yet now he was seated in the boat while other men did the rowing for him. His fingers and feet were red and cold from the water, and he was shaking all over. Filthy water dripped down his face, down his body, and down to the bottom of the boat, which was already covered with water that sloshed rhythmically as the boat swayed. The opposite bank was still a vast whiteness.

The four were silent, reluctant to exchange words. Suddenly he saw, in the opposite direction, a boat edging its way toward them along the bank. When the boat drew near he saw a man in a raincoat standing between the two paddlers. It was the mayor. All smiles, he stretched out a hand to the boatman, who merely looked at him, as if in a trance.

Many people had gathered on the bank, but it was only when the boat neared the shore that the size of the crowd impressed him. Some were in new-style raincoats and some in old, but all were looking at him. From the time he'd noticed them gathering, they had been looking at him. Suddenly he saw a woman standing in front. It was she, with no bamboo rainhat or raincoat, soaked to the skin. Her hand still clutched that water pail as if it were part of her. Up to her knees in the muddy water, she, too, was looking at him with an unwavering gaze.

Grandfather had told him that, of all the townsfolk of Old Town, only he had ever plunged into the Ta Sui Ho in defiance of a raging storm. Now his grandson had had that experience, too. If Grandfather had been alive, he would surely have said that of all the townsfolk of Old Town, only he and his grandson had had the experience of plunging into the Ta Sui Ho in defiance of a raging storm, one dragging back a pig and the other saving a man. The pity was that, despite his great experience with the river in tempestuous weather, some years later Grandfather was caught in a light rain, fell ill, and died shortly after. People later attributed his abrupt death to his senility. If he had not died, he would surely have said that, of all the townsfolk of Old Town, only he and his grandson had gone into the Ta Sui Ho in defiance of a storm.

V

He sat at the stern of his boat, his bamboo rainhat pulled down over his face. He wanted to snatch some sleep, yet sleep would not come. The river ran clear again and could provide water for doing laundry. Actually one could have washed clothes in it three days earlier. He again waited for her to come out.

Early in the morning when he saw the thick white smoke rising out of the chimney he started to count time. Little by little, the white smoke yellowed and finally blackened. The river flowed and kept flowing. He kept his eyes on that tightly closed door, that old door; his heart pounded and pounded, and he himself could hear the pounding. They were going to give him another award, and it was said that the mayor would send some of his assistants to be present at the ceremony, too. He wanted to break the news to her. He had not yet decided whether he should go, but if it pleased her, he thought he would. He did not know whether or not she was pleased, but he must see her and talk with her. In five years they had never exchanged a word. The water was flowing. Thirty minutes had passed, thirty minutes: his instinct told him he could not be mistaken about this. Yet that door was still tightly closed. The water was clear again, yet she still did not appear. This was the first time in five years she had not come out, at the hour when she should have come out.

What's the matter with her? he thought. He kept his eyes on that door, on that old door where once a streamer of red cloth had hung. For three days he had watched that door. He could picture her standing before him. The rain was falling at a slant— hard and fast—on her body, on her face. Her hair clung to her cheeks, the ends curling up slightly. The wind was howling. Her rain-soaked clothes stuck to her body, and still she held in her hand the water pail, as if it were a part of her. He recalled how she stood in the water. The muddy water kept washing against her legs, and bits of grass stuck to them. The muddy water was washing against her legs, and those bits of grass were moving about.

He could picture her standing there, expressionless, her lips slightly parted. Water was dripping down from her hair, from her cheeks, from her eyebrows, from her chin. Dripping? No, pouring. The wind was howling. Her hair stuck to her cheeks, her clothes to her body. She was looking at him, expressionless, her lips slightly parted, red, shaking all the while. She was standing in the water shaking, and the water was flowing around her.

The water was moving now, but mostly it was clear. His eyes rested on the river, and he saw, drifting on the surface, some foam, thin foam. He was seated very low, so the face of the river seemed to him all the more broad and far away. The water flowed toward him as if attracted by something, rippling faster and faster until it dashed against the side of the boat, shattering into a fine spray.

The water passed under the boat and gushed up at the other side and gently rolled away to someplace beyond the hills and far away. He put his feet into the water as if in an attempt to stop the flow, though he knew he could not. The water was cold. He drew back his feet, only to thrust them into the water again. The water flowed past. He pushed his bamboo rainhat back a little, and still the door remained shut, as if it had been so ever since he had caught sight of it years ago.

He looked and waited. That familiar chimney was belching cooking smoke again in the early morning light. What will she be dressed in? he asked himself, and his heart began to pound again. He had waited a whole day, a day full of uneasiness and anxiety, yet she had not come out. It was the first time she had not come out when he thought she should have appeared. Yet today he was positive that she would come out. He looked at the chimney, at that cooking smoke, and thought how he would break the news to her the moment she appeared. For the last twenty-four hours, that was all he had waited for. While he waited, he considered what he would say to her first, trying out possibilities, repeating the words over and over in his mind.

Almost thirty minutes had passed. He looked at that door, feeling as though he would suffocate. Any minute now she will come out, he assured himself. Never before had that door seemed so huge to him. When she came out, what would he say to her? Second after second ticked away; his heart pounded faster and faster and more violently. Thirty minutes . . . maybe it hadn't been thirty minutes yet. Maybe his own sense of time was not so good. It was the first time in five years that he had lost confidence in his sense of time.

What on earth was the matter with her? He recalled her again, standing in the rain staring vacantly at him, a water pail in her hand. Her hand was so fair and appeared a bit thin. Then that dream. The dream in which she fell into the water. But even falling in the water couldn't make her look any worse than she had standing in the rain, could it? In fact, ever since the day he had seen her standing there in the rain, that image of her hadn't left his mind. He looked at that door again. What should he say to her? Should he break the news? He'd spent a whole day—yesterday—preparing his part of the conversation, but now, looking at the door, he'd forgotten everything. Forgotten. What difference did it make? Everything would be all right if only she would come out. Now this was all he could hope for, he thought. I'd go and accept the award if only she would come out. I would do that—no, not only that. I would do anything if only she would come out, anything to please her. And still she did not appear.

Tomorrow would be the day of the award ceremony. Yesterday someone had come to congratulate him and said that the newspaper had carried a long story about him. The first award ceremony flashed in his mind again, and so did those incomprehensible words, those unfamiliar faces, and those huge, sweaty palms. If it pleased her, he would go to receive this second award. But surely it wouldn't please her much. So it was better to put the matter—the acceptance of this second award—out of his mind. She was all that mattered to him, he thought. If only she would come out, if only he could see her once again! Now even the desire to speak to her appeared too much of a luxury to him. His only hope was to see her once again, the woman before she fell into the water, the water in his dream.

At long last—after those seemingly interminable forty-eight hours—that door opened, noiselessly. She came out. It was time for her to come out. And he had believed all along that she would.

He saw her walk slowly to the flight of stone steps and then suddenly heard the clop-clopping of her wooden sandals. All at once it occurred to him that she always removed her wooden sandals and carried them when she walked down the stone steps. He gazed at her. It was not her! Actually he had known this since the moment she'd opened the door and become partly visible, only he had never considered the possibility that the person who opened the door might not be her.

The wooden sandals clop-clopped on the stone steps, raising a wisp of pale gray dust. Suddenly she stopped, took off her wooden sandals, and held them in her hand. She carried a basket in one hand and the pair of wooden sandals in the other. But it was not her!

She laid her laundry down and sat on her haunches. But it was not her. She started to do her washing, occasionally raising her head to look at him. He looked at her, too. The hair, the figure, the complexion, they all resembled hers; still it was not her. She scoured, beat her laundry with her wooden bat, shook it over the water, and then let it fall and sink into the water. She looked toward him, and he toward her and the sinking articles of clothing.

They were white as she washed them, yet in the water they turned dull yellow as they sank. She stood up, looking at him. He looked at her, too, and at the sinking articles of clothing. He was holding his pole, yet he did not make any move.

He held his pole in his hand, with one leg dangling over the side of the boat. What was going on? In the past two days she had not come out, but he had not worried. Now this morning, when he saw another woman bearing so much resemblance to her, he began to feel uneasy. What had happened? He had watched day and night by the river, yet he'd noted no change. There was no change. Yet when he saw this woman who took her place, he no longer believed she would come out. The water flowed past his leg; suddenly he felt how very cold the water was. He had not been aware of the water's coldness when he put his foot into it a moment ago. He looked at the beach, on which the sun cast slanting rays. The mist that had hovered there a moment ago had now disappeared. He ran his eyes over the stretch of beach. The water flowed straight toward him carrying foam and the debris of broken grass past his foot—and hers. Her foot was so snowy white that the broken grass sticking to it looked very much like leeches. Suddenly the sight of a piece of broken grass drifting by made him draw up his foot.

He looked up and saw a man carrying a black leather case enter that door. The man looked like a doctor, but he could also have been a dealer in used watches and clocks; he could not tell. Soon the man came out, and the door slammed shut again and, like the flowing water, left no traces that someone had come and gone. His eyes followed the departing man, whose head swung slightly. He was walking in the direction of the temple of Matsu, his feet slowly disappearing behind the levee, sinking slowly as if into a body of water. Looking farther across the levee, he saw only the upturned eaves of the temple and two dragons fashioned out of green tiles on the roof.

The Mosquito

Half sitting, half lying in his chair, Ch'iu Yung-chi stretched out his legs, crossed them on another chair, and drew deeply on his cigarette. There were three different newspapers on his desk, as well as two copies of the evening edition. The manager was already gone, the assistant manager was in the process of locking up the vault, and aside from a few employees who were finishing up the accounts for the day, almost everyone had left the office.

His eyes stared blankly at the smoke he exhaled. He had already read several of the newspapers from front to back. He had read the larger ads, every word of them. There were a lot of advertisements for restaurants, and although he had never been to any of them, he had memorized each ad like a child memorizes television commercials.

Ch'iu had been promoted to the position of deputy manager more than two weeks before. He was still at the same branch of the bank; the only difference, he felt, was that there seemed to be less work to do. Although the position of deputy manager was said to be a springboard to the manager's position, it would be a long time before he got there.

"Mr. Ch'iu, you're still here." The assistant manager had just finished locking the vault.

"I'll be leaving in a minute," said Ch'iu.

"What are you reading that's so interesting?"

"Nothing really."

The assistant manager laughed and, without waiting for Ch'iu to make any further remarks, stuffed the keys into his pocket, waved good-bye, and left. Being a bank employee these days, all one asked was that no unexpected disasters occur. Ch'iu put out his cigarette and leafed through the newspaper again, hoping to discover something different in the news articles, which all seemed so much alike. Many of the news items in the evening paper he had already seen in the morning paper. He found a connect-the-dot game and, using a ballpoint pen, followed the numbers in the correct order, connecting one dot to another. He was rather disappointed at the outcome. The picture would certainly never be a source of much excitement in the world.

He opened the drawer of his desk. A customer had lent him a copy of *Playboy* magazine that afternoon just as one of the female bank employees was approaching him with a question. He had stashed the "material" into his desk drawer and had almost forgotten about it. He opened up the brown-paper cover and leafed through the magazine until he came to a photo of a blonde, nude woman. The picture wasn't bad. The choice of model, the pose, and the photography were all first-rate. He raised his head and looked around. There were only a few people left at the counter.

He walked over to the main office, placed the magazine face down on the Xerox machine and pressed the button. The green light flashed once, and suddenly a red light on the side of the machine started blinking and a buzzer sounded. One of the overtime workers turned around and looked in Ch'iu's direction. Ch'iu quickly turned the machine off. He could feel himself blushing.

"It's out of paper," said the overtime worker, who hurried over to the machine and bent down to look in the paper tray.

"That's okay, I know how to fill it."

"All right, but press the button again just to make sure it's working."

He pressed the button. The picture he had Xeroxed just before turning the machine off came out first, followed by another copy. The prints emerged face down. He felt very grateful to the person who had designed the machine. What if the second copy hadn't come out then, and the first person to use the machine the next day just happened to be a woman?

He went back to his desk, put the magazine into its folder, tossed it into his drawer, and locked it. It really wasn't worth the trouble, he thought, as he put the things on his desk in order. He looked at his watch. It was just past seven, still too early to go home.

He went to the men's room and looked at himself in the mirror. He thought he looked comical, like an ape. He blinked at the man in the mirror, took out his comb, and began combing his hair. His hair really wasn't long, but it could still stand a trim. The last time he had gone to the Three Phoenixes Barbershop a girl named Chin Feng had been pretty nice to him. Her uniform was a pale yellow sheath dress with a mandarin collar, the name of the shop embroidered in blue over her heart. The material of the dress was so thin that he could almost see the color of her underwear through it. He didn't have the nerve to look directly at her, but he could see her quite clearly in the large mirror in front of him. When she was shaving him, her belly had pressed against his elbow, which rested on the arm of the chair.

The Three Phoenixes Barbershop was in an alley right across

from the bank. He walked over to the front of the shop only to discover that today was the twenty-fifth of the month, and it was closed. Barbershops usually closed on the tenth and twenty-fifth of each month.

He sighed, feeling suddenly aimless. "I'll go downtown and walk around," he thought vaguely to himself.

It didn't matter what time it was; the downtown district was always throbbing with people. This was the world of the rich and the young. Pushed and nudged from all sides, Ch'iu worked his way into the crowd. Tonight was the same as many previous nights: he had absolutely no plans. Sometimes he would stop and watch the hawkers shouting, or he would stand in front of the stores and look at the colorful window displays. Sometimes he would squeeze into the crowd, rubbing against the bodies, or sometimes he would just let people push him around. Sometimes he would dodge to one side and watch the crowd, avoiding contact with people; other times he would purposely stick out his foot and let people step on him.

It was such a noisy, bustling scene. He felt very small in the crowd, yet still he felt himself to be a part of it.

He turned down a little alley lined with coffee shops. This was a completely different world. He hesitated a moment. He had been to this sort of place in the past. Today was no different from any other. Heavily painted women stood in front of a few of the shops, while others hired men in their twenties or thirties to stand out front and solicit customers for them.

"Come in and sit down!" they called to him.

He smiled. He knew that, as a civil servant, he couldn't go into places like that. Just looking was enough, he thought, as he walked the whole length of the alley.

A long time ago, before the government had become so strict with its workers, Ch'iu had made the acquaintance of a woman from one of these shops. She wasn't bad looking, and you could even say that she had a pretty good head on her shoulders. He just couldn't understand how she had gotten mixed up in that kind of place. At the time he had wanted to ask her if she wanted to go with him.

Suddenly Ch'iu realized that without knowing it he had already walked all the way home. The iron security gate had already been pulled down over the shop front. He wormed his way through a small opening in the door, looked up at the electric clock hanging on the wall, and saw that it was exactly nine o'clock.

The family ran a hardware store on the ground floor below their apartment. Lai-chih managed it. To be exact, the Wu Fu Hsing Hardware Store was started by Mr. Wu, Lai-chih's father, forty or fifty years ago. Lai-chih's father had retired, so she managed everything now. The location was good, and Mr. Wu had always advocated dealing honestly with customers, so business had grown steadily.

As Ch'iu Yung-chi walked in, Lai-chih was waiting on a customer. The shop closed around eight o'clock, and the clerks could go home then. After that, Lai-chih took care of any remaining business. Ch'iu decided that the person at the counter must be a supplier collecting payment for some goods since he noticed Lai-chih was writing out a check and handing it to him.

The building had four floors altogether. On the second floor was the kitchen, the dining room, the bathroom, and his mother-and father-in-law's room. The third floor belonged to Ch'iu Yung-chi and Lai-chih, and the children's study and bedrooms were on the fourth floor.

Ch'iu's mother- and father-in-law were up on the second floor watching television as he came in. There they were, the two of them, sitting shoulder to shoulder. They could almost be rolled up into one person, thought Yung-chi. He felt that they made it a point always to appear especially intimate when he was around. He didn't know why, but he firmly believed they

31

did it on purpose. At their age, it really was rather unusual. Maybe this was their way of hinting that he and Lai-chih ought to get along as well as they themselves did. They probably wanted to set an example. Perhaps they did it to show how, with their united strength, they could overcome the enemy. And in this family, if they had an enemy, it was him.

"Mom. Dad," he greeted them.

"You're home," they said in what seemed like one voice. "Hurry up and eat."

His mother- and father-in-law were always polite and thoughtful. No matter how late he came home, they always told him to go eat, as if it was the only thing in the world that mattered.

"Ah-chin, the master is back; hurry and heat up his dinner."

Ch'iu Yung-chi went upstairs to the third floor, changed his clothes, washed his face, and sat down and relaxed for a moment. There was a Sansui stereo set on the third floor that his friend had persuaded him to buy. He reached over to turn it on and then decided against it. Originally, he had hoped that he and Lai-chih could listen to it together, but she didn't seem to be interested. He suddenly hurried down to the second floor, worried that his mother- and father-in-law would be waiting for him to come and eat.

Although Lai-chih and her parents' faces didn't show it, he had a feeling that they were upset with him. Every meal was always divided up into several shifts. The children ate first, then his mother- and father-in-law, next the servant, Ah-chin, and then it was his turn. Sometimes Lai-chih ate before him, and sometimes she ate after he did.

There was a plate of pork on the table. It was his favorite dish, but no one else in the family, including Ah-chin, liked it. From the looks of it, there was too much for him to eat by himself. But he knew he had better finish it all up. If he didn't, they would ask him if he was sick. On the other hand, if he did, the next time they served it, he would have to eat just as much. Once he told Ah-chin not to make so much. She told him she was just following instructions from the mistress of the house.

"Mom, Dad, why don't you have something to eat?"

"We've already eaten. Hurry up and eat or your food will get cold."

"I'm going to call Lai-chih."

"Never mind, she's waiting on a customer."

He sat down, ate a little, and suddenly felt thirsty. What he really wanted was a little wine, but he didn't dare ask for it. After a couple of minutes Lai-chih came upstairs. Her customer must have left.

"Have you eaten yet?" he asked her.

"No, but I'm not very hungry."

She looked so small and thin. Who would have guessed that she managed all the affairs of the household, from the first floor to the fourth?

"Were you busy today?" she asked. She sat down. She always asked this question. Actually, she knew quite well who was the busier of them. And if he came home late, she never called the bank anymore to ask why he hadn't come yet.

She scooped some rice into her bowl, only two or three mouthfuls. There were rust marks on the hand with which she held the rice bowl. He didn't know whether she hadn't washed her hands yet or if the rust stain just wouldn't wash off. He wanted to reach over and give her a squeeze, but he felt embarrassed to do so in front of her parents. The impulse quickly died.

"I wasn't that busy," he said. He wanted to tell her about his promotion, but he didn't feel like talking either.

"Do you want some wine?" she asked.

"No."

If he was going to drink, he preferred to do it alone. She finished eating and continued sitting there. They sat together silently.

"Take your time, I'm going back to the accounts," she said.

As soon as she left, he quickly finished his rice and stood up.

"Are you full?" his mother- and father-in-law asked anxiously. "You should eat a good dinner, you know."

"Yes, I had enough," he said. Even though they were watching television, they seemed to be paying close attention to him the whole time.

Lai-chih was on the third floor finishing the accounts. Her fingers moved across the abacus slowly. She had made progress, but as far as he was concerned, she was still slow at it. He was an employee of the bank, and his skill with the abacus was considered to be better than most of his coworkers.' Once he had told her that he could take care of all the work requiring an abacus. But she had answered that since there wasn't much calculating to do, it didn't matter how quickly it got done. After that, he never asked her again about the accounts, and she never asked him for help.

"Aren't you going upstairs to see the children?" she asked.

They had five children, two boys and three girls. The first three were girls. When they were born, Ch'iu's mother- and father-in-law were not very happy. Afterward, two boys were born, and the tense atmosphere at home eased considerably.

Before he married into the Wu family, they had come to an agreement, through the intermediary of a matchmaker, as to how the children should be named. They had even prepared a contract. Originally, it was agreed that the first child would be given the surname of the mother: Wu. All the children after that would have their father's surname: Ch'iu. Later, Lai-chih's parents changed the agreement, giving the first, third, and fifth child their surname, and the second, fourth and sixth child the father's surname.

According to this agreement, the first child was given its mother's surname, and the second child should have taken its father's surname. But when it turned out to be another girl,

Ch'iu's mother- and father-in-law were displeased, so Lai-chih suggested compromising by giving the child their own surname. The third child, another girl, was also named Wu. The fourth child was a boy, just what Lai-chih's parents had been longing for, and they claimed that since this was the first male child, he should be surnamed Wu. Ch'iu Yung-chi had never really placed much importance on the business of surnames. After all, he had married into a woman's family and did not have to take charge of the household. If the children were named Wu or Ch'iu, what difference did it make? They were still his own children. The fifth child was also a boy, and since Ch'iu did not protest, the child was registered under the surname Wu.

The children's world was contained within the confines of the fourth floor. Their tutor hadn't left yet. All the children were doing fairly well in school, especially the girls. The eldest had been accepted into the foreign languages department of a national university, and the two younger girls had gotten into a prestigious high school. The two boys, who were in middle school, were also high-ranking students and would have no problem passing their high-school entrance examinations.

According to the bank's regulations, the children were all eligible for scholarships, but Ch'iu had never applied for one. This was because he had once heard one of his coworkers refer to him behind his back as "Brother Pig," a term used for male swine hired out for breeding. Ch'iu put out his own money to pay for the children's education.

The tutor stood up, and Ch'iu nodded to her.

"Our children are fine in school; we just want you to be here with them while they do their homework. Give them some pointers on how to prepare their lessons. You can bring your own homework along and do it here, too." Every time they hired a tutor, Lai-chih explained the job this way: supervision was more important than teaching. Both Ch'iu and the children agreed with this, especially the children. One time the youngest child had remarked that another "prison warden" had been hired.

As soon as Ch'iu Yung-chi reached the fourth floor, his eldest daughter, Hsiu-ling, turned away and went into her own room. Hsiu-ling had been avoiding him for several days now.

About a month ago Hsiu-ling had come to the bank looking for him.

"Dad, do you want to take me out for lunch?"

"Okay," Ch'iu felt that there was something a little unusual about this. "Where would you like to eat?"

"How about a Western-style restaurant? I've never been to one before."

He took her to a new Western-style restaurant that had just opened on Heng Yang Road. He showed her how to use a knife and fork.

"Dad, is it all right for me to have a boyfriend?"

"I don't object, but . . ."

"But I had better ask Mom about it, right?"

"You know . . ."

The two of them ate in silence for a moment. Then Hsiu-ling suddenly opened her wallet, took out a photograph, and handed it to him.

"Dad, what do you think of him?"

"Very nice looking."

"Dad, I'm asking you again. Do you think I ought to start dating? I want your opinion."

Ch'iu remained silent.

"Dad, you still haven't said anything!"

She got up, wiped her mouth with the napkin, threw it on the table, and, without looking back, walked out. Ever since that had happened, Ch'iu had felt depressed. The fact that his daughter had asked for his opinion showed that she still had some respect for him.

Why, he thought to himself, why couldn't he say how he felt, even for his own daughter? Her contempt showed how hurt she was. He had been trying to find an opportunity to talk to her about it, but if she kept avoiding him, he didn't think he would ever have a chance.

"Lai-chih," Ch'iu called to his wife.

It was almost eleven o'clock, and Lai-chih was still on the third floor finishing the accounts. He lit a cigarette and sat down next to her. He wanted to talk to her about Hsiu-ling.

"Today's newspaper said that smoking is harmful to your health." she said to him.

He abruptly snuffed out his cigarette. "What did you do that for? I only said that there was another article in today's papers about how harmful smoking is. To get angry so often is just as bad for your health."

Ch'iu Yung-chi changed into his pajamas and went down to the second floor to take a bath. His mother- and father-in-law had already turned in for the night. He went into the bathroom; the tub had already been filled. Every time he went into the bathroom he thought about gas leaking from the water heater, even though Ah-chin always ran his bath for him.

After he finished bathing, he went back up to the third floor. Lai-chih was just getting ready to come down for her bath. In the past, he and Lai-chih would occasionally bathe together. But that was something they hadn't done in a long time, and he knew it wasn't entirely because the children were grown up now.

"You look tired," Lai-chih said to him. "Why don't you go on to bed?"

He sat down on the couch and wanted to smoke a cigarette, but he thought of what Lai-chih had just said about smoking.

He let out a long sigh. Should he go to sleep now, or should he wait for Lai-chih? She had said that he looked tired. She often said things like that. Actually, she was the one who should be tired. But that wasn't what she said.

He turned on the little light above the bed and lay down. Go to sleep, he thought to himself. A while ago, there was a girl he used to know. At the time, Lai-chih had just given birth to their youngest son. The girl was an accountant for one of the bank's big clients. She came to the bank every day depositing and withdrawing money. He had had a couple of dates with her. They had gone to the movies twice. He had told her all about his family life. She had said she was willing to marry him, willing to give birth to his children, children named Ch'iu. He was ready to give up everything, including his job at the bank. But then her parents intervened and made her leave him. The customer who employed her blew up over the matter, withdrew all his money from his account, and deposited it in another bank. The head of the bank had confronted Ch'iu about this and made him apologize to the customer.

He never saw her again after that. He didn't know whether she was married or not, whether she had any children, whether her life was happy and secure.

His mind was drifting. Suddenly he heard a mosquito buzzing incessantly above his head. He tried to determine what direction the noise was coming from. Then he made a violent swipe at the insect. Did he hit it? He opened his eyes and looked at the palm of his hand. It was empty. The buzzing stopped for just a moment and then started again. He swung again with even more force than the first time. His hand smashed into his temple. His head jerked, and then he felt it fall forward, sinking down and down.

It seemed as if he could still hear the buzzing sound. He didn't know if it was the sound of a mosquito or if it was his ears ringing. He lifted his hand again and struck out violently.

THREE

Betel Nut Town

The graduation ceremony was yesterday morning. Some class-mates had taken the afternoon train home, and some had left that evening. Others were going to leave this morning. Only a handful still remained in Taichung.

Hung Yueh-hua went downtown by herself to buy her parents some souvenirs before returning home.

She had been a student in Taichung for four years. Now, as she walked along the street, by all the familiar places—the park, the library, the theaters, the cafés—she suddenly realized that she might be seeing them for the last time. So she could not help lingering as she passed each familiar spot.

Suddenly she thought of the classmates she'd come to these places with. Most of them were girls, but occasionally one or two boys accompanied them. Ch'en Hsi-lin, however, was not one of them. He never went out with his classmates.

He had not attended the graduation ceremony yesterday. He hadn't even shown up to say good-bye to his classmates or autograph their yearbooks.

Why hadn't Ch'en Hsi-lin come? After four years of college, what could possibly have been more important? No one had seen him since the last exam. Could he be sick? Remembering his muscular build and deep tan, she just couldn't imagine him being ill.

He had been a strange person at school, hardly making friends with anyone. He worked hard at his studies, and his grades were quite good.

Hung Yueh-hua had only talked with him once, and that had been last year when they went to the farm for field training. They'd been assigned to the same section. They had talked quite a bit, but since then, he'd become a virtual stranger. She just couldn't understand him; but then, she had never really tried.

Why was she thinking of him, today of all days? Was it because he hadn't come to graduation?

She walked to the railway station, checked the timetable for trains to Taipei, and then looked at the schedule of the south-bound trains.

Maybe she should go to see him. She bought a third-class ticket for a train going south. Why am I doing this? she asked herself. But the ticket was already bought; it would be silly to go and ask for a refund.

The train was about thirty minutes late, and the trip itself took more than an hour. It was well past one when she finally arrived. The sun was dazzling. Only a few passengers got on the train, about as many as were getting off.

Although she had never been here, the name of this small stop had stuck in her head for more than two years. During winter vacation of their sophomore year, she and her classmates had been coming home from their tour of the south. She was sitting beside the window and when she glanced toward the western sky, she saw a huge red sun about to sink below the horizon. "How gorgeous!" She and her classmates had all exclaimed at once.

Just at that moment, she noticed a rectangular farmhouse in the middle of open fields, surrounded by tall betel nut trees that seemed to be supporting the magnificent setting sun. Betel Nut Town, this lovely name flashed through her mind and became inseparably linked with that beautiful sunset.

Their train soon left Betel Nut Town far behind. The sun sank below the horizon. The sky was a flaming crimson. She had looked at her watch; it was five thirty-five.

She had closed her eyes, trying to retain that beautiful image. Then suddenly the train had stopped. Calling out the name of the station, the conductress had explained that they were waiting for another train to pass. She had opened her eyes, and the name of the small station had become engraved in her memory.

As she was leaving, the conductor's eyes followed her. This would never happen in Taipei or Taichung. She had the impression that everybody was staring at her, especially the girls. Was her skirt too short? Were the heels of her shoes too high? She suddenly felt herself blushing.

Betel Nut Town. It had been over two years since she'd seen it through the train window. How was she to get there?

She knew Ch'en Hsi-lin lived in Betel Nut Town. He had told her that last year when they were working on the farm. He had also told her many things about the planting of betel nuts.

"Betel Nut Town, such a beautiful name! It's just as beautiful as those watercolors of peaceful rural villages that artists paint. But actually . . . I really hope you'll be able to come sometime and see it for yourself."

"You'd really let me come?"

"Why shouldn't I?"

But he had never invited her again. Actually, he had never talked to her again after that.

In the second semester, they had fewer required courses and were able to take more electives. She chose less rigorous classes, but he continued taking hard ones, so there were fewer opportunities for them to run into each other. Even when they did happen to meet, he seemed intent on avoiding her and would just walk away.

Soon after, they finished their final exams, and everybody graduated. But he didn't even come to the graduation. Could he have forgotten he'd invited her to visit Betel Nut Town?

She hadn't forgotten. Right now, her only problem was how to get there. She knew the general direction. All she had to do was to follow the railroad tracks south, and she would be sure to find it. However, judging from how long the train had traveled, she estimated it must be about a four-mile walk.

At the time, she hadn't thought to ask Ch'en Hsi-lin how to get there or if there was a bus.

As she left the train station, she saw two long rows of shops. Some were selling cigarettes and sundries, others were selling fruit, and still others were selling fish and pork. There were even six or seven snack shops, including a cold-drink stand. The narrow streets and walks seemed to reflect the peculiar color of the earth here, an ashen gray.

As late as it was, there were still some customers in the shops. She could hear the sizzling sound of food frying and could see steam escaping from the large pots.

She also saw a shop that sold desserts. It had peanut soup, red bean soup, and sweet rice congee. A narrow-spouted tea kettle whistled continuously. Through the window she saw some pancakelike pastries and some twisted-dough fritters. There were two or three people inside eating.

All of a sudden she remembered that she hadn't had any lunch. She'd boarded the train on an impulse and had completely forgotten about eating.

A glass jar of fried flour caught her eye. It brought back memories of eating fried-flour paste at the stand in front of the temple when, as a child, she went to the countryside to visit her grandmother. She rarely went to her grandparents' house since Grandmother had passed away and even more rarely saw anyone selling fried-flour paste.

She ordered a bowl. She would never have expected to be able to eat fried-flour paste in a such place.

The shopkeeper was a short, portly woman, probably in her fifties. She poured some of the fried flour into a bowl and mashed it expertly with a spoon. Then, picking up a tea kettle with a narrow spout, she poured in boiling water with a flair, raising and lowering the tea kettle as she poured. The flour had already started to bubble. Then she stirred it lightly with the spoon.

"There's a house near the railroad tracks that has betel nut trees planted around it," she said to the shopkeeper. "Could you please tell me how to get there?"

"Which house?"

"They have a son who went to Taichung to study."

"Is that Ch'en Hsi-lin's family?" asked a young man sitting at a table across from her, drinking peanut soup with twisted-dough fritters in it.

"Do you know him?"

"He's our local agricultural expert. Whenever we have problems with seeds or fertilizers, we always go to him."

"How can I get there?"

"If you'll wait a minute, I'll take you on my motorcycle."

"Isn't there a bus or something that goes there?"

"There is, but it's not very convenient. The buses don't run that often, and after you get off the bus you'd still have a long walk, and you probably don't know the way. It's better if I take you."

"It's too much trouble for you."

"What trouble? Every time I run into someone from the city, I get the feeling that they don't trust anybody."

"I . . ." she stammered and felt herself blush.

43

"Are you his schoolmate?"

"Uh-huh."

"Let me go next door to pick up the things I bought. I'll be back in a minute."

His name was also Ch'en. They sped down paths between fields. On both sides of the paths, the fields were a fertile black, and by now most of the soil had already been turned in preparation for the next crop.

The white-hot sun was hanging high overhead. After they had ridden for about fifteen minutes, they arrived at Ch'en Hsi-lin's house. This was it! This was the grove of betel nut trees that she had seen from the train. The only difference was that it seemed smaller than she had imagined.

She stood at the entrance gazing east. There was the railway embankment stretching out into the distance.

As it turned out, the young man who had brought her on the motorcycle was a distant cousin of theirs.

The house was made of red bricks and had been built quite a long time ago. There was a cement courtyard in front for drying grain, dotted with droppings from the ducks and chickens. There were two rings of betel nut trees around the house, most of them higher than the roof. Several smaller ones looked as though they'd been planted sometime later to fill the gaps. Some trees were flowering, and some had begun to grow nuts. Ch'en Hsi-lin had told her that the betel palms were valuable as a windbreak as well as for their nuts and leaves.

Ch'en Hsi-lin wasn't home. His mother came out, saying that he had gone to work in the fields, and asked his cousin to go look for him. But Hung Yueh-hua wanted to find him in the fields herself.

The rice paddies were right behind the house, opposite the railway, toward the west.

The sun was glaring down mercilessly. She walked behind the house and saw nothing but rice paddies stretching out before her.

Some were already filled with water and looked like gigantic mirrors reflecting the azure color of the sky.

In the distance, she could make out a few figures walking back and forth in the paddies. It looked as if they were chasing something, sometimes taking large strides, sometimes short, hurried steps. It was comical, and it also looked like fun. Some of them were women, wearing bamboo hats draped with brightly colored cloth to protect them from the hot sun. These hats hid their faces, but, judging from the shape of their bodies, one of them seemed very young. Who was this girl?

Hung Yueh-hua's face suddenly turned red. Why had she thought such a thing?

The path between the fields was only about a foot wide and sometimes the heels of her shoes sank into the mud. One careless step, and she would fall.

As she drew closer, she saw Ch'en Hsi-lin. Ch'en hadn't gotten sick. She saw him stop and turn to look at her. He seemed a little startled at first, and then, taking the shortest path, he walked over to her. He was wearing a short-sleeved cotton shirt, but it didn't hide his broad shoulders and muscular arms. He was much more tan than he had been at school.

His mud-coated feet made it look as though he were wearing knee-high boots. Mud was splattered all over him.

"What a surprise!" Ch'en Hsi-lin took off his bamboo hat.

"What are you doing?"

"Burying rice stalks."

"Burying rice stalks?"

"Haven't you seen that done before? We step on the leftover rice stalks to bury them in the mud so they will rot there. There's so little time between the first crop and the second crop. That's why we have to bury them in the mud."

"Oh, I never knew that."

"It's not your fault. You couldn't possibly have learned this in class or at that farm where we went for field training."

45

"Why didn't you come to the graduation ceremony yesterday?"

"Too much to do at home. Everybody is busy transplanting the rice seedlings."

"Will I be disturbing you?"

"Not at all."

"May I try it?"

"It's very tiring."

"I'd just like to try it."

"Aren't you afraid of getting your dress dirty?"

"It doesn't matter." She blushed.

"Then you should put on a hat. The sun is so strong," Ch'en Hsi-lin said as he took off his own hat and gave it to her.

"What about you?"

"I've got this." He fished a cap out of his pant's pocket. "I'll get you a piece of bamboo to use as a walking stick."

"You don't use sticks."

"We're farmers."

"I studied agriculture, too. I graduated yesterday, but this could be considered a way of earning some extra credit."

It was true that she had studied agriculture, but her case was entirely different from Ch'en Hsi-lin's. She had been assigned to the Department of Agricultural Science on the basis of her college entrance exam scores. As for Ch'en Hsi-lin, he had gone into this field because of his single-minded desire to learn what he needed to improve his farm.

Hung Yueh-hua took off her shoes and stockings. Although her skirt was already above her knees, she carefully pulled it a bit higher as she stepped down into the rice paddy.

Ch'en Hsi-lin introduced her to the people who were working in the paddy. The young girl was Yu-lan, his younger sister. She was a student at the Normal College in Taichung. One of the others was his sister-in-law.

As soon as she stepped into the rice paddy, she felt her whole body sinking. It was a strange feeling. Now the muddy water was almost above her knees, and it seemed like the mud kept pulling her deeper. She quickly hitched her skirt up a little higher, revealing her pale thighs; she blushed again.

She watched the others stepping on the rice stalks. Their feet were rapid and accurate. Ch'en Hsi-lin stayed by her side. He offered her the bamboo stick again, but she refused.

She saw a clump of rice stalks in front of her. She wanted to step on them, but her feet seemed to be stuck in the mud, and no matter how hard she tried, she couldn't pull them out. Then, with one surge, one foot did come out. But she almost fell down in the process.

Ch'en Hsi-lin handed her the bamboo stick and insisted that she use it.

She stepped gingerly. This was the first time she had ever tried to walk in a rice paddy. Each time she put her foot down she almost lost her balance. And just as she managed to steady herself, her legs would sink halfway down into the mud again. How small she suddenly felt!

Here and there throughout the freshly turned mud, there were clumps of rice stalks sticking up. Some were sticking straight up, others were at various angles, and still others were upside down in the water. Since the rice had been cut rather recently, the rice stalks were still quite sharp. She smelled the mud. Although she had never smelled it before and could not describe it, she knew she recognized this unmistakable smell of mud.

She aimed carefully as she stepped on the rice stalks, burying them in the mud. Still, sometimes she was a little off target, and the rice stalks remained stuck halfway out. When this happened, she had to lift her foot and step on them a second time. Sometimes, a rice stalk stuck straight up or was buried in such a way that she didn't see it. Then the soles of her feet got pricked sharply. This could hurt so much that she bent over in pain.

47

Sometimes, the mud was so sticky she had trouble lifting her feet. Other times, it was so slippery, it felt as if leeches were wriggling around. Once in a while, the mud squirted up her legs, staining her skirt and her thighs. She stepped slowly and cautiously, afraid she might fall down.

Ch'en Hsi-lin worked a much broader area, while the area she worked was a more or less narrow, if crooked, line.

Each time she took a step, the mud squeezed up between her toes and spread them apart. She noticed that Ch'en Hsi-lin's toes were spread wide and the bottoms of his feet looked broad and thick like a duck's. She wondered how he managed to get his shoes on.

A little after three o'clock, they stopped for some refreshments. In the country, this is known as eating five meals. The refreshments consisted of rice congee with sweet potatoes and salted black beans and chopped dried radishes to accompany it. The men just rinsed off their hands and feet and ate standing on the paths between the paddies. The women followed suit. Ch'en Hsi-lin's younger sister, Yu-lan, asked her some questions about the city and kept complimenting her on the texture of her skin.

She had never eaten these foods before, but they seemed to taste better to her than anything she had ever eaten, especially those yellow sweet potatoes in the rice congee.

Their break was very short. Actually, they only stopped long enough to eat. She looked down at her feet. There was still some mud on them, and where the mud had dried, her skin felt a little tight. Much of her nail polish was already gone, and with mud caked under them, her nails looked like crescent moons.

Her arms had started to turn red and felt a little burned.

After finishing eating, they returned to their work. Ch'en Hsi-lin wanted her to rest, but, her cheeks burning, she insisted on going back into the paddy.

The sun was still scorching hot. Sweat streamed down her

forehead, stinging her eyes. Her mouth was dry, and her throat was parched. Her back was wet as well. Gradually her steps became slower and slower. Her back was getting stiff, making it more and more difficult to straighten up. She had never perspired so much in her life.

As her steps slowed, the strip she was able to manage grew narrower, and Ch'en Hsi-lin had to cover even more area to maintain the pace. Sometimes when she would miss a stalk or not get it entirely buried, Ch'en Hsi-lin would come back and do it over again for her.

"I'm very happy you came to see me."

"Oh." Again her face turned red, and she seemed to perspire even more.

"Actually, I wish some of our other classmates could have also come with you."

"They've all gone home."

"What are your plans after you go home? Are you going abroad? Will you get married or find a job?"

"My father has already found a job for me."

"What kind of job?"

"A trading company." She blushed again.

"A trading company?"

"They export handicrafts. It's only temporary, because I couldn't find a job in my field."

"It's okay. But you know, I've been thinking how many people there are who would like to train in this field and can't get in, while other people who aren't interested and really don't need the training, squeeze their way in and take up all the available positions."

"Sometimes I feel that way, too. Especially when we were about to graduate, and I was looking for a job and finding it so hard. Then I really felt it. I understand exactly what you mean. Actually, I often feel that I made a mistake."

"It isn't necessarily your fault. Everybody has a right to study,

49

and they can study anything they want. It's only that there are some people who are really serious, and they just don't get the opportunity. Take me, for example. I took the exam three times before I could get in, while some of you were assigned to this department because your exam scores were too low in other areas. It wasn't because you were really interested in this field. You remember the first time you went out to the farm for field training? You all acted like you were on a picnic. You stood around and talked; some of you even brought radios and tape players along and listened to music while you watched the hired hands work."

"There were some farmers like you among us. Several of them did quite well in their studies and really wanted to go on to the experimental agricultural farm or find other opportunities for more training."

"But we were a small minority. Most switched fields as soon as they graduated. And these conditions don't just affect the individual; it's a loss to our society as a whole."

"But what can be done about it? I worked very hard at first, too. Every one of us wanted to do well in the exams, and we all felt this was better than not going to school at all."

Hearing this, Ch'en Hsi-lin's expression turned grave. After a short pause, he continued, "Forgive me. I really shouldn't have said that to you."

Hung Yueh-hua was just about to say something, but when she heard this, she swallowed her words. She felt very embarrassed. Blushing, she lowered her head. Her steps became even more sluggish, and her back more sore. She stood there in the mud as if she were stuck, unable to extract herself. She forced herself to straighten up, and, eyeing a clump of rice stalks about half a yard away, she jerked her foot as hard as she could, wrenching it free. But as she did so, she lost her balance. She teetered, trying to regain it, but fell backward, and landed sitting in the mud.

The mud was so soft and sticky that when she tried to pull herself free, she sank even deeper. Using her hand, she tried pushing herself up, but her hand also sank. She was still clutching the bamboo stick with her other hand, and it flailed uselessly in the air.

"What happened?" Ch'en Hsi-lin rushed over to her side and pulled her up. Her arms and skirt were covered with mud.

"I really should not have said that to you." He helped her up to the path between the paddies. "I'll have Yu-lan take you back to change your clothes."

"I'm sorry. I've slowed down your work."

Yu-lan heated some water for her.

There was no bathroom in their house; the place where everybody bathed was in a corner of the kitchen. There was no screen or anything for privacy, and it was still bright daylight. She was a little hesitant.

"It doesn't matter; we all bathe like this. I'll watch for you," said Yu-lan as she went to the doorway to sit down and act as a lookout.

The kitchen had only one small window, and even though it was closed, she could see some green shadowy forms swaying. "They're probably those betel palm fronds," she thought to herself.

Yu-lan lent her a dress to change into and took her dirty one to wash. Yu-lan was shorter but slightly broader than she was, so she was able to get into the dress. Pulling it on, however, her skin felt strange. Was it the material's texture or whatever had yellowed it and given it that alkaline smell, perhaps the minerals in the laundry water? It felt as if there was something crawling on her skin, especially around her neck, shoulders, and arms. Perhaps she had been in the hot sun too long, for these areas were all sunburned.

Once the mud was washed off, her skin was white again from her calves down. But the caked mud under her nails would not wash out. She discovered a number of scratches from the rice stalks above her calves. They were red and itched.

"I like you very much," Yu-lan said.

"I'm so sorry. My coming here has only made extra work for you all."

"Never mind. You are the first classmate of my brother's to come here to visit. He must be very happy. We all hope that you will be able to come back and see us again."

"Today I'm going back to Taipei. I honestly don't know when I can come again. Still, I'll never forget today for the rest of my life."

Yu-lan took her on a tour of the house. She told her that those betel nut trees had been planted to replace the bamboo windbreak that had originally grown there. They had been planted ten years before, when her brother had first entered Agricultural High School and had urged her father to switch to betel nut trees. At the time, her father was set against the idea, but, by counting off the many virtues of the betel nut trees, her brother had managed to persuade him.

A little more than an hour later, Ch'en Hsi-lin and the others all returned. They had finished burying the rice stalks.

She had originally intended to hurry back to Taichung and then on to Taipei, but Ch'en Hsi-lin, Yu-lan, and the others kept insisting that she stay for supper. His mother had even killed a chicken in her honor and offered her a drumstick. The usual custom of country folk was to give the drumsticks to the youngest. Hung Yueh-hua felt herself blushing again.

She felt embarrassed to eat it and embarrassed not to. Gazing down at the chicken leg in her bowl, she picked at her rice. Ch'en Hsi-lin's mother, however, insisted that she eat it, repeating over and over that country chickens were so much more delicious than the ones you got in the city. She even loosened the meat from the bone for her and dipped it into the soy sauce before returning it to her bowl. If she didn't hurry up and eat it, she declared, she would have to force her to.

Ch'en Hsi-lin's mother was probably already in her sixties, and she was fairly short, but her movements were still quite agile, and she was very strong. Hung Yueh-hua had seen her using only one hand to carry a large wooden bucket of slop to feed the pigs.

With her chopsticks, Hung Yueh-hua delicately pulled off a strip of meat from the chicken leg. Then peeling the skin with her fingers, she placed it on the table. She never ate chicken skin.

When Ch'en Hsi-lin saw this, he reached over with his chopsticks and nonchalantly popped the skin into his mouth. Her face flushed again.

After supper, Ch'en Hsi-lin asked her if she'd like to walk over by the railroad tracks to watch the setting sun.

"Oh no, we don't need to do that."

"Well, since you're here, don't you want to take one more look?"

"I think I should go back."

"In that case, I'll take you to the train station on my motorcycle."

The sun had just gone down, and the western skies were still fiery red. Sunset in the country was, as always, so very beautiful.

The motorcycle whizzed along between fields as the paddy water mirrored the colors of the sky. With both hands, Hung Yueh-hua clung tightly to the leather seat strap. Her head was right behind Ch'en Hsi-lin's back. The motorcycle was going very fast, and there was a lot of wind. Should she press a bit closer? As this thought occurred to her, she blushed.

Her hair was flying in the wind. Suddenly, something flew into her eye. She kept trying to blink, but whatever it was refused to come out, and tears streamed down her face. She didn't dare let go of the leather strap, so she tried to rub her eye on her shoulder. The more she rubbed, the more her eye hurt.

She wanted to cry out for them to stop, but she kept thinking they would be at the train station in a few minutes and she could probably bear it just a little longer.

By the time they arrived at the train station, she could no longer open her eye. Her whole face was stained with tears.

"What happened?"

"Something must have gotten into my eye." She sounded as if she had a cold. The tears had even gone into her nose.

"Let me take a look." He used his fingers to pry open her eyelid. "You've got a mosquito in your eye."

"A big one?"

"A little one. Hold still," he said. And moving closer, he blew hard into her eye and then pulled her eyelid back again for another look. "Okay now?"

"A little better." She blinked her eyes over and over again. She wiped her face with the back of her hand and said, "I've really been a nuisance to all of you today."

"Why do you keep saying things like that? I'm very happy. It never occurred to me that you would really come. I'm really very happy to see you again."

"From now on, whenever I pass this way by train, I'll think of you."

"From now on, whenever I see a train pass by, I'll think that you might be on it, especially if the sun is about to set."

A Fisherman's Family

The ashen sky hung low over the ashen sea. The rain had stopped, but it would soon begin falling again. Waves swelled like gigantic tongues, lapping violently against the shore. The roar of the waves was low, turbulent.

On a beach at Taiwan's southern tip, fishermen were preparing to put out to sea. Uncle A-ch'un and his son carried the boat down to the water's edge on heavy bamboo poles. The waves surged onto the shore and then retreated, dispersing white foam, which hissed as it sank into the sand. One wave subsided, only to be followed by another.

Aunt A-ch'un followed silently behind. Her two young granddaughters, one on each side, clung loosely to the slightly curved lip of the stern. The fishermen carried the boat to the water's edge. They studied the waves, preparing to push off into the water. A-kuo put down the poles and turned to lean down and kiss his two daughters. This was something new he had picked up while in the army.

He stood up and looked at his mother. She smiled, revealing

a set of uneven, gaping teeth. Her smile wasn't beautiful, but it was warm-hearted. When she wasn't smiling, her cheeks caved in, making her chin look too long. From her forehead and temples down to her chin, her face was etched with creases.

It had been over thirty years since she had married into Uncle A-ch'un's family. For all that time, except when she was in labor, she had always seen him out to sea. It had become her habit. She stood silently at the shoreline. She didn't need to speak. He knew she wanted him to return as soon as he could.

Fishermen who worked the coastal waters, like her husband and son, seldom ran into trouble. Their only worry was how many fish they could catch. But this wasn't the case with the women. They felt secure only when their menfolk were by their side. Sometimes, when they saw the weather suddenly turning bad, they would race down to the shore, forgetting even to take in the clothes, and stand there gazing out in the distance at the minuscule dots bobbing on the waves. They would watch while the black dots slowly moved toward them. At times, they might start shouting wildly, but even if they screamed themselves hoarse, it wouldn't make the least bit of difference. This rarely happened; maybe once or twice a year. Though, of course, there were some who never returned.

"Don't forget to hoist up the red banner." They had already agreed that if A-kuo's wife gave birth to a son, Aunt A-ch'un would hoist the red banner up on the hilltop.

Before A-kuo went into the service, his wife had given birth to two daughters. After he returned from the army, she had become pregnant again. They all hoped she would give birth to a son this time. Aunt A-ch'un had made pilgrimages to temples all over the island to make vows so that this would come true.

A-kuo stood up in the boat, his hands grasping the oars. He looked back at his two daughters, giggling and chasing the foam left by the waves as it disappeared into the sand. He

smiled wistfully. If only they had been boys, how nice things would be, he thought.

The old man gave the boat a push, but his first attempt missed the mark. He was an experienced fisherman; perhaps his strength was failing. He pulled the boat back, eyes riveted on the waves that came crashing around him. He pushed off again. The small boat slipped into the water with the rise of a retreating wave. A-kuo pulled on the oars. The old man turned around to remind his wife once again not to forget to hoist the red banner. She nodded and then took her granddaughters by the hands and led them home. Her daughter-in-law had been in labor for two days already. The midwife was at the house waiting, but still Aunt A-ch'un had wanted to see them off to sea. It was her habit.

A-kuo strained to row out to sea. The old man half squatted in the stern. The wind lashed steadily at his long, wispy silver beard. He was over sixty years old. If Aunt A-ch'un's first child had been a son, and if his first grandchild had also been a son, he could have retired long ago.

He looked up at the sky, as was his habit. They wouldn't be out on the sea very long today. Lurching forward, the boat slammed against the waves. Waves broke over the sides of the boat in a steady rhythm.

A-kuo took off his jacket. His vest hugged his broad chest. The muscles on his upper arms bulged and rippled. They hadn't caught large fish for a long time. Yesterday, during a break in the storm, their neighbor had caught a lot of fish. When it rained, large schools of fish swarmed into the shallow coastal waters to feed.

His wife was about to give birth. It wasn't her first child; why was this birth so difficult? Her belly was unusually large. The midwife said it was certain to be a boy. They had waited at home all day yesterday for the boy's arrival. They had waited in vain and hadn't caught a single fish. They couldn't afford to miss the opportunity to catch fish today.

Before leaving, A-kuo had gone to see his wife. She was moaning softly. He placed his hand on her forehead beaded with cold sweat. She gazed at him helplessly, looking weak and fragile.

Before he had gone into the army, she was still young and strong as a water buffalo. During his years in the service, she had gone to sea with her father-in-law. The sea sun and wind had robbed her of her youth and vigor. Like an ox, she had worked all day without a word of complaint. Within two years, her skin had turned dark and wrinkled.

Dark clouds spread lower and lower over the horizon. Uncle A-ch'un tossed the net into the sea with a practiced hand. The buoys bobbed wildly in the ash-green waves.

Theirs was a fairly primitive method of fishing. Since gasoline-powered fishing boats had come to the coastal waters, their livelihood had become threatened. However, they weren't willing to give it up. They believed the fish in the ocean were inexhaustible.

After spreading out the net, they looked around and began hauling it back in; silvery and speckled fish caught in the net struggled to free themselves. The largest were a palm's width. A-kuo remembered the first time he had gone to sea, when he had watched his uncle haul in a large fish. He had insisted on taking it out of the net himself. His pleasure at the time had been pure and innocent, free of any of life's worries.

"Let's go back. It's going to rain," the old man said, looking up at the sky.

"No," A-kuo replied resolutely. The red banner hadn't been hoisted up onshore yet. For the past few months they hadn't run into any large fish. His wife was very weak now and needed additional nourishment. Her last birth had been very dangerous; she had almost died. At that time, they were catching very few fish and hadn't been able to give her any additional food.

In fact, he hadn't wanted her to give birth again, though they really needed a son. But she had wanted another child. She always looked at A-kuo apologetically, as if not giving birth to a son were her fault. Even though she had been able to bear heavy physical labor, she wasn't able to bear shame.

He had to catch more fish. The fish were right under him, near the net. They couldn't escape once they came into the net. He hauled the fish in one by one. The bottom of the boat was already completely covered with fish. The waves surged around them, rising and falling, beating furiously against the sides.

He thought of his wife once again. He remembered her standing alone on the beach, gathering driftwood. They had been only seventeen or eighteen at the time. He had raced over with a fish weighing more than two pounds and thrust it at her, saying only, "This is for you." Startled, she had thrown the fish on the beach and run off. Even now he blushed when he thought of that scene.

"Let's go back. Take in the net." It was now A-kuo's turn to urge his father to return.

"No." The old man had become more and more excited. "Thirty years ago, I once caught this many." He pointed to the hold of the boat. "It looks like we could break that record today. We probably won't get another chance like this."

"Everyone else has gone back in."

"No. The red banner hasn't been put up yet."

They both believed she would give birth to a son this time. The midwife couldn't be wrong.

Raindrops as large as peas began to strike the ocean's surface. The wind and waves were growing stronger. The father and son hurried to haul in the net. Their clothes were already completely soaked.

A-kuo rowed hard. The wind blew straight into their faces. Waves kept breaking over the bow. Before them spread an expanse of mist and spray. Sometimes, the tiny craft would ride

the crest of the waves; other times, it would burrow into the wave itself. A blurred stretch of sea still lay in front of them.

Water spilled and spilled into the hull. Uncle A-ch'un bailed the water out ladle by ladle. The bulwarks sat low in the water. Indifferent, the water surged over the sides and into the boat.

"Throw out the fish!" A-kuo held the oars steady as he shouted. Uncle A-ch'un's superstition was that live fish shouldn't be thrown out, or they'd go back and warn the other fish, and he'd never catch any fish ever again.

"Throw the live ones out, too!"

"No!"

But their squabble didn't matter in the least. The rain continued to fall, and the wind continued to blow. The ocean kept curling its large tongue, licking at the boat over and over again.

"Give me an oar!"

"No, squat down, squat down!"

The wind blew harder. Now they could just barely make out objects on the shore. The betel nut tree waved at them like a gigantic hand. They were saved.

An hour later, they brought the boat ashore. They were exhausted. Two or three neighbors helped them pull the boat up onto the sand. They didn't see Aunt A-ch'un or the red banner hoisted on a pole. Did she give birth to a daughter? They hoped she hadn't given birth yet.

"Your wife's already given birth to a boy!"

"A boy! A boy!" The father and son shouted in unison. But when they saw the neighbor's somber expression, they knew something was wrong.

Could she have died? A shadow flickered across their hearts. But the two didn't dare ask.

They returned home. Several neighbors had come to look in and see how things were. The newborn baby was large and plump. He sucked vigorously on a plug of cotton soaked in honey stuck in his mouth. His mother lay exhausted on the

bed. Her face was ghastly pale, and her lips were completely colorless. She slowly opened her eyes and looked at A-kuo. She didn't speak. She had never spoken much. Aunt A-ch'un was sitting on the side of bed, stroking the sick woman's hair.

A-kuo came into the bedroom, and his mother hurriedly got up to give him the seat. His wife gave him a wan smile, as if to say she hadn't let him down. Then she closed her eyes wearily. He held her hand, hoping she wouldn't die.

In front of the bed, draped over a low cabinet, lay the red banner. No one paid any attention to it.

FIVE

The Last of the Gentlemen

Uncle Ah-shou decided that he would attend the funeral service for Uncle Chin-teh despite the fact that he could not walk too well. After all, Uncle Chin-teh had been his friend for over sixty years.

After searching for it, he found his white suit, which had been custom-made for him over forty years ago from top-quality linen. It was somewhat faded, but now, after proper ironing, it looked quite nice. He remembered that Chin-teh had also had one made, which he had not worn for a long time either. He doubted that Uncle Chin-teh's children would have thought of burying him in it.

He also found his white hat. It did not look new anymore, but after dusting it off, he found it could still be worn, though the lining was somewhat frayed.

It was very strange, however, that he could not find his white shoes. They had probably been thrown out during a thorough house cleaning. Someone should have told him, though, before throwing them away. Maybe they had, and he had forgotten.

Maybe the shoes were still around. Maybe they were under his bed or somewhere on the second floor. Actually, he could buy another pair; maybe he ought to. Now that he had found his white suit, it was only right that he should have a pair of white shoes to go with it. Chin-teh dying so suddenly was really quite unexpected.

Sunshine came through the window. The winter sun was not very strong, but it did warm him a little.

He put on his white suit and stood before the mirror looking at himself, front and back. He felt the fabric, smoothing it out with his hands, and took out a black bow tie from his pocket. A white suit, an outdated white suit, was hardly the proper attire for winter. But Chin-teh would surely have appreciated it.

Forty years ago, when he walked down the street or rode in a rickshaw wearing his white suit, white shoes, and white hat, everyone he passed, especially the women, would stop and look at him. He looked especially nice in a Western suit, better than most, for he had long legs, longer than an average person's. He had heard that a person with long legs and a short torso would have a somewhat shorter life span. But now he had outlived Chin-teh. Was it perhaps because his name meant longevity?

The suit was a little big. It had been custom-made for him. Maybe ironing had stretched it out a bit. No, he had shrunk. He had heard that, as a person gets older, he tends to shrink, just as clothing does. But now, it was the person, not the clothes, that had shrunk. Furthermore, the older you got, the faster you shrank, as if sooner or later, you could disappear entirely.

With the help of a cane, he got to the street. It was an English cane. In the old days, in fact, the cane would have been hanging from his arm, in the aristocratic manner of an English gentle-men. Now, it served to support him.

Still, he straightened up as best he could. His legs were long, a fact that had always made him proud. He was willing to pay the price of a shorter life span for them. But now his pants were too long. It seemed as though they were trying to make things difficult for his feet. He thought of rolling them up. But, no, that would make him look like a farmer. He preferred to step on them.

It was a traditional funeral service. The status of Old Town had been raised. It was now considered an old city. Still, there was no funeral home. A temporary tent was set up for this purpose. Everyone said that Uncle Chin-teh had died too soon. He disagreed. He thought Chin-teh had not died soon enough, because a person of Chin-teh's stature should have had his funeral service held in a public hall or some such place. The public hall had now become a theater.

He found a place to sit in the back. Immediately, someone came and helped him make his way to the front. It was right that he should be seated in the front; why had it not occurred to him? Perhaps it was because he did not like to be helped, or perhaps he thought the noise of the drum and the gong would be too much for him. He stared at the picture of Chin-teh. Could he bear it?

In the old days, both he and Chin-teh had joined the orchestra. In those days, among the twenty thousand inhabitants of their town, no more than five or six played instruments well enough to join. At that time, Chin-teh expressed his distaste for wind instruments and drums. Wind instruments belonged in bands, not in orchestras; harmonicas, of course, were out of the question. Chin-teh had said that the instruments for gentlemen were the strings. Both he and Chin-teh played violin.

After the incense had been offered, the person in charge of the service came over and told him he could go home now. No, he wanted to walk a distance with the funeral procession. Again and again he was urged to turn back, but he insisted on following the custom of walking all the way to Haishan Tou, the traditional spot at the end of the street. It had been quite some time since he had walked the whole distance; there was no one left in Old Town for whom he had to do this.

Only after he got there did he realize how many new buildings had been erected, taller than the old ones. He had not come this way for a long time. The road had been extended farther, but people who followed the funeral procession still turned back at the traditional spot.

Leading the procession was the band. When they reached Haishan Tou, the bandleader gave a signal, and they all put down their instruments. The other people also relaxed, turned around, and headed back, as if they were out for a stroll. It seemed to Uncle Ah-shou that they were as casual and careless about this as if it were an everyday event.

Well, he was not going to do that. Although he could not walk too well and had to go slowly, he was not just going to turn casually around and walk back. He tried to stand very straight, but his feet kept making him tilt to one side, one shoulder higher than the other. He kept his eyes on the coffin moving ahead. Very slowly and solemnly, he bowed. That was the proper etiquette. This had dawned on him once when he had seen a friend in a high position do it. Would there be anybody following his example today? People these days were so terribly crude.

From a distance, the coffin looked very low and very small. Heavy pedestrian and motor traffic along the street soon obstructed his view. Thus Chin-teh departed. All Ah-shou could hear were the sounds of the drums and gongs, sometimes clearly, sometimes indistinctly, as the distance increased. Would Chin-teh have been satisfied?

Chin-teh really had left too suddenly, without settling any-thing. Did his children have any idea what was on his mind? Uncle Ah-shou knew that if he had been the one who had de-parted today, it would have been the same with his children. For a long time, he watched the coffin disappear. Only when he started to turn back did he realize the others were all gone. He leaned on his cane and walked back the way he'd come, dragging his feet step by step.

He had not come this way for a long time, and if he hadn't had to see Chin-teh off, he most likely would not have come this way today. It was not far, but there was no reason to come here, and, too, he never thought of walking in this direction. Perhaps the next time he came this way, he would be carried along, just as Chin-teh had been carried today.

The street was full of people. Peddlers spread their wares along the street, and there were also many parked cars. Probably more people owned cars today than had owned bicycles in days gone by. He noticed that modern buildings had replaced the old ones on both sides of the street. In the old days, it was believed that the *fengshui* of Old Town was like that of a bamboo raft. In time of flood, when the river rose, flooding the surrounding areas, Old Town would be able to weather it, floating like a big bamboo raft. Tall buildings were not allowed. Actually, there were people who did not believe this and went right ahead constructing buildings with many stories. They either met with bad times or ran into other kinds of misfortune.

Now nobody seemed to believe in *fengshui* anymore. He, for one, did not believe and had never believed in it. Though his house, too, had more than one story, it wasn't like the ones along this street. This street was so narrow, it felt as though those tall buildings might collapse. It all made him very uncomfortable.

He was in front of the temple of Kuan Ti, the god of war.

"Cheap! Nothing is cheaper than this!"

He recognized a woman who was the granddaughter of the Third Master, the last person from Old Town to pass the old provincial examination. The granddaughter had been to college, but now she was peddling ready-made clothes.

"Two dollars for this. You couldn't even buy the material for that price."

She held a microphone in one hand and, in the other, a piece of clothing that she held up high, waving it back and forth. A large group of people had gathered in front of her, busily picking and choosing.

This was how she had been able to buy back the house her father had sold. The whole town was singing her praises. Her father had sold the house for over ten thousand dollars, and she had bought it back—the same house, ten years later—for one hundred thousand dollars. This was partly due to inflation and partly because the seller had given her a hard time. That alone put her beyond reproach. Still, he could not bear to see a woman screaming at the top of her lungs.

Not only could she scream, sometimes she even cursed and fought. She was short but powerfully built. When peddlers from out of town blocked the entrance to her place with their stands, she was quite capable of taking a broom to them and chasing them away. Some called it a mother hen's protective instinct toward her chicks. To protect her chicks, a mother hen would fight an eagle, risking her own life. Nowadays, money was to people what chicks were to a hen.

He had seen her after she'd been beaten up by the street peddlers. She had a black eye and was missing a front tooth. In the end, however, she'd gotten her way. Hers was the only store in front of which no peddler dared to spread his wares. Did it really have to be like this? In the old days, not many people from Old Town went to college, not even men, to say nothing of women. In the old days, a college student would not kneel down when he was out on the streets.

Uncle Ah-shou walked in the middle of the road. In the old days, he often felt uncomfortable when walking in the streets. The English walked on the left, and the French walked on the right. The Japanese copied the English, and after the war the Taiwanese switched to the right. Only much later did he realize that these weren't the same rules that drivers followed.

67

Walking in the street, one needed to keep close to the curb. This was especially true when one was with a woman; one must be sure to let her walk along the curb. He suddenly recalled that he had never walked side by side with his wife. When they did go out together, they did it the Japanese way, the man in the front, the woman following behind. He had heard it said that Japan had copied all the rules of etiquette from China. In those days there were few cars, so he always walked in the middle of the road. Today, however, things were different. The sidewalk was crowded with people, the road with vehicles, mostly motorcycles. He saw a motorcycle coming toward him, with its headlight on. Why a headlight in broad day? In the old days, he went around in rickshaws, but only the bright and shiny ones. He would not settle for anything less. That motorcyclist was approaching very fast and was headed straight for him. Perhaps the driver realized there was nowhere for the old man to go; begrudgingly, he went around him, turning back only to give him a dirty look. "You'll get yourself killed!" he swore. That was no way for a civilized person to talk!

In the old days, when he walked down the road, everybody in town would either greet him or move to let him pass. That man must have been an out-of-towner.

He was not walking fast, but he still kept stepping on his cuffs. He wanted to stick his chest out and keep his legs straight, but he could only manage a step or two before he would revert to his old shuffle again. Occasionally someone would turn around and look, but most people seemed to show little interest in him. The stores along the street had now been taken over by the next generation or by new owners who most likely did not know him. He was almost halfway home now, and he had run into very few acquaintances.

Those who did acknowledge him eyed him oddly. They acted like children staring at some old grandfather or a stranger. What was that look in their eyes? Hadn't they recognized him?

Was it respect or frightened curiosity? Or were they looking at him as they would a monkey with a chain around its neck? Was it because of his suit? Was it the way he walked?

Before, when he was walking in the funeral procession, he'd been sheltered from the pedestrians' view by the crowd. Now, all alone, he imagined this was how a naked woman might feel. Did he look ridiculous? Was he disgracing himself? He didn't care. No, it was not that he didn't care, but that he shouldn't care. He couldn't care. Forty years ago, when he had walked down the street in this same suit, everyone had stopped to admire him, especially the women. Some even whispered to their sons, "Look at that gentleman." Countless women wished their lovers, husbands, or sons to be so distinguished. How old were those sons now, and where had they gone? Had they forgotten their mothers' words? Had they ever understood them in the first place?

But it was not only the sons. Even the mothers did not know exactly what a gentleman was. They could not have known there were English gentlemen, French gentlemen, and American gentlemen. Most women did not understand the term at all, and even those who had graduated from high school could not necessarily distinguish among its various representatives.

He stood in front of a shop with electronic games. He did not like the light, much less the noise. The noise gave him a funny sensation in his teeth and made his heart skip. He had heard that this was a form of gambling. He had gambled, but not like this. To gamble was to get together a few well-bred acquaintances, drive to a hotel in Peitou, and gamble quietly, without complaints if you lost or smiles if you won. Even if one wished to smile, it should only be done inwardly.

This wasn't the way to gamble at all, crowding around like ants piling on top of one another in a sugar jar. How crude, how low, to gamble in broad daylight and right off the street. He glanced at the people inside. They were young or middle-aged. Could some of these middle-aged men be the sons of those mothers who had pointed him out as he walked down the street in his white suit?

He felt something at his feet. It was a dog sniffing at his heels. He shifted his cane slightly, and the dog quickly walked away. Even the dogs were different now. In the old days, dogs were more timid. When they saw people carrying a stick, they stayed away, only barking from a distance. They did not dare to come near. He had even heard that, nowadays, cats no longer caught mice. The dog walked over to a telephone pole as if nothing had happened. It lifted its hind leg and began to urinate, but only a little bit. Maybe it was scared after all.

Ah-shou felt himself blushing. He looked around to see if there were any children about. There were, but they did not seem to have noticed him and the dog. Children nowadays seemed neither curious nor naughty. In the old days, children would have noticed his legs and the way the dog lifted its leg and would have imitated them both. It was probably just that children today were concerned with other things, not that they were better behaved.

He reached the square in front of the temple of Matsu.

"Three for a dollar!"

The last time his daughter had come home, he and she had bought nine apples from this peddler. Three had been rotten, and the other six had had bad spots. They had not realized that the peddler had switched apples on them until they got home. Peddlers in front of the Taipei railroad station switched fruit regularly, he'd heard. His daughter had thought that since this was a small town where everybody knew everybody else, they would not dare to do this. Who would have imagined the practice finding its way here, too? It probably came with changing the status from town to city. His daughter had wanted to take the apples back. He had said it was not necessary, but she'd insisted. Even if the peddler refused to exchange them, she said, she still wanted him to know she was on to him.

At first, the peddler not only denied it but swore at them. He said if Ah-shou hadn't been so old, and his daughter hadn't been a woman, he would have let them have it. His daughter was angry and wanted to get a policeman.

"Go right ahead. We have an arrangement that only three citations get issued every month," he said as he took out some papers and waved them about.

"You must be Ah-t'ien's son." Uncle Ah-shou said.

The peddler was taken aback at first.

"Yes! But so what? We don't owe you any money. Times are different now, and people are different, too."

Ah-t'ien had been a guileless and honorable fellow. At one time, he worked as a janitor in the office. Once at the wedding dinner of a coworker, someone had told him that the dishwater was a bowl of soup, and he had actually drunk it. That Ah-t'ien's son should turn out like this came as a shock. Maybe it really was true that times had changed, and people were different, too.

He had tried to talk his daughter into going back home, but she had refused.

"It's all right with us if you won't exchange them. We're just going to stand right here and see how you conduct your business."

Sure enough, the daughter's strategy worked. Whenever a customer came along, she fixed her gaze on the peddler's hands to see if he would make a switch.

"Will you go away?" He was half pleading and half threatening. "Get the police to write me a citation," he begged. "OK. I'll exchange them," he conceded.

"Didn't you claim none of your fruit was bad?"

"Do you want to exchange them or not?"

"No."

She would not yield an inch. Finally the peddler begged her to go and agreed to give her two extra apples.

Ah-shou did not approve of his daughter. He had instructed

her on how to behave like a lady, had set stringent rules for how she should talk and act. Maybe it was true, what someone had once said: survival is primary; living is secondary. But what is survival, and what is living? Who among the people alive today had ever had to eat dried shredded yams? During the war years, he was considered a fairly important person, yet he had had to eat dried shredded yams every day.

Now Uncle Ah-shou saw the peddler again. A customer was there selecting apples. The peddler saw him, winked, and stuck out his tongue. Was he cheating people again? He wanted to hit him with his cane. No, it was not in his nature or his upbringing to do so. In the past, this cane had been a symbol of his high position; now it served to support him. The thought of using it to hit someone should never have crossed his mind.

Ah-shou turned away. Seeing the peddler today made him uncomfortable. As he turned, he sensed something strange in the peddler's look. Maybe he was seeing things. Old people tend to imagine things. He looked back at the face again. It still wore that mischievous grin. He regretted turning back to look.

Suddenly he noticed that the peddler had grown a mustache. Only a few days had passed since he'd last seen him, and now he was sporting a mustache. What's more, it was exactly like his own except for the color: the peddler's was black; his was white.

What was the meaning of this!? Was he imitating him? Was he trying to put one over on Ah-shou's daughter? He could just hear the peddler saying to his daughter, "Doesn't my mustache look just like your father's?"

"What a buffoon!" he stormed to himself. "Like a monkey washed and dressed up." He nearly said it out loud. If a sage could say something like that, surely he could, too.

His was the mustache of a poet, a musician, a gentleman. "Who do you think you are?"

The peddler held a plastic bag open with both hands so his

customer could put the apples inside. Ah-shou was shaking with anger. There was a sly look on the peddler's face.

"What a clown!"

Actually, who was the clown? He or the peddler? The peddler was obviously imitating him. Did he really look like that? Could an image that had taken six or seven decades to cultivate be so easily shattered? The more he thought about it, the more he resented it.

"Go home and shave!" he stormed to himself. He thought he must look terrible. No, he must not shave it off, no! It would be even more ridiculous if he did.

Uncle Ah-shou returned home. The only thing that gave him any comfort at all these days was the face of his daughter-in-law. Before he'd reached his house, someone from the funeral party had sent a messenger with an invitation to dinner, which was the local custom. He didn't feel like going, nor did he feel like eating. If he had to, he'd rather eat his daughter-in-law's cooking, and his daughter-in-law was in the kitchen. The sound of the spatula lightly scraping the bottom of a pan was very pleasant to his ears.

This daughter-in-law had been in his family for more than twenty years, he figured. He had always liked her cooking. It was not a matter of getting used to it.

He not only liked her cooking, he also liked to look at her. He had had this feeling the moment she married into the family. Her presence had a calming effect on him, especially since his wife's death.

Although he was aware of her soothing effect on him, he never looked directly at her. That was how it had always been, and it was still like that today.

The first time his son had brought her home, he had had a feeling that she was going to be a good daughter-in-law, good both for his son and for the family. She had come from a good family, but many girls came from good families. She did not wear heavy makeup, nor did she fuss over her wardrobe. Her look was simple and refined. She took large steps and held herself erect when she walked. She talked softly but clearly. When she handed someone something, she always did so with both hands, her heels together.

He was not alone in this; his wife had liked her, too. When his wife was ill, the daughter-in-law had cared for her diligently day and night, even through the critical period. She'd lost weight; still, she always looked neat from head to toe, and not even a trace of annoyance ever showed on her face. His wife had said she was a better daughter to her than their own daughter. Maybe that was why his wife was able to manage such a smooth departure. He could not bring himself to face his daughter-in-law these last couple of days, and the days seemed unreal when he did not see her.

His daughter-in-law had told him that his son was deeply in debt after losing the election. Could they sell the house? He knew this was his son's idea. Ah-shou had been considering it for the last few days. The only reason he considered it at all was that his daughter-in-law had been the one to bring it up. He was well aware of this.

His son had narrowly lost the election; he'd come in only a little more than one hundred votes behind the last elected councilman on the ballot. The vote buying had gone amiss. His son had given money to the district leaders, and some of them had pocketed their districts' shares. The voters did not know this; they thought he was to blame for the discrepancy in their payments.

After losing the election, his son had disappeared. Ah-shou had not seen him for several days. Every day, someone came looking for his son. They were all his son's creditors. Some of them even came to him.

These demanding creditors displeased him. In the old days, when he lent money, he was always very patient. He never dared to ask for payment. One must simply wait, and while waiting one must exhibit no anxiety or worry.

If his son did not show his face, they said, Ah-shou would have to pay his debt. If he didn't, it would be to his son's "disadvantage." Disadvantage? Did that mean they'd sue? Or use force? Well, why had they lent him money in the first place, Ah-shou wanted to ask, but he didn't. Quite a few of the creditors had urged his son to run.

He had tried to talk his son out of running. There was nothing worthwhile about being an elected official. To win such a position, one had to yell at the top of one's lungs and beg. How was this different from the beggar on the street? When he had served as an official, he had been asked to do so. At one time, he had been the head of a district encompassing six villages and towns. Among them, two had since been elevated to the status of city.

His daughter-in-law had also tried to talk his son out of it, but he would not listen. He seemed to be under a spell. Not a single word of advice would he hear. And then he even turned around and asked her to campaign for him. At first, Uncle Ah-shou was very much against his daughter-in-law's going door-to-door begging for favors, screaming until she was hoarse.

But she did not scream herself hoarse. She reasoned with the voters and told them stories. Uncle Ah-shou was told that she was very persuasive. If she had been running she might have been elected by a large number of votes.

His son, however, blamed her for not doing her best. This was really unfair. She even prayed to the gods for his success. Not only that, she also begged Ah-shou to pray for his son, too.

Uncle Ah-shou never prayed to the gods. Some said he was not a believer. In fact, it had nothing to do with believing or not believing. He would not beg from the gods simply because he would not beg. In the old days, when he was head of the district, he had prayed for his constituents. Especially during

75

times of drought, when he even put on a coconut fiber raincoat to pray for rain. That was an exception; that was not begging for himself or for his own family. Begging was not the act of a gentleman.

He had no intention of reprimanding his daughter-in-law; he even did as she asked, for he saw that she was completely selfless when she prayed. When he prayed for his constituents, he was like that, too.

He was merely praying; he did not want to get anything out of it. He knew that an election was like a war; both were equally barbaric. In warfare, there had to be a winning side and a losing side. Even though the loser was sure to be miserable, the winner would not necessarily be happy. That was how he thought about it. His son had lost, and that loss had greatly affected the whole family. This change was a terrible blow to him. It hit him harder than the death of his wife.

After the election, things calmed down, on the surface. He could tell that everybody was tired. He was tired, too.

Before the election, as a matter of fact, the family had worried about its effect on him. They were afraid it would be too much for him and that he might have a relapse, so they set up the campaign headquarters on the street. But he could feel the tension in the air.

When the election results were made final, his son just collapsed. His face turned ashen, and he couldn't speak. His daughter-in-law cried. Women cry easily, but he had seldom seen her cry. She had cried once when his wife died; now she cried again.

Once he had told his wife that he did not like to see women cry. She had understood. She never cried in her life; she only shed some tears when her illness reached a very painful stage. But it wasn't because of the physical pain; it was the pain of bidding farewell. It wasn't crying either; it was shedding tears. Actually, his daughter-in-law's crying was not crying either; it, too, was shedding tears. The brave don't shed tears lightly. He had shed some tears, too, when his wife passed away, but he'd done it alone in his own room. He'd had a good cry. Afterward, he wiped the tears away and looked into the mirror to make sure there were no telltale signs.

Unaware of all this, some people thought him cold. They did not know him and did not understand him, but he knew that his wife understood him, so he didn't care what the others thought.

His daughter-in-law, however, was not like his wife. There were certain things he could not come right out and say to his wife. A daughter-in-law like this was more than one could hope for. He doubted his own daughter could outdo her.

His daughter-in-law brought out the dishes. There was the hint of a smile on her face. The dishes were prepared according to doctor's orders. If she had not gone with him for physical therapy, he would never have recovered so quickly. He glanced quickly at his daughter-in-law. Her head was bowed; her mouth still almost smiling. How could a woman like this have campaigned in an election? How could she have told him his son wanted to sell the house? Otherwise, she'd said, his son would commit suicide.

Was this a threat? He realized his son had told her to say this. His daughter-in-law had only one fault, he thought, and this was the way she blindly followed her husband's wishes. Here, again, she differed from his own wife.

But it was the men, not the women, who were different. He would never have asked his wife to do anything against her wishes. So the problem wasn't with the women but with the men. In any event, now that the daughter-in-law had raised the question of selling the house, he must give it serious consideration.

Chin-teh's family again sent messengers urging him to come to dinner. Some took him by the arm, some nudged him toward the street, making it look like he was being disrespectful by refusing. These people were all his juniors; they ought to be less bound by convention than he was. Didn't they know any better? Didn't they know that forcing a person against his will was also disrespectful? He wanted to tell them to go away, but he forced himself to put up with them. How could they know of the close relationship between Chin-teh and himself? What kind of a friend was he, after all, if he had to be dragged to dinner? He explained to them politely that he had already eaten and now he had to rest.

He wanted to take a nap but could not fall asleep. His sleeping habits had been disrupted since the start of his son's campaign. Lately it had gotten worse. Was it because his son had lost or because his daughter-in-law had asked him about selling the house? He really couldn't think of any other reason. As all these thoughts were running through his mind, he fell asleep. He couldn't sleep when he wanted to and fell asleep when he didn't want to. This came with age, but it still made him feel strange.

He opened his eyes and found it was already dark outside his window. An afternoon nap should not have lasted so long. Now he was worried about not being able to sleep again that night.

His room used to be upstairs. He had moved downstairs after his illness. Upstairs, he used to look out over open fields, although now it was all apartment buildings there anyway.

After dark, business started up in the night market behind his house. All kinds of noises could be heard. Where the stands were now, there used to be a ditch seven or eight yards wide. Some four years before, it had been covered over. In the daytime, it served as the local market; at night, the night market took it over.

His neighbors were very happy when the ditch was covered, because their only way in and out used to be an old wooden bridge at their back door. Now that it was covered and the ditch had become a marketplace, they had chopped down a huge tree, set up stands of their own, and gone into business. Uncle Ah-shou considered chopping down the tree barbarian. Many people opposed chopping it down because they believed a spirit resided in it. He was against it for other reasons entirely, the most important being his distaste for those peddlers who made so much noise. It was the magic of modern times that had allowed the ditch to be covered, and most people welcomed it. He, on the other hand, felt like the injured party.

Then he heard another sound, television. His granddaughter had come home. This girl had just been admitted to the best high school in Taipei. She always watched television while she ate, so as not to waste time, perhaps. She turned the volume up high because of the noise outside. She kept it especially loud during commercials. As one grew older, one's hearing was supposed to deteriorate, but this noise was too much for him. How could she stand it?

His granddaughter was very pretty. She took after him in one particular aspect: her long legs. But when she ate a bowl of food standing in front of the television set, she did not take after anyone at all in the family. He knew his daughter-in-law had scolded her about this, and he had, too. Either she couldn't change or she wouldn't.

Actually, not much slipped by her. One time he had reached for a piece of food from the platter with his chopsticks, and the food had slipped. When he reached for it again, he missed and took another piece instead, because his hand was trembling. He shouldn't use chopsticks to help himself, she had pointed out, it wasn't sanitary.

He had a grandson, too, who was older and studied medicine. He was very pleased with him, not because doctors made so much money, but because, of all the professions that paid well, only doctors were thanked while being paid.

But times were changing. A while ago, a doctor in their town had been called in for tax evasion. Another doctor had been hit by a patient for being abusive. He'd heard that a doctor out of town somewhere had even got himself killed. It was hard to believe things had reached such a state.

Despite all that, medicine was still the ideal career. No, the problem with his grandson was not his profession. His grandson sometimes came home very late, whistling. In the old days, Ah-shou had considered it crude even to play the harmonica. That was nothing compared to this. What pained him most was that the boy never closed the bathroom door behind him. What kind of a doctor would act that way? When his daughter-in-law admonished him, he said he was at home and who cared?

Ah-shou recalled that when his grandson had been away at school and had had to address an envelope for the school to send his report card home in, he had not even put "Mr." in front of his father's name. He had asked him about that; his grandson said that was the way the teacher said to do it.

He was not sure he believed his grandson; still, he asked himself, was this modern education?

After dinner, more people came, the creditors. In the old days, when he had lent money, he hadn't even asked for receipts. Nowadays, a receipt wasn't even enough; money was lent using checks that had to be endorsed on the back. Were people less trustworthy these days? Indeed, people in the old days couldn't have imagined all the ways people now tried to avoid paying debts.

He realized that if all had gone well and his son had been elected, this wouldn't be happening. Could winning or losing really make such a difference? The way it looked, the house would have to be sold.

Actually, the house itself was not worth very much. But the land it sat on, close to six hundred *p'ing* of land, was worth quite a lot. What he valued, though, was the house. A house like his was a landmark in places like Old Town. All the other houses lined the street in a row and were two or three courtyards deep. Only his stood by itself. It was big and spacious with an open area all around it, and it was a perfect square. It was the talk of the town at the time it was built. No one had ever seen anything like it. He had never told anyone, but it was a copy of French architecture. He had selected all the bricks at the brickyard himself. While supervising the construction of the second floor, he had liked to go up there and look around. He had picked the spot with the best view for his room. There were always orchids in front of his window, and he would sip tea as he looked out at the fields and the farmers working there. Sometimes he went for a walk in the fields, mostly very early in the morning or at dusk. He would pause every few steps and turn around to look at his house. Now apartment houses had gone up where the fields had been. There was no place to go for a walk anymore. Most of the apartment houses were taller than his house, and he could no longer watch the sun setting from his bedroom window. After his illness, for everyone's convenience, he had moved downstairs, making his world even narrower.

Ever since his illness, he had often dreamed about the fields and the view from his window. Sometimes he saw them clearly in his dreams; sometimes they seemed mixed up with other things. He also dreamed of his wife. Immediately after her death, he often dreamed about her. Then she appeared less frequently in his dreams. Lately he had begun to dream about her again.

She was still elegant and refined, and she smiled that smile of her younger days. In his waking hours, his memory of how she looked was blurred, but she appeared very clearly in his dreams.

He also dreamed about walking out in the field and looking back at his house. It was the most unique and beautiful house in the entire township; it was like the castle of a European nobleman. This was the house his son wanted him to sell, this house in which he'd been born. How could he feel so little attachment to it?

Clearly, the house could not be saved. The view from the second floor used to span long distances, but the landscape had changed drastically over the last decade or two. All the land had changed hands, and there were only his six hundred *p'ing* left intact.

And what would it mean to keep the house? At best, he could hold on to it for however long he had left to live. As soon as he was gone, it would be gone, too. The price of land was very high now, and maintaining a house like this was no longer economical. Once the land was sold, the house would be torn down to make room for new buildings. It was only a matter of time. He did not like to admit it, but he could feel things changing with his daughter-in-law. Still, she had been the one to bring it up, and he would just as soon give her his consent.

His daughter-in-law brought him a glass of water. It was time for his medicine. There were dark circles under her eyes, which neither enhanced her beauty nor hurt her looks. Not only was his son deeply in debt, he had also disappeared. They said he had a mistress. It was proper for a French gentleman to have a mistress, but in this respect only did his son resemble a gentleman, French or otherwise. They said his mistress had campaigned very hard for him and won him quite a few votes. He was probably hiding out at her place. He had called home to contact his wife, but he would not tell her where he was or give her his telephone number.

He, too, had had affairs, but his were conducted strictly along French rules.

He had read Byron when he was young. Both the poet and his poetry were very romantic. Byron might be an Englishman, but he was an English rebel. He felt he knew Byron and imitated him, and in this he was more like a Frenchman. That was how he saw it, anyway. He felt, in matters of the heart, he had conducted himself superbly, and his wife had done the same. As for the consequences, he again considered the difference to be with the men. His wife had dealt with his affairs superbly, better than his daughter-in-law, because he had conducted himself superbly, better than his son.

Once again, he thought of his wife. Already she had been gone a few years now. Sometimes he remembered her very clearly, and other times his mind was a blank.

As a rule, women live longer than men, and usually the husband is older than the wife. Accordingly, the woman should be the one left behind. Now he was the one left behind. Which circumstances ought to be considered normal and fortunate?

One had to go sooner or later, except some had their partners there to see them off, while others had to see their partners off. Really, he should be above this sort of thing. Whether anyone was there or not to see one off should make no difference. The important thing was that both parties conduct themselves with dignity.

His wife went that way. She had never cried, even when she was in dire pain; never even moaned. The nurse even admitted she was moved; never had she seen such self-control. Would he be like her? This was what worried him.

Their illnesses were entirely different. His wife had died of cancer, and she was lucid until the last moment. In this respect, she was lucky. He had had a stroke, and he knew he would not be so lucky. He might be able to endure pain, but to be mentally disabled and dependent on others? No longer to be responsible for himself and under his own control? If that could be avoided, why not avoid it?

While alive, one should conduct oneself graciously; when departing, one should do likewise. The best way was through an overdose. He could wear his white suit. Chin-teh had left too suddenly and did not have time to decide what to wear in the coffin. The cut might be out of style, and the color was not ideal either, and it hung on him too loosely, but it was his favorite suit. He could lie very still and wouldn't even wrinkle it. In this respect, he was better off than Chin-teh.

He brought out the pills he had stashed away. They did not look like they had been touched.

He looked at the pills, and his thoughts turned to his house. Though he had only one son, he had three daughters. Should he depart like this and leave the children to decide about the house? Wouldn't it create conflict among them? If so, they would blame him, and that would not make for a gracious departure.

Actually, at the moment, his son was the one with problems. He ought to leave a little more to him than to the others, but then he would have to leave a will. He'd have to specify in his will why he was leaving more to his son. And that would hardly be fair.

How could he be fair about this? He had never thought it would be so difficult. How would a French or English gentleman handle the situation? It was a pity that he had learned only how they lived and not investigated how they died. He had never realized before that, although it only took an instant, dying could be as complicated as living.

He turned it over and over in his mind but could not find a good solution. To have no solution was the best solution. He was not satisfied with this, but he could figure out no other way.

He swallowed all the pills and drank the water his daughter-in-law had brought him. This glass of water was the last favor given to him in his lifetime, and he was very grateful. He was also very moved because his daughter-in-law had brought it to him herself. She had held it in both hands and put it down on the table carefully. She never forgot the proper behavior, even in a very difficult moment.

He lay quietly in bed, waiting. He heard a noise. At first, he did not know what it was; it sounded like a dog howling. The locals gave this sound a special meaning. They said it was a sign of imminent death. He did not believe it; nor did he care to be sent off by such an inauspicious sound.

No, it was not a dog. It was the sound of the gambling machines he'd seen today on the street. He knew he often imagined hearing things. Could it be that he was not gone yet?

He also heard the sounds of certain insects. These were sounds he liked. They came from the fields. In the old days, during the quiet of the night, he could always hear the water and the insects. Now that the ditch had been covered up, he was never able to hear the sound of water. The fields, too, were now built over. No, the sound must come from the yard around his house. Since the ditch had been covered, they could not water the flowers, so all the flowers in their yard had died, leaving only weeds. In one corner, there was a weed that grew taller than a person. He did not like these weeds at all, but he did not have the energy to get rid of them. The sound of insects could often be heard coming from their direction.

No, that was not possible either. Since the night market had sprung up, the sound of insects was blotted out by the noise of men. Was he imagining hearing the insects, too? No, he not only could hear the insects, he could also see them. They belonged to the cricket family. He could see himself, too.

He saw himself lying on his bed, wearing his white suit. The sun was shining on him, and his suit was meticulously clean; he looked elegant and refined. He even had on a pair of white shoes. He was dead. Someone was crying. Who? His daughter-in-law? His wife? There was a faint smile on his lips, though. He was at peace. He was satisfied. What a gracious death!

He had the feeling that he could not move. He ordered himself not to move. Still, he wanted to move, to get up. He woke and found his hand trapped under his body. He struggled to free it and woke completely. He felt an urge to urinate.

So it was a dream. He did not want to wake up from it, but he did. It really was a dream; he was not dead.

He wasn't dead; he really wasn't. He felt pressure in his lower abdomen. He now remembered that he had forgotten to go to the bathroom before his nap. He wanted to get up, but he felt weak in one leg. Was it because of the way he'd slept, or was he having a relapse? What if he had a relapse, and it didn't kill him but left him like a zombie or a vegetable? How awful that would be! What a disgrace! He felt he could not control his bladder. He urinated, only a little, but what a disgrace!

He felt his pants; only his underpants were wet. He noticed that his pants were not buttoned. If he had died, who would have been the one to find him with his pants unbuttoned? His son or his daughter-in-law? If it were his daughter-in-law, would she have buttoned them for him?

He tried again and managed to prop himself up. He went out to the bathroom. He suddenly remembered the dog he'd seen that morning, lifting its hind leg.

He returned to his bed, and just when he was about to lie down again, he heard the sound of running water. He had wanted to flush the toilet but had turned on the faucet instead. How could he have made such a mistake? It was not the first time, either. The modern toilet was a part of Western culture. Of course, he could handle it. He went back out to turn off the faucet and flush the toilet.

He felt a numbness in his leg, but it did not feel like a relapse. He had a feeling that he would sooner or later have a relapse. Since taking pills could not solve his problem, apparently he would have to resort to other means while he was still able to decide on his own fate.

But none of the ways he considered were any good. None of them could be called an elegant way to die. The most elegant way was still an overdose. But it hadn't worked. He wasn't sure whether the druggist had given him the wrong medication, or whether his daughter-in-law had switched them. Well, if they wanted him to live, he'd live.

He had no confidence left in either life or death.

He lay back on his bed again and closed his eyes. After the trip to the bathroom, he felt much better. Again, he saw himself in his white suit and stretched out on his bed. Sunshine poured through the window. How very peaceful.

Secrets

I

Shu-fen and Chien-jen had walked back and forth along the river six times already. Side by side, they kept a good five to ten inches between them.

Chien-jen had finished three cigarettes. Each time he would flick the smoldering butt into the water, the glow arching into the darkness, landing with a tst.

December brought few people out, aside from the three or four young couples who passed them.

Wind rippled across the water, the waves lapping at the banks. The ocean tides left a taste of salt in the air. Shu-fen was quite warm from walking, despite the chill wind.

Shu-fen and Chien-jen had seen each other almost twenty times now over the past two months. They had gone to movies and spent time together in coffeehouses, but Chien-jen had not made any further moves toward Shu-fen. And he had yet to say anything affectionate, like "I love you" or even "I like you."

He certainly wasn't a man of many words. She could hardly

believe he could ever have sold cars or that now he was assistant sales manager of a car dealership.

"Your lips are quite thin," he commented for the fifth or sixth time. She wondered if this was the way he described an automobile's special features to customers. If he would only say he liked thin lips, perhaps she could consider marrying him.

She was twenty-eight; he was thirty-six. Their ages were compatible enough. She had assumed that, at this stage of the game, she probably wouldn't marry at all, or, if she did, she could not hope for much romance. Yet he was proving a disappointment to even her minimal expectations.

She moved a little closer to him. But before she knew it, he had already shifted ever so slightly away. Again, she edged toward him, and again he edged away. He was sandwiched between her side and the water, and she was seriously tempted to just push him in.

He seemed completely unaware of her feelings and took another pack of cigarettes from his pocket.

"May I smoke?" He asked politely.

She certainly wasn't expecting this kind of courtesy. Every time she came home from a date with him she told herself that it was the last time. But when he called again, she felt she couldn't refuse. Why was that? She often asked herself that very question.

"Mm." She had already decided if nothing happened before he finished this cigarette, she would just walk away from him and this wretched river once and for all, not caring whether she saw him again for the rest of her life.

"Your lips are very thin," he repeated. "I've heard that people with thin lips are good talkers."

"What would you know about good talkers?" she wanted to scream at him.

He took another pull from his cigarette and flicked it into the river.

"We should leave," she kept telling herself, yet her feet matched his pace, step for step.

Why was that? Could it be tonight's moon? Or was it that she liked him? Or was it just that she was twenty-eight and not married? She certainly couldn't think of anything she liked about him. Perhaps the most she could say was that she didn't dislike him.

He was merely a man, plain and ordinary and, what's more, already thirty-six years old. Perhaps he made a good salary. Aside from that, aside from that . . .

The moon illuminated his wide forehead and receding hairline. It also revealed a few gray hairs. In contrast, his eyebrows appeared even more thick and coarse.

Why doesn't he mention how pretty the moon is tonight? He said she was good with an abacus. Did he mean this as flattery or criticism?

If you were in the securities business, you had to know how to use an abacus. She'd heard it said that those who worked in securities were even more money hungry than bankers. When he said she was good with an abacus, he must have meant she was proficient.

"I'm only at grade two or three. You couldn't really say I'm good."

Exhausting. This was a date? So this was what dating at twenty-eight was like? She wanted to turn around and leave. Leave forever.

"May I smoke another one?" He never forgot to ask.

"Please."

The first time she went out with him, she was afraid he would try to take her hand. Back then, she had wondered what she should do if he tried that. Should she withdraw it? Now she was wondering why he didn't take her hand. After two months of seeing someone, was this progress? If he took her hand now, would that be some kind of proposal?

SECRETS

But all he held in his hand was a cigarette. His cigarette hand was always the one nearest her.

So, was this love? They had been introduced to each other two months before. Was being introduced an impediment to love?

He was so aloof. Was that his personality? Or was it because he had had a failed love affair? There must be a reason he wasn't married at the age of thirty-six. She had thought of asking one of her coworkers for advice, but then, if things didn't work out, wouldn't that just be one more person who knew about it?

"The moon is very pretty tonight."

Hearing this, her heart jumped. This might be the high point of the evening.

She turned and looked at him. His eyes seemed thoughtful as he gazed into the distance. The moonlight made them look even more deep and solitary than usual. Perhaps he was thinking about the moon. No. He always had that look. Perhaps that was why she couldn't leave.

"Yes, it's really beautiful."

She couldn't believe she couldn't come up with a better response. This was the moment she'd been waiting for, and this was all she had to say. Infuriating. She felt like crying.

Perhaps a good cry would be the best thing.

After her last disillusioning affair, she'd decided that she had had it with men.

She didn't meet her classmate Hsueh-ching's brother until she was a junior in high school. Although she'd been to their house several times, he had never been there. She'd heard he was quite a talented guitar player. The day she met him, she had heard him strum a few songs. When she went home, he was all she thought about. That year, she didn't make it into college. Then, not long after that, he left for the United States to study. She decided the only way for her to be near him would be to study hard, get into college, and then go to the States for graduate school. Even now she regretted wasting that year. Never had she imagined that within a year he would have married an American girl. She heard that the American girl had also been drawn in by his guitar. She tore up the proof of her virginity, resolved never to marry, abandoned her college plans, and went to work for a securities firm. She hated her demeaning job but chose to accept it as her part of her punishment.

As time passed, she began to realize she had done a foolish thing. Love should be a two-way street. Although friends and relatives introduced her to some eligible bachelors, none of them compared with Hsueh-ching's brother, and she couldn't make herself go out with them.

One year after another passed. It became increasingly difficult even to get introduced to men. People told her that this was life's most crucial period, but for her it remained a blank, waiting to be filled.

So was this her aborted affair? Had Chien-jen also been through something similar? Did men also bury such experiences in their hearts?

"Should a person have secrets?" As soon as these words left her mouth, she felt she'd said something silly.

"What?" He sounded a bit surprised.

She'd really just been asking herself, but now it sounded like she was questioning him.

"Some say the moon likes to keep secrets for us." She thought she could cover her slip by adding this, but her companion still heard it as an inquiry.

"Some people like the moonlight for hearing secrets; others like the moonlight for telling them. But even when they've been told, they are still secrets, aren't they?"

She never expected to hear something like this from him. She was almost moved to tears. So this day wasn't a total waste, after all. As a matter of fact, this life wasn't either.

"Everybody has secrets," he continued.

SECRETS

"No, please, you don't need to say anything," she quickly interrupted him.

"Over ten years ago, I was teaching in the countryside."

"Please, don't."

He stopped and looked up as if tonight were the first time he had ever seen such a beautiful moon. This thought by itself was enough for her.

She believed everyone was entitled to secrets. It wasn't that she was worried she'd have to tell hers if he told his. It was just that, if everything was out in the open, it would seem as bald as a scrubbed radish. When her father suggested that couples who had been together for a few months should look into each other's background, she had objected furiously. She felt this would be stooping even lower than working at the securities firm.

"Isn't the moon beautiful?" He turned back to their old subject.

The reflection of the town's scattered lights stretched across the wide river toward them, twinkling in no particular pattern. The silhouettes of boats bobbed up and down.

"Too bad we can't see the reflection of the moon in the water."

Above their heads, the moon was just starting to go down behind them.

"Those people out in their boats can see it."

"Maybe if we lean out over the water we can see it." As she said this, she leaned as far as she dared out over the bank, craning her neck.

"Can you see it?"

"Not yet."

She thought he was going to take her hand so she could lean out a bit more. What was wrong with this guy? Was he incapacitated somehow? And if that was so, why did he keep on asking her out? Even if she fell into water, she wasn't sure he would reach out to save her.

They started walking along the river bank again. Now that he had brought up the moon, she wasn't going to let the subject drop. This was the first time they had ever walked as far as the river bend. But still they could not see the moon reflected in the water.

"Look over there."

Beside a small shed ran a black pipe that extended out into the river.

"We could definitely see it from there," she said, taking off her shoes and walking across the sand.

Suddenly, for no reason, this seemed more important than even the moon itself, as if only seeing its reflection could save the evening from being a total loss.

"Will you break the pipe?"

"I don't care," she answered as she stepped unsteadily onto it.

"Be careful," he shouted. "Can you see it?"

She didn't answer. Looking at the pipe extending into the middle of the river, she felt she just had to walk to the end of it. And suddenly that seemed more important than seeing the moon.

"Wait a second," Chien-jen called from behind, trotting after her. "Hold onto my hand."

Perched on the pipe, almost afraid to believe her ears, she shifted her feet carefully. The wind was blowing from all sides. She felt cold and shivered slightly, but she still wanted to get out there. Turning a bit, she grabbed hold of his hand.

"Now can you see the moon in the water?"

"A long time ago, there was a poet called Li Po. He wanted to dive into the water to retrieve the moon."

"So I've heard."

"I've got this urge to go into the water, just like Li Po." Looking up, she could see the moon in his eyes.

He said nothing.

"I feel like following the moon with my eyes, up, up, up, and then falling backward into the river. That would be beautiful."

"The water's deep. And it might be cold, too."

"No. Right now I forbid you to say anything about how deep or cold the water is. I even forbid you to tell me if you can swim."

"I can't ask any questions?"

"No questions. In Kaohsiung, the Love River is completely foul, but it's still the Love River. As long as there's moonlight, the moon is still the moon, even if man has already landed on it. Just look up at the moon and fall in."

At this point she realized his hand was sweating. She had been holding on tightly all along, but now he was holding on tightly, too.

"Don't say anything or ask anything, okay?"

"Mm."

For that split second, when she felt herself hovering in the air, only one thing was on her mind: the moon was exceptionally bright and large.

II

Shu-fen entered the emergency ward. It was filled with patients, some on IVs, some breathing through oxygen tubes, some bandaged and quietly resting, some crying out. Many doctors and nurses milled about, some bustling busily, others taking their time.

Hsiang-hua said she hadn't found out anything.

Hsiang-hua was her coworker at the securities firm. This was all her idea.

Not long after Shu-fen and Chien-jen had gotten married, Shu-fen noticed that Chien-jen would either leave the house early or would come home late. Sometimes when something would come up, she would call his office and be told he had already left.

When she asked him where he'd been, he always came up with some excuse. Sometimes he'd met a friend or bumped into an acquaintance. Sometimes he'd been with a customer. Sometimes, he said sheepishly, he'd just been out walking, or he'd gone to the park to watch people practicing tai chi.

Sometimes, after she'd asked him where he'd been, he would come home a bit earlier or leave a bit later. But after a few days, he would go back to his old routine.

Tailing him was Hsiang-hua's idea, and it had Shu-fen very upset. To do such a thing after less than two months of marriage! She wasn't the kind of person to tail a man or to work in securities! She had said as much to Hsiang-hua. But Hsiang-hua had insisted. There must be another woman. A woman had to protect herself. Furthermore, Hsiang-hua was willing to follow Chien-jen herself on her scooter.

Hsiang-hua followed him three times, once in the morning and twice in the evening, and discovered nothing. Twice, she saw Chien-jen enter the emergency ward in the hospital, walk toward the surgical ward, and exit from the rear. Another time, it was just the opposite: he entered from the rear, passed through the surgical ward, and exited via the emergency ward. Although the direction was reversed, the path was exactly the same. That time, it had been morning, and he had stopped at the hospital shop, bought a bottle of milk, and read a newspaper. Once, in the evening, he had gone to a park to admire the flowers. All three times, he didn't even so much as nod to anyone.

Although she hadn't seen anything, Hsiang-hua insisted something was wrong. Especially since he'd taken the same route. That had to mean something, and it probably involved another woman. Most likely, it was a nurse. According to Hsiang-hua, some men had a thing for nurses dressed in white.

Following Hsiang-hua's observations, Shu-fen prepared to go to the hospital, walk to the rear, and then walk back through to the emergency ward.

Chien-jen and Hsiang-hua had only ever seen each other once, and that was at the wedding, so Hsiang-hua only needed to wear sunglasses to disguise herself. But Shu-fen couldn't get away with that. She could only go at some time of day when Chien-jen wouldn't be there, when there might not be anything to see. But Hsiang-hua said that was better than nothing.

She did, of course, have some misgivings about Chien-jen.

She still remembered their walk along the river. He hadn't seemed in any rush to get close. This had made her suspect he had some kind of psychological or physical problem. But his behavior indicated he was simply playing hard to get with her.

She had almost been taken in by his "water's deep" and "might be cold, too." When she hadn't let him ask if she could swim, she gathered that he couldn't swim either but would be willing to jump into the water with her. Actually, he was an accomplished swimmer. He had entered several swimming competitions and had won a medal.

Perhaps he had noticed someone following him; a woman wearing sunglasses in the hospital wouldn't be hard to miss. But Hsiang-hua had said he hadn't; she was willing to swear to it.

She should, of course, trust Chien-jen. On the other hand, weighing Chien-jen's silence against Hsiang-hua's suspicions, how could she know what to believe? Chien-jen was gentle and quiet and honest, certainly not salesman material. Yet he must be an outstanding salesman, otherwise how else could he ever have risen to assistant manager of the sales department?

Turning this over and over in her mind brought no comfort.

Up till now, she had noticed nothing, but Hsiang-hua's suspicions had shown her the light. Just like the last time, she seemed to be the initiator when in fact she was being manipulated like a puppet. This made her even more determined to be on her guard.

Thinking back to when she had gone into the water, it seemed she'd set the whole thing up. She didn't admit this to anybody.

Back then, she'd been rather reckless. Romance was something everybody was entitled to pursue. For a woman to experience love once: was this asking too much? But what was love? A river of freezing water? A river of freezing water was certainly an unforgettable experience. She had a hard time thinking of it as a ploy.

The more she thought about it, the more uneasy she felt. She'd been so cold, she had shivered, and he had taken her home. Dropping her off, he'd kissed her lightly, and she was his. Not a word of proposal was ever spoken.

He seemed warm and considerate. She considered him faultless. But according to Hsiang-hua, warmth and kindness were a man's weapons. If they seemed exaggerated or self-conscious, one should be especially careful. Hsiang-hua was right.

She walked to the courtyard behind the gate. In the courtyard was a pond teeming with carp and beside the pond grew several palm trees. Under the palms were a number of shoots, perhaps palm seedlings, which resembled a miniature grove.

Hsiang-hua hadn't said anything about a pond. Shu-fen didn't stop. She walked to the surgical ward and, following Hsiang-hua's instructions, turned into the central hallway. Doctors, nurses, patients, and visitors were all milling about. Some of the patients were in wheelchairs, some were being walked around, some lay on stretchers, some were carrying their own IV bottles, which dripped into their veins. She saw one patient with a hole in his temple. Frightened, her head suddenly started to swim. She groped for the wall and closed her eyes.

She stood there for a moment before opening her eyes again and continuing toward the hospital shop. The whole hospital was full of doctors, nurses, and patients. Only she was an alien in this little world. On second thought, perhaps she belonged to it somehow through Chien-jen.

The cashier in the shop was very pretty. She wore white just like the nurses. So it was here that Chien-jen drank his milk and read newspapers. Hsiang-hua said he didn't even look up.

So why did he come here? She agreed with Hsiang-hua: there had to be a reason.

She lingered by the shop for a moment and then continued toward the rear. There she found a parking lot and a basketball court. Beside the basketball court was a garden full of flowers, including roses and cherry blossoms, brilliant in the light.

She liked cherry blossoms. She didn't want to stay there too long, so she just walked around a bit. Again, she discovered nothing. Maybe it had something to do with the time of day.

Turning from the garden, she looked at the parking lot. Just as she was planning to head back, she saw a small group of people coming quickly toward her.

Two men whizzed passed with a stretcher holding a person swaddled in a white sheet. At first, she wondered why this patient was all wrapped up. And why was the head wound so tightly it resembled some decapitated character out of a Peking opera? Two women, weeping, followed the stretcher, but there were no tears, perhaps because they were walking so quickly.

She saw the procession turn toward a corridor where a sign read "Mortuary."

Feeling faint again, she reached out to lean against a pillar. She thought she might vomit.

So she had come all this way to find answers, and all she'd met with was a corpse.

III

"Tse-tse."

"Zinga!" The cicadas were crying.

Shu-fen gazed out the window. The eucalyptus tree across the courtyard touched the railing of the fourth floor. So the cicadas were up there.

These seemed to be the first cicada sounds of the year. Summer had arrived a bit late. The cicadas on the ground were getting impatient, which meant their cries were even louder.

She had heard that there was one type of cicada that lay in the ground dormant for seventeen years and then climbed out of its hole, lived for three or four weeks, cried for a short time, and then quietly died.

Was this what life meant? Shu-fen turned to look at Chien-jen. Chien-jen was lying in bed, his mouth slightly open, sleeping, breathing rhythmically.

He had already lived thirty-six years, twice the cicada's hibernation period. She looked at his face. His forehead lost its three small furrows when he slept.

Today was Sunday. Sunday was the only day he didn't visit the hospital; Sunday belonged to her alone. But she did not dare to feel self-confident.

Thinking over her visit to the hospital, she felt increasingly uncomfortable. All she'd discovered there were the remains of some poor departed soul headed for the mortuary.

The more she thought about it, the angrier she got. But Hsiang-hua had said she was right to go to the hospital; what's more, she should do it again. No! she protested to herself. Just thinking about it made her want to retch. There was no way a man could be thirty-six and never have slept with a woman. She had to find out what was behind all this, Hsiang-hua urged, promising to do anything further she could to help.

Why on earth did Chien-jen go to the hospital? To look at corpses?

Impossible. He had to have a reason. But what? He alone knew.

She wanted to come right out and ask him. The night before, she had made up her mind to do just that. She couldn't stand it any longer.

A woman had a right to some romance when it came to love. But this unmentionable secret of her husband's was another matter. On the one hand, getting to the bottom of it could damage their relationship; on the other, if it did involve another woman, what did she have to lose?

She took another look at Chien-jen. He was sleeping soundly, mouth still slightly open. The whirring of the cicadas outside had no effect on him.

She reached out to touch his lips but decided against it and slowly drew her arm back again. The sun had already turned things a golden yellow. It was time for him to get up. It was time for her to clear up the mystery.

Why was he going to the hospital? There had to be an explanation. Should she ask him? Or should she listen to Hsiang-hua and continue having him tailed? She felt that stalking him wasn't right, wasn't proper. What's more, she couldn't stand it any longer.

"Tse-tse!" The dry whir of the cicadas was unrelenting. She raised her hand. She wanted to smack him on the cheek but then stopped herself. Sometimes, she actually considered striking him. She wanted to wake him, to ask him why he went to the hospital.

Ever since she'd learned about Chien-jen's visits to the hospital, she'd felt there was something standing between them, even when they were being intimate. Maybe his going to the hospital meant nothing at all. No, that was impossible. Who would go to the hospital for no reason?

She tapped him. Too lightly. No, too hard. She seemed to be losing control of herself.

Startled, Chien-jen opened his eyes. Should she ask him or shouldn't she?

"Oh, it's only you. What time is it?" He blinked his eyes as if looking for something.

"Eight-thirty."

He reached out and took her hand.

"I think everyone should have a secret."

"What . . . are you talking about? Sounds like you have something on your mind."

"Well, even husbands and wives need to keep their own secrets."

"Are you saying I have some kind of secret? Don't you remember that that night I had wanted to tell you something?"

Thinking of that night, she remembered how she'd thought Chien-jen was even harder to figure out than a stock certificate. As for herself, that night she had felt like a cat dragged out of water. Now he embraced her, wanting to kiss her.

"No."

"What's the matter?"

"Chien-jen, I'd like to ask you something."

"What?"

"A friend told me she's seen you going to the hospital a few times." She went on, "But if you don't want to say anything, we can forget it."

"Shu-fen, there's nothing that can't be said. That night, I really wanted to tell you, but you didn't let me. Now you're asking me."

"You don't have to tell me."

"Don't you want to know?"

"Don't tell me if you don't feel it's necessary."

Then he told her how, ten years before, he'd gotten a teaching position in a small town outside of Taipei. Taipei's urban sprawl hadn't quite reached this old village, despite its proximity. The residents were still fairly rustic. He got to know a girl who worked in a small store. Their relationship had reached the point where they were discussing marriage, but the girl's family had balked at his being a teacher. Teaching didn't have any future, they said, and protested strongly.

He loved her, and she loved him. He decided he would make love to her, thus claiming her, so her family wouldn't be able to object. Originally, he wasn't planning to tell her, but then he didn't want to trick her like that. At first, she was afraid; eventually, she consented.

He took her to a hotel. If he had taken her to one in Taipei, their plan might have worked. But he hadn't counted on her family being on their guard. That little town had only two hotels. As soon as they checked in, someone alerted her family. They brought along a whole gang, beat him up, and even called the police.

Although the girl was of age, this was a small, conservative town. The news spread like wildfire. He was an elementary school teacher, a role model in the community. There was no way he could stay.

Immediately, he resigned, went to Taipei, and began working for a relative. He resolved to forget about the girl, forget that place, forget the whole affair.

About six months later, he got a call from her unexpectedly. Her father wanted to marry her to a local businessman involved in construction. But she was defiant; she'd rather run away with him.

They had made their arrangements, and she had asked a relative to give her a ride to Taipei. But on the way, along Chung-hwa Road, they had had a collision. The relative died at the scene. She was taken to the hospital. After five hours, she died, too.

He, in the meantime, had no idea what had happened. He waited at the place where they had agreed to meet. Hour after hour passed. He waited late into the night, but there was still no sign of her. He considered every possibility, but hadn't they made a pact? That should have outweighed any obstacle. Once more, he felt like a fool. And this time it was even more outrageous. He cursed her. Who would have thought that, at just that moment, she was drawing her last breath?

Outraged, he banished her from his thoughts. It was about three months later that he heard the news of her death, that he learned she had died for him. She'd been taken to the hospital and prepared for surgery, he learned, but before anything could be done, she'd died.

After that, he started visiting the hospital. Although he had also visited her town's cemetery, there were so many graves there, it was impossible to find hers. He could pay homage best at the hospital, where she had spent her last moments.

"So that's my secret. It's really quite commonplace."

"Commonplace?"

Yes, commonplace. A story that could happen anywhere, anytime. But she couldn't let it go. He said he had taken the girl to a hotel. She was still unclear about what had happened there, but she could not ask any more questions.

"So, for the past ten years, you haven't cared about any other women?"

"It's not that I haven't, it's just that . . ."

"Just that you can't forget her."

"Shu-fen, I go to the hospital to forget her." He paused and then continued, "Shu-fen, I hope you believe what I've said."

Still silent, Shu-fen slowly turned her gaze to the window.

"Zing-z zing-a!" The cicadas were crying again. They sounded even more frantic now. A shadow darted by the window. A sparrow caught a cicada in its mouth and sped off.

IV

Already seven o'clock, and no sign of Chien-jen. Was he at the hospital again? Yesterday and the day before he hadn't come back till seven. She'd asked if he'd gone to the hospital. He had said no. Even though he denied it, did he think he could conduct this affair openly now that he'd confessed his secret?

Shu-fen seated herself in front of the dressing table mirror and adjusted the wig.

After Chien-jen had revealed his secret on Sunday, she assumed he would stop going to the hospital. But, although he denied going there, she couldn't believe him.

Well, Hsiang-hua had told her Chien-jen had a problem. Now, she didn't need anyone else to tell her that; she knew it herself.

"Bzzzzz!" The entrance bell rang.

She looked at her watch one more time, straightened the wig, and went to the door to greet him.

His footsteps on the stairs were as heavy now as they had been two months ago when they were first married. Tired? They were on the fourth floor, it was true, but he was only thirty-six. Was coming home that bad? Or was it another sign that he was finding pleasures elsewhere?

She remembered that her parents didn't altogether approve of their marriage. There must be something wrong with a man who wasn't married by thirty-six.

From the outset, they had advised her to find out a few things about him, but she had adamantly refused. That would be too much like an arranged marriage. And if they tried to ask around, she said she'd cancel the wedding plans. If there was anything wrong with him, she wanted to find it out for herself. Although they'd been introduced to each other, she wanted it to be just as if they'd met on their own.

She opened the door, set out a pair of slippers, and took his briefcase.

"Thanks."

For the past two months, every day was pretty much like this. She'd told him from the start that there was no need to thank her. It seemed so formal. He'd said there was no need to get his slippers. But she got off work earlier and got home first, she said; getting his slippers was nothing. They'd never really reached a resolution. So it became their pattern for one to bring slippers and the other to express thanks. Today, when she squatted down, she tried to keep her back straight as she looked up. Her posture felt completely unnatural; she didn't know whether he had noticed anything.

"How do you like my hair today?" She didn't mean to say anything, but it just slipped out.

"Hm." He barely glanced at her.

Dinner was ready, she told him.

"Okay, let's eat."

From what he said and did, she tried to guess whether he'd gone to the hospital. His voice and actions were the same as ever. Was this proof that he had gone? Or that he hadn't?

He didn't eat much, but he wasn't particularly picky. In this respect, he was easy to take care of. At first, she had thought he'd eat anything, so long as she had made it. But now she thought the opposite was probably just as true.

After dinner, as always, he watched television. For over two months, the same routine, day in and day out. Smoking, watching television quietly. The day the Pope was shot was the only time he responded to it out loud, cursing softly.

Did he want a shower? Would he like her to turn on the hot-water heater? No, he said, it was too hot outside. Cold water would be fine. This meant he wasn't interested in taking a shower with her.

Maybe he didn't know she was pregnant. She hadn't told him she couldn't take a cold shower because she was pregnant. She only said she didn't like cold water. At first, she had wanted to tell him, but maybe this could be her secret.

While Chien-jen was bathing, she stood by the window looking out, gazing at the dark shadow of the eucalyptus tree across the garden. The cicada's zinging had stopped. Three days before, a sparrow had eaten it.

She patted her wig. It felt a bit strange wearing one.

Sometimes she had to admit that letting Hsiang-hua tail him had been going too far. But if it weren't for Hsiang-hua, she'd still be in the dark about a lot of things. In fact, she believed there was still at least one thing he was keeping from her.

Everyone should have secrets, she thought. But some are tolerable, and some aren't. What Chien-jen wasn't telling her was the core of his secret. Because he wasn't telling her the most important part, she had to suspect his whole story.

When he emerged from his shower, he'd watch television if there was anything good on; otherwise, he'd read the papers. The first thing he did in the morning was read the papers. Then he'd go to the office and read the papers some more. Hsiang-hua had seen him reading the papers at the hospital store. When he got home, he'd keep reading the papers. She had heard that men were like that these days.

She ran hot water in the shower, although it was summer. Her face was too pale. Hot water would bring out a little color.

She took off the wig before bathing. She caressed her freshly shaved scalp. This afternoon, when she'd had her head shaved, the skin had shimmered with a bluish tinge like a billiard ball. But her hair was already starting to grow back, and her scalp felt a little fuzzy.

Standing in front of the misted mirror, she wiped a circle clear. A reflection emerged. Perhaps because of the light or the time of day, the bluish tinge was fading. But it was still such a ludicrous sight. In Hong Kong, she had been told, people ate monkey brains. The monkeys were still alive, but they were rendered unconscious. The crowns of their skulls were cut off, and their brains eaten with little spoons. First, though, their heads were shaved. She looked like a shaved monkey._

Today, she had finished her accounts early and gone to her beauty salon, where she asked to have her head shaved. Incredulous, the hairdresser had asked her twice to repeat herself.

"Shave it. It's none of your business why. Just get to work."

Everyone in the salon had turned to stare. She had just closed her eyes and kept silent. She'd wanted to cry but saved her tears until she got home. Her heart was breaking. After the

107

hairdresser finished, she had taken a wig from her purse and fitted it on in front of the huge mirror.

The wig looked very much like her real hair. Chien-jen had barely responded to her question. Maybe he just didn't notice her hair. At least he didn't notice anything peculiar.

She emerged from the shower wearing only a sheer gown. Perhaps because the water had been so hot, she continued to perspire; her gown stuck to her body.

Chien-jen was sitting at the desk reading *The Dream of the Red Chamber*. She used to think he wanted to be a *Red Chamber* scholar. He collected various editions of the *Red Chamber* as well as various commentaries and critiques. She thought this was a good hobby for someone to have, something out of the ordinary. At least, it showed some culture. Only yesterday had she finally unveiled his secret.

After hearing his story, she felt there was still something he wasn't telling her. When he wasn't home, she carefully went through his belongings. He didn't keep a diary. She watched how he read the *Red Chamber* and thought she might find an essay or something folded between the pages. She flipped through the books. There weren't any marks on them. Then she noticed some had bookmarks, all placed in the section with Miao-Yu, the Buddhist nun character in the book. And all the books were well thumbed in that same section.

Why? Why did he only read about Miao-yu? At first, she was baffled. Then she remembered his scrapbook containing pictures of Buddhist nuns clipped out from newspapers and books. Most were movie stars dressed up, although some really were nuns.

Why? Why? She kept asking herself.

Then she suddenly remembered how, when she was in the corridor leading to the mortuary, the head of that corpse had been swaddled with a sheet. Was it a man or a woman? There was no way to tell with the hair wrapped like that. Maybe there wasn't any hair.

So did Chien-jen go to the hospital to look at dead people? To bring back the memory of that girl entering the mortuary?

Yes! That was it! The girl hadn't died immediately after the collision. She remembered she had even been prepared for surgery. Shu-fen's own aunt had had all her hair shaved when she had to have brain surgery.

That was it. That had to be it.

"Chien-jen, you should come to bed." She spoke in her sweetest voice. It sounded a bit artificial even to her own ears.

"You go ahead."

"How do you like my hair?"

"Nice. It's nice."

"Did you get a good look at it?" She swept off the wig.

"Shu-fen . . ." Chien-jen choked on his words, completely stunned.

"Chien-jen, am I beautiful like this?" Her eyes closed, she heard him get up, his chair falling backward.

"What are you doing?"

"Are you angry?"

"I just don't understand."

"Would you say I look like Miao-yu or not?"

"Miao-yu?"

"The nun in *Dream of the Red Chamber*. Would you say I look like her?"

He said nothing.

She went on, "People should have secrets. I'm not against secrets. I'd just like to break down some of these walls standing between us."

"Since you're the one who brought it up, now I want to ask you if you ever slept with another man before me."

This was exactly the question she wanted to ask him but had never had the chance. Now, ironically, he was asking her. She felt his eyes boring into her, her skull, her breast.

"No," she replied, not hesitating.

"So you're a woman without secrets?"

"No. A person can't be without secrets. And now I'll tell you a very important secret."

"An important secret?" His eyes were still boring into her. She had never seen this look before.

"You're going to be a father."

She lowered her head, and the corners of her mouth quivered. She felt like smiling, but she knew this wasn't a smile.

SEVEN

God of Thunder's Gonna Getcha

T'ien-sung's wife had spread out a large square cloth on the bed and was slowly straightening the corners. Her fingers were short and rough. Her fingernails were hard and thick, with dirt-lined cracks that never washed clean. She laid her clothes on the cloth piece by piece, smoothing each one out with her hands. Tears ran down her cheeks. She couldn't remember how many times A-chin had kicked her out, but she had never cried before.

Yesterday she had come in from the countryside. She had been afraid that A-chin might kick her out again, so she wasn't even going to unpack. But she had really wanted to stay for a few days.

In the past, A-chin had kicked her out, but never as fiercely as today. It was all the fault of A-hsueh. A-hsueh must have said something bad about her to him. She didn't know what A-hsueh had said. But she was sure that was what had happened.

Smoothing out her clothes piece by piece made her feel a little better. A-chin had changed. It seemed he got annoyed just looking at her, so seeing him made her afraid.

"Go back! Go back, today!" he had said to her sharply.

She had come a long way, and she should have stayed for a few days at least. It wasn't that she liked the city, but she had hoped to help out for a while. Who would have thought he'd kick her out again? He wanted her to leave today. The way he had spoken to her did not leave her the choice of staying. A-chin had never spoken to her like this before. Even if he had wanted her gone, had told her it would be better if she went back to the countryside, he would always let her stay for one more day.

In the past, it had never been like this. A-chin had always listened to her. She still remembered when he was small and didn't dare not listen. She remembered a time A-chin and his friends had gone swimming in the creek. When she had found out, she had taken a bamboo stick like the kind used to herd water buffalo and hurried to the creek. She'd unhooked the pants he'd left hanging on a pandanus tree branch and called him over.

"You can do anything else you want, but you must stay away from water and fire. They can kill you. I forbid you to go swimming, especially in this creek, which flows so fast." That was what T'ien-sung's wife thought about water and fire. Stark naked, A-chin had run all around her, clamoring for his pants. Losing her temper, she had lunged at him, but he had darted off and started running home. She had chased after him, still holding the bamboo stick and his pants. She hadn't caught up with him till she'd reached home; A-chin had had to kneel while she'd smacked him twice with the stick.

"God of thunder's gonna getcha!" she had sworn. In those days, she'd often yelled at him that way. It had always hurt her to beat him, so she would yell this at him. And when he wouldn't let her catch him to beat him, she would also yell this at him. But she would never yell anything worse than this.

"God of thunder's gonna getcha!" The phrase seemed to

resound in her memory. She repeated it to herself as she smoothed out her clothes.

"God of thunder's gonna getcha!" How long had it been since she'd used this expression? She had almost forgotten it entirely. And she couldn't remember when she'd given it up.

"The god of thunder is going to get you." The more she said it, the clearer and louder it became. Saying it made her feel a little better.

One time, while they were eating, she'd seen A-chin drop a grain of rice. She had told him to pick it up. He had taken one look at her and then stomped it into the dirt floor. She hadn't said a word. She'd just taken the stick from behind the door and smacked him twice, hard. She'd tried not to look at the two red marks on his legs. She'd just kept saying, "God of thunder's gonna getcha. God of thunder's gonna getcha. Who taught you to tramp on rice?"

After that, A-chin did not tramp on any food. And after that it seemed she had never had to hit him again. What a long time ago that was. She couldn't remember if she had ever even yelled at him again after that. But now, now, she wanted to yell at him. He was her son; how dare he not listen to her? As she said this to herself, she thought back to waving her bamboo stick and chasing A-chin along roads among the fields again. And she thought of when she'd hit him. There was A-chin running naked along the road. And she could still see those two red marks on his legs. He had always listened to her. That's how he was as a boy, and nothing could have changed. Yes, she remembered, A-chin always listened to her. If it hadn't been for A-hsueh, A-chin wouldn't have kicked her out. And now A-chin said he wanted to marry the woman.

"God of thunder's gonna getcha. If you dare marry her, the god of thunder's gonna getcha."

"What are you saying?" She hadn't realized that A-hsueh had come in and was standing behind her.

"God of thunder's gonna getcha," she said, as if to answer her but also still talking to herself. There was no need to answer her, but why not yell at her? She'd yelled at A-chin. Why not at this woman who was only hired help working in A-chin's restaurant?

"What?"

"God of thunder's gonna getcha."

"What?"

A-hsueh didn't understand. A-chin understood. He'd heard this familiar curse since he was a child. It must be that A-hsueh'd never heard the expression. This girl didn't even speak her language. A-chin had already asked T'ien-sung what he thought about A-hsueh, but T'ien-sung had never given him a clear answer. By the way things looked, though, A-chin must like her very much. But she didn't understand their language. How could a daughter-in-law not understand a mother-in-law? For half her life, each day, she had made an effort to understand her mother-in-law. In her opinion, a mother-in-law was more important than anyone else.

Even though she had hinted to T'ien-sung that she did not like this girl, he expressed no opposition. T'ien-sung was not involved in the restaurant anymore, but A-chin still listened to T'ien-sung on many matters. If T'ien-sung expressed some disapproval, would A-chin still marry her?

She didn't understand why T'ien-sung didn't disapprove. Nor did she understand why T'ien-sung didn't fully approve of her coming to Taipei. He had argued against every trip she had made here, saying she would only be in the way.

In the past, she had brought the grandchildren with her, but now she refused. She was afraid that they would turn as bad as their youngest uncle. It wasn't easy to be good. Turning bad was so much easier. A-chin was a perfect example of that.

"You cannot be always throwing away good things," she had told him. This was something she just couldn't stand.

GOD OF THUNDER'S GONNA GETCHA

"Not throw away junk? Keep it around just to take up space? Don't you see how small this house is?"

She just couldn't understand. In the past, she'd always been told to save everything. Now she was told to throw everything away.

"Before, many things were made by hand. Things were scarce, and we knew it wasn't easy to make them. Now, many things are made by machine. It's easy to make them. There are lots of things and not much space. We have to throw them out." If he were in a good mood, A-chin would explain this all to her.

If he were in a bad mood, he would just say, "You don't understand."

"When the thunder comes, there won't be any place for you to hide." People who tramp on things and aren't good to their parents get struck by thunder. But was it that in the city you could run inside, and the god of thunder couldn't find you?

She hoped that A-hsueh would ask again. She would say that this was the way she used to yell at her son. But, much to her surprise, A-hsueh didn't ask. She didn't show any interest in the expression. How unpredictable things were.

"Are you leaving?"

She wondered if she was being kicked out again. What was it to her if she left or not? She tied two corners of the cloth. She tied them as hard as she could, as if she meant to flatten all the clothes. Or rip the cloth.

"A-chin asked me to give this to you."

Each time she came to visit, A-chin would give her a little money.

"I don't need it."

If A-chin wants to give me money, she thought, he should give it to me himself. He always gave it to me himself before. Who is this A-hsueh? What's she doing here, hanging around like she's glued to me? It wasn't really that she didn't want the money, but she didn't want to tell A-hsueh that.

"You don't want it?" It seemed that A-hsueh was reading her thoughts. "A-chin said to give it to you."

"I don't need it." Since she'd said this once, she might as well repeat it. This time, though, she spoke more softly.

Ignoring her, A-hsueh put the money on the edge of the bed. T'ien sung's wife squinted at it. The four dollars were for her own use, and the other one was for the bus. The travel money she could save. It was just a little after noon, so she could walk back and arrive home before dark.

A-chin told her every time that she should take the bus. He said time was more valuable than money. If someone would pay her to walk—give her a certain wage for it—she'd be willing to think of it the same way she did working in the fields, and each day she would walk to and from the city. If she walked, she didn't have to worry about those gasoline fumes giving her headaches. This way she could save a dollar. She would put away half of it and make the rest into change for the grandchildren. She imagined having all those kids around her clamoring for money.

As she picked up the money, she thought of A-hsueh again, who had already left. She hurried to the door. She often felt like A-hsueh was spying on her. She did not like A-hsueh. She hadn't always felt this way. It was only after A-chin had told T'ien-sung that he wanted to marry A-hsueh that she began to feel A-hsueh was taking advantage of them and of A-chin. She had told T'ien-sung this, but he hadn't responded. She had told A-chin, too, who hadn't responded either.

A-chin had always been an obedient child. At thirteen, after he had finished grade school, he had come to Taipei with T'ien-sung to help run the restaurant. Now T'ien-sung had handed the business over to A-chin and returned to the countryside.

A-chin didn't do things the same way as T'ien-sung at all.

The first time T'ien-sung went to Taipei, he carried home a wooden ladder and door. Each night, he would take a leisurely walk home after the restaurant closed. The next day, he would hurry back to Taipei at noon. When he came home again, he would bring all kinds of good things that he had collected.

A-chin was different. He threw everything away. The cardboard boxes, bamboo baskets, wood, and tin cans aside, the food he threw away each day would be enough to fill a banquet table.

Hired help like A-hsueh weren't willing to eat the customers' leftovers. They must have food cooked just for them, three times a day. She had once reprimanded A-chin about this. Not only did he not listen, he accused her of not understanding things now, and, worse, he did so right in front of the hired help.

"Why eat other people's leftovers?"

"Why not?" she had countered.

In the country, women did not eat with their men, did they? And sometimes, when the men left a little of their vegetable soup, wouldn't the women pour it over their rice to finish it off?

Sometimes she would get upset with the customers. Why did they leave leftovers? If they couldn't eat it, they should have ordered less, especially those young ladies. The fingers of those young ladies were as long as chopsticks, and so slender and white. When they ate, it was as if they were afraid to put the food into their mouths. Usually they left more than half their food; almost none of them cleaned their plates.

If the hired help wouldn't eat the leftovers, it could be brought home for the grandchildren. She started thinking that even if she spent six or seven hours a day walking back and forth for the leftovers, it would still be economical. And she was more than willing to do that. It would be a whole lot better than quietly sitting at home. It would even be better than making bamboo hats.

She proposed her plan to A-chin; she was sure he would approve. To her surprise, his answer was one word: "No." He wouldn't even give her a reason.

A-chin really had changed. He was never like this when he worked with T'ien-sung. Hadn't he helped T'ien-sung to bring home bag after bag of leftovers? Now, he wouldn't do it himself and he wouldn't let her do it either.

She really couldn't understand how they could spend so many hundreds of dollars just on lights. She had asked him how long it would take to earn this money back if he charged just a dollar more per meal. Again, A-chin blurted out that she didn't understand. Sometimes she thought that she really didn't understand. There must have been a good reason for A-chin to yell at her like that.

A-chin not only told her she didn't understand; he didn't permit her in the restaurant either. She really didn't understand how they could spend thousands of dollars to decorate a restaurant. She must try to find out why. Sometimes, she wanted to study all the customers to see what made them so different from country people. But actually, what she wanted most was to do something to help A-chin and the others. At home, whenever the neighbors needed help, they would ask her. She was very responsible. She could clear the tables. She would be good at that. She was confident she could do it better than A-hsueh and the others. At least she wouldn't break as many dishes as they did. And she would be happy to do it. This is her son's place. At home, everyone said how capable her son was and how much money he made. Sometimes she wondered how much more he would be making if so much wasn't wasted and tramped on.

But A-chin didn't allow her in the restaurant. He had said that she could come see him and go wherever she pleased as long as she didn't interfere with the restaurant. He didn't want her in the dining room, and he didn't want her in the kitchen. But she didn't come to Taipei to go out. And she couldn't help being concerned about the place. She just couldn't stand to see how A-chin and the other cooks threw away food. Sometimes she would see them cut one piece out of a fish and throw the rest away. At home, fish soup was a treat.

They would give the best part to the customers, who would leave most of it on their plates. And then the leftovers would come back into the kitchen and be thrown in the garbage. One time, she saw an entire king prawn brought back, something she had never eaten in her whole life. It wasn't that she wanted to eat it; she just couldn't stand to see it thrown away. She'd grabbed it, removed the shell, and stuffed it into her mouth. She wasn't a pig, but she had never had a chance to eat a prawn like that in all her life. She wasn't complaining about that, no; it was just that she thought that a king prawn should be eaten and not thrown in the garbage.

A-chin happened to see her do this; he told her not make a fool of herself in the restaurant.

She only went into the dining room because A-chin had forbidden her to go into the kitchen. A-chin had told her to go back to the countryside. That was the first time A-chin had kicked her out.

Each time after that, before she came to Taipei, she would make a promise to herself not to go into the kitchen or dining room. But it just wasn't possible. That's where she wanted to go, where so many things were being tramped on. She always felt that the people in the restaurant were tramping on things.

Sometimes, when she helped them clean vegetables, she felt that the hired help threw too much away. What the hired help threw away, she went and picked out of the garbage, and then they threw it away again. They were all A-chin's hired help, but they never listened to her. Sometimes, they would even criticize her in front of A-chin, especially A-hsueh. She didn't know how often A-hsueh had criticized her in front of A-chin. A-hsueh was half the reason A-chin was kicking her out. She really didn't like that A-hsueh. But A-chin liked her. So the same thing had happened to both A-chin and T'ien-sung when they'd left home, hadn't it? This all had something to do with the city and all those people around them. Especially that A-hsueh.

God of thunder's gonna getcha, she thought, just like before when she was chasing A-chin in the fields, shouting at the top of her lungs. But now, in this little building, the only place where there was any room was in the restaurant; everywhere else was so cramped. If you spoke up at all, someone would hear you. Of course, she thought, A-chin wouldn't remember that expression. And what difference would it make if he did? He really had changed.

She pressed the clothes a little flatter and tied the other two corners, pulling them tight enough to rip the cloth. She loosened the knot, thinking she might really rip it. How strong she used to be. The entire village had praised and admired her for her strength. But what good was it to be strong? City people don't seem to need any strength. Look how little they ate, especially the young ladies. They just took a little rice with their food; sometimes they didn't eat any rice at all. How could they get strong like that? They seemed afraid of being strong, especially strong enough to work. She hardly had the strength anymore to tighten knots in cloth.

"Hey."

"Who is it?"

"A-chin said you should go out the back way." It was A-hsueh again.

"Why?"

"The restaurant is full of customers now."

How could A-chin have said such a thing? It must have been A-hsueh's idea. The heck I'll go out the back, she thought. I'm going to see A-chin. But she was afraid to see him. He might really have said this. He'd kicked her out before. If he got mad, it would be the same thing all over again.

A-hsueh is wrong to think I'm afraid of her, she thought. It's my own business if I'm afraid of my son. But I'm not afraid of that little witch. At least, I can show *her* that I'm not afraid.

She picked up her bundle and followed A-hsueh.

She opened the little door going into the dining room where quite a few customers were eating their lunch.

She heard both A-chin's and A-hsueh's voices saying, "Come in! Come in!" How refined and sincere they sounded.

They were greeting their customers. At first she'd been really frightened. Their voices sounded so loud, they'd taken her by surprise. She thought they were yelling at her.

A-chin and A-hsueh hadn't noticed her yet. There were quite a few customers. Some were waiting; others had just finished eating. There were a few empty dishes.

A-hsueh was going over to greet some customers. T'ien-sung's wife scurried behind her so as not to be seen. She was not afraid of A-hsueh, but it might be better if she didn't see her. It might be better not to let A-chin see her either.

Two customers were just standing up. The man had eaten almost everything, but the woman had left quite a bit on her plate. When the couple wasn't looking, she reached over and grabbed a chicken leg. It wasn't that she was hungry, she just couldn't bear seeing it go to waste.

"A-chen, hurry up and clear that table." It was A-chin's voice, speaking calmly but firmly.

Then she knew A-chin had seen her. And she knew that he was angry. A-chin sometimes used this tone to kick her out. Though he wouldn't make a fuss in front of the guests, and he had not spoken loudly, there was no disobeying him.

Quickly she made her way through the customers, through the beaded screen, and out onto the street. She didn't look back. A-chin and A-hsueh would be glaring harshly at her.

EIGHT

Autumn Night

This happened fifty years ago.

It was the eighth month, the night of the sixteenth, the first night after Mid-Autumn Festival. Auntie was lying in bed, unable to sleep. Auntie was Mother's younger cousin, and that day was her husband's birthday.

Auntie's mother-in-law slept in the bed by the door. There were two beds in the room. The first bed was a simple one with only a bed frame: no mirrors, decorative glasswork, or carved railings. The bed faced the door, and this was where Auntie slept. The other bed by the door was made of bamboo, and this was where her mother-in-law slept. It was as if she slept there just to keep Auntie under constant watch.

Auntie was the third daughter-in-law. Actually, her two sisters-in-law had both undergone the same treatment. They had all slept on that same bed.

Auntie was thirty-eight years old. In her time, the year spent in the womb counted as the first year of one's life.

Her father-in-law had passed away when her mother-in-law

was thirty-eight years old. Therefore all the daughters-in-law were asked to sleep alone, separated from their husbands, when they turned thirty-eight. It was this way with the first daughter-in-law, as well as the second. Now it was Auntie's turn.

"Look at that Ah-hsiu next door! She's approaching forty and almost a grandmother, but she is still sleeping with her man, even allowing him to make her belly swell. Doesn't she have any morals?!" Mother-in-law repeated this many times. Auntie knew that it was for her benefit.

Actually, in those times, many people were like Ah-hsiu. Many uncles were younger than their nephews.

Her sisters-in-law accepted this rule. First Sister-in-law not only followed the rule; she even acted as watchdog for Mother-in-law, spying on Second Sister-in-law and Auntie. Second Sister-in-law followed in First Sister-in-law's footsteps, outdoing her predecessor. Second Sister-in-law often flung warnings at her, her words sometimes stinging with sarcasm.

"Now you won't be able to go after each other like a pair of wild cats, howling all night."

Who would have suspected Second Sister-in-law would change her tune later on?

Auntie lay quietly, staring at the rectangular skylight in the roof. It was a small window, but through the mosquito net moonlight still glimmered.

Her husband had once told her that the moon was biggest and brightest the night *after* the full moon. The previous year, he had even come home from school just to share it with her.

She stared at the skylight, and for some reason the moonlight aroused in her uneasy, anxious feelings.

Her husband taught in the school of the neighboring village. He had wanted her to move to the village with him, and she wanted that, too. Mother-in-law, however, had objected, saying that the family needed her to help with the farming, since they were short of hands already. The family property had not yet been divided among the sons. So not only did she have to help her sisters-in-law with the cooking and feeding the pigs, she also had to work in the fields.

Mother-in-law wasn't asleep yet, she knew. Mother-in-law tossed in bed and feigned a cough. She knew Mother-in-law was about to get up to use the chamber pot. Mother-in-law usually had to get up three or four times during the night. It was probably because of her age.

The chamber pot was between the two beds. Most of the time she was not aware of the smell; she had gotten used to it. But when someone used the chamber pot, the strong odor of urine filled her nostrils.

She got out of bed quickly, put on her wooden clogs, and walked out. It wasn't the smell of urine, however, that made her leave the room.

She didn't know how she'd gotten into this habit. It may have been because Mother-in-law didn't want her to hear the splattering or because she didn't want to hear it. No, it was probably Mother-in-law, because otherwise she wouldn't have the nerve to get up and go out.

Of course, if she were asleep, she wouldn't get up and leave the room when Mother-in-law relieved herself. Sometimes, when she was too tired to get up, she would pretend to be asleep even if she wasn't.

Tonight, however, she was feeling stifled, and this was a good opportunity for her to get some fresh air, to soak in the moonlight flooding the rice paddies, and to go to the out-house.

Auntie did not like to use the chamber pot, especially when her mother-in-law was in the room.

She walked along the rice paddies and then headed toward the outhouse.

Outside, the moonlight illuminated the entire countryside. She could see the bamboo trees behind the house, their branches

bending over the roof, swaying gently in the breeze. The roof was thatched with straw.

The outhouse adjoined the pigsty. She had to pass the pigsty on her way to it. The outhouse had actually been built for storing pigs' manure.

The pigs heard her approach. They thought someone was coming to feed them and started making quite a commotion, snorting through their noses. The more impatient pigs stuck their snouts into the pig trough.

She did not light the lanterns. There were no lights in the countryside then, and the country folks did not light lanterns when it wasn't necessary. Not only could they save fuel that way; they could also save themselves trouble. In fact, the moonlight shone through the slats of the pigsty that night, illuminating everything inside.

She went in and came out again. The pigsty grew quiet as she left.

She walked back toward the rice paddies and looked at the rooms of her sisters-in-law. No lights were shining through the windows. No one lit lamps at this hour, even if they were awake.

From the outside, the windows all looked alike. But she could sense a pair of eyes watching her every move behind First Sister-in-law's window. The same was true for her mother-in-law's.

She looked up at the moon. It had not yet climbed to the center of the sky, and the sky was cloudless. The moon seemed as bright as it had been last year. But the weather was not as cool as it had been then.

The year before he'd taken her for a walk along the Hou-bi Canal. That was quite unusual for country folk.

In the country, men ate before the women, and very often the women ate only the men's leftovers. In the evenings, when everyone sat outside by the rice paddies to talk, the men sat on high stools with their legs propped up, talking about the weather, the harvest, and sometimes the war. The women sat on low stools some distance away. The women rarely talked; they just sat quietly, waving their bamboo fans to chase away mosquitoes. They rarely had the chance to be with men, except in the privacy of their own rooms.

The year before, when he'd taken her down by the Hou-bi Canal to bask in the moonlight, had he foreseen that they would be separated soon? Only a year had passed between his two birthdays, but everything had changed.

That morning, she'd brought him some duck meat. They raised ducks on the farm. She'd also brought two pies and a grapefruit, offerings to the moon from the festival the day before.

Usually, Auntie's son ran such errands, by the decree of her mother-in-law. That prevented them from meeting. Her son was away for the day, so she was sent instead. She put down the things and turned to leave.

"It's my birthday today, I want you to stay."

"No, I can't."

"Then just stay for a little while. Go back after lunch."

"I can't."

"Why?"

"Auntie told me to hurry back before noon." In those days, many country people referred to their parents as aunt or uncle.

He tugged at her hand.

"No . . ."

"Do you really mean it?"

Without answering, she turned and ran as if she were running for her life.

She ran, but his words lingered in her ears. She remembered his gaze and the sensation of his hand holding hers.

"Why? Why did I run away from him? Isn't he my husband?"

She walked from the rice paddies toward the gate. She could

sense the eyes of her mother-in-law and sister-in-law following her every step. She paused for a moment and then opened the gate. Not far from the gate was the Hou-bi Canal.

She walked toward the canal. The year before, they had taken a walk here. Today, there wasn't a soul in sight. She walked slowly along the canal bank.

The road along the canal was the only one leading to the outside. If you walked opposite the current, you reached the main street. If you walked with the current, you passed a small brook and eventually ended up in P'ing-ting.

Her mother used to tell her that, once married, a woman belonged to her husband's family. Once married, if she should feel wronged, she could only hide in her room, cry to her heart's content, and then wipe away her tears.

Now, she didn't even have her own room where she could hide and cry her eyes out. Maybe the Hou-bi Canal was a more appropriate place. There wasn't a soul here, just the moon in the sky.

The thought released her tears, which kept pouring out. She cried until the moon became a blur.

Suddenly she wondered if she had been gone too long. Mother-in-law must be up and awake and waiting for her.

She wiped her eyes, but the tears kept coming.

In the daytime, the Hou-bi Canal came to life. Many women did their laundry here in the morning. In the evening people washed vegetables, and in the afternoon water buffaloes soaked themselves.

Looking into the canal, she could see moon shadows floating on the water. The current wasn't strong, but she could hear it flowing.

She walked back and forth along the canal three times and wiped her eyes again. He was in P'ing-ting. P'ing-ting was more than two hours away. If she hurried, she could reach the place in two hours.

What time was it? Back at home, she had not lit the lantern

so she hadn't been able to see the clock. She looked up at the moon. The moon could tell her the time.

She looked in the direction of home; nothing stirred. In fact, not a light could be seen in the whole village right now.

She walked a few steps along the canal, following the current, and then stopped. She took a few more steps, walking past the little brook and up a hill that would take her to P'ing-ting.

The path looked almost white, glimmering under the moonlight, stretching straight ahead. There wasn't a human soul in sight.

She stared ahead in the direction of P'ing-ting. She had married him at eighteen; twenty years had passed since then. And that's where he'd been all that time.

She was still wearing her wooden clogs. The path became more narrow and winding. She took off her clogs and held them in her hand.

She knew that there were plenty of snakes along this path, some of them poisonous. One was very likely to come across snakes on a humid night.

With a swish, some creature darted into the shrubs. It could have been a frog; she had only gotten a glimpse of it.

She stopped and picked up a bamboo stick. Like a blind person, she tapped the path ahead of her as she walked.

There was heavy dew. Under the moonlight, one could see drops forming on the grass by the roadside and the rice stalks in the fields. The dewdrops glittered under the moonlight. The long stretches of rice paddies soon gave way to a grove of jequirity trees.

Should she enter the woods? She still remembered about ten years ago, when a village woman had hanged herself in the woods. Actually, there had been several incidents like that. The ghosts of these women were often said to appear, and, it was true, the souls of those who hanged themselves did linger, looking for other bodies to inhabit.

Looking back, she realized that she had already walked a long way. This was the only road that led to P'ing-ting.

She stepped into the woods. Above her, the leaves of the jequirity trees were sometimes thick and sometimes sparse, sheltering the road. Moonlight poured through the foliage. Shadows mottled certain sections of the road where the branches weren't as dense.

Moonlight danced across the trees. Looking up, it was as if crowds of people were moving about. Would the ghosts of those women who hanged themselves appear? She looked down and walked faster.

Suddenly, in front of her, she saw a bamboo pole. No, it was a rope draped across the path. She'd once heard that ghosts used ropes to trap people, and one must not step over them.

She looked at the rope and tried to walk around it by stepping into the shrubs along the side of the road. Then she noticed that the rope seemed to emit a faint glimmer of light.

What was it? A live rope?

Or it could be snake. Judging from its sheen, it could be a poisonous snake.

What could she do? She waved her bamboo stick, and it fled. Her hands were shaking.

Some ten minutes later, she found that she had put the woods behind her. At the other end of the woods, there was a cliff about thirty feet high. The villagers called it the village god's cliff. A little brook ran below the right side of the cliff, and on the left side a tall camphor tree grew. Under the tree, there was a little temple for the village god. There were no lights, no candles, and no incense. It was just a tiny little village god's temple.

The camphor tree was said to be very old. It was so old that there was already a huge hole near the base of its trunk. In the moonlight, the hole appeared as black as ink and bottomless. Villagers claimed that a vixen was once seen running into that hole, and it never came out again. It was said that vixens could transform themselves. If that was so, the vixen might have turned into a spirit. Would it come out now to catch its prey?

Her eyes fixed on the hole, she walked around the tree. She paused for a moment, clasped her hands together, and made three bows to the village god's temple.

Whoosh!

The sound came from the brook below the village god's temple. What could it be?

Two birds flew past. They could be owls or some other night bird.

Past the village god's temple, to the left, was the cemetery. The cemetery was full of graves. This was a poor region, so the graves were very small. Some didn't even have tombstones; they were marked with only a rock from the riverbed. Reeds growing among the graves swayed gently in the breeze.

She had walked down this road many times. But she had never walked down it alone at night.

Fireflies sparkled over the graveyard like flowing water. No, they couldn't be fireflies. She'd once heard that ghost fires appear in graveyards. Was she seeing ghost fires?

Ghost fires were supposed to be green. Red fires were supposed to be the fires of the village god. People had seen the village god's fire chasing away the ghost fires. The village god's temple was close by. Why didn't his fire come out to chase the ghost fires away?

Suddenly, she noticed two large green lights shining side by side on a grave close to her.

Was she seeing ghost fire? She backed up, retracing her footsteps.

No, it was not ghost fire. She looked closely and saw a pair of eyes. It was a black dog standing on the grave mound, ready to attack her. She could see the dog's ears standing up and its tail out straight. Under the moonlight, its eyes glared like steel.

She wanted to run. No, she couldn't do that. You must not let a dog know that you are afraid. In one hand, she had her clogs; in the other hand, she had a bamboo stick. Her two weapons may have kept the dog at bay.

Barking dogs don't bite. That dog didn't bark, and it was black. Also, it didn't make any noise when it moved. That was the most terrifying part. Was there only one dog? Wild dogs were said to travel in packs. She looked around quickly but did not spot any other dog.

She straightened up and walked on, dragging her bamboo stick. She tried to make as much noise as she could with the stick. She knew the dog might be following her, but she also knew she shouldn't look back.

Past the graveyard, the road headed downhill. She saw something climbing up the hill from below. On nights like this, all noises seemed muffled. As the thing drew closer, she could hear creaking sounds.

It was a person pushing a bike. This stretch of road was winding, bumpy, and muddy. In the daytime, many water buffalo grazed at the graveyard and trampled the road. When it rained, the road turned to mud. And when the mud dried, it became very bumpy.

The figure appeared so suddenly, it was as if he'd sprung from the dark. A human being appearing at this moment, in this place! Before she saw it was human, she was afraid it might be another dog, an even larger dog, or even one of the unlucky things.

It was said that the unlucky things had only a shadow and their feet did not reach the ground but only floated in the air. Dogs were supposed to be able to detect such things. The dog did not bark. Dogs were supposed to bark and howl when they saw them. Country people would say that "the dogs were blowing on their conches."

The shadows moved strangely. It looked as though a whole lot of things were moving together. Later, she realized the bicycle created this effect.

A new sense of uneasiness came over her. No, it wasn't just uneasiness; it was fear. This was different from the fear she had felt walking through the woods or passing the graveyard.

A person. The first person that came to her mind was Ho T'ien-ting. Not a lot of people owned bicycles. Could it be Ho T'ien-ting?

If it was Ho T'ien-ting, that would be more terrifying than meeting a dog, especially here and now, when there wasn't another person in sight. That could even be worse than running into an unlucky thing.

Ho T'ien-ting belonged to the Ho family. He had graduated from the agricultural school and worked as a vet on the main street. He was one of the few educated members of the family.

The main responsibility of vets in those days was to pair animals for mating and assist in deliveries of livestock, including dogs, horses, sheep, and imported breeds of pigs. Of course, vets also gave injections and administered medicines to sick animals, and some even did blood tests and made serum. Respectful farmers addressed vets as "Doctor," just as they did physicians. But there were others who were not so respectful and called them "the ones who lead the pigs."

Every year, after the annual castration of the water buffalo, Ho T'ien-ting would bring home their huge testicles to fry with sliced ginger and wash down with liquor. He considered that his privilege and his greatest moment.

Could this be Ho T'ien-ting?

Ho T'ien-ting was probably one or two years her junior, and he was her husband's cousin.

She remembered an incident that had taken place about six months before, when the sun was midway up the sky, and she was coming home from the market. She had been alone then, too, and was carrying an empty basket.

Ho T'ien-ting had caught up with her, ringing his bicycle bell. She stepped out of his way to let him pass. He jumped down from his bike.

"Sister-in-law, look at your hair. Your hairstyles keep getting more and more old-fashioned. What a pity, with hair as black as yours!" Ho T'ien-ting leaned over and looked right into her face.

She did not respond but lowered her bamboo hat. Her ears were burning.

"Your skin is so white, the whitest in the clan. Why are you going around barefoot? You can afford shoes. I get it: you want people to look at your white feet, right?"

In those days, the country folks, both men and women, usually went around barefoot. Ho T'ien-ting stooped down, and with one hand on his bike he tried to touch her feet with his other hand.

"What are you doing?" She brushed his hand away.

"I've heard that you no longer sleep with Brother Ah-chin. Do you miss him?"

She didn't respond.

"It's cruel for Auntie Ah-man to force widowhood on all her daughters-in-law just because she's a widow."

Again, she didn't respond.

"Everyone is saying that you are still so young and pretty, you mustn't let your little Mary get moldy!"

"Don't fool around with me. I'm going to tell Uncle Ah-yuan to give you a good smack on your head with his pipe!"

Auntie was furious, and she felt like crying.

Everyone said that Ho T'ien-ting was a handsome chap. He was taller than most men, with a boyish face. Many people called him "a handsome black dog," but to Auntie he seemed more like a stupid lovesick hound.

But Auntie had not told Uncle Ah-yuan, and she came to regret that. Still, how do you tell people about such things?

The affair involving her second sister-in-law happened two

months later. It occurred to her that if she had told on Ho T'ien-ting, she might have prevented it.

One day, a dozen villagers, both men and women, climbed the mountain to collect firewood. Second Sister-in-law was small of stature and not terribly strong, so she fell behind. This wasn't unusual, and no one suspected anything. Later, the group noticed that Ho T'ien-ting was missing, too. Someone went back to check and found Second Sister-in-law sitting on a rock with her bamboo hat off, her feet dangling. Ho T'ien-ting was standing in front of her, very close. The person who caught them claimed that Ho T'ien-ting was touching Second Sister-in-law's face.

"We weren't doing anything. I have a mosquito bite, and he was putting ointment on it."

It was true. Everybody could see the little red spot on her face and traces of ointment. First Sister-in-law reported the incident to Mother-in-law. Second Sister-in-law used to be the watchdog; now she was watched. Mother-in-law berated Second Sister-in-law right to her face.

"You're already over forty! You think your face is so tender? Letting other men touch it like that . . . you're . . . you're . . . !"

Actually, Second Sister-in-law was only a year older than Auntie, making her thirty-nine. Mother-in-law exaggerated on purpose, saying that she was in her forties.

That seemed to be the end of the incident. Who would have thought that three days later something even worse would happen? That night, after dark, the two of them were seen at the far end of the rice paddies, walking into Uncle Ah-fu's grass shed.

Auntie understood how Second Sister-in-law felt. Mother-in-law summoned her second son.

"You take the proper measures to deal with this matter!"

Second Brother gave his wife two hard slaps on the face. He was a strong man, and she was tiny. She staggered and fell onto the ground.

That night, Second Sister-in-law swallowed poison and almost died. Fortunately she was discovered before it was too late. They made her swallow putrid water and saved her. Now Second Sister-in-law followed a strict vegetarian diet and seldom left the house unaccompanied.

About a week after that incident, Ho T'ien-ting was ambushed on the street, and his leg was almost broken. Some speculated that Second Brother had attacked him, while others guessed that Second Brother had had someone else do the job for him. Ho T'ien-ting may have known who his attacker was, but he kept his mouth shut.

Which were more terrifying: dogs or men? She looked back. The black dog had disappeared. So, the dog was afraid of people.

The figure walked past her, pushing his bike. Soon he was out of sight. She didn't know him. But she saw clearly that he wasn't Ho T'ien-ting.

As she kept walking down the road, her legs felt weak. She did not have that reaction to the snake or the dog she'd run into. If that had been Ho T'ien-ting, she didn't know what she would have done.

She walked down the hill, toward the brook, and stepped across the rocks that formed a bridge over the water. After a long steep trek, she finally reached P'ing-ting Village. She was sweating from the brisk walk uphill. She wiped her forehead with the back of her hand.

P'ing-ting was a small village with only one short main street. That street was deserted, with not a single pedestrian. There were no cars either, just a few dim yellow streetlamps in the distance. Under the lamps, several mosquitoes buzzed about.

It was probably very late. The houses were shut tight, only a little light escaping from cracks in a door here and there. She looked up at the moon.

Today was his birthday. Was he celebrating with someone? Or was he asleep already? She wiped the sweat off her forehead.

She'd heard rumors that he'd become friendly with a female teacher in the school. Was it true? In those days, it wasn't uncommon for married men to have other women as well.

She walked toward the school. A gray cat in no hurry at all crossed the street. It emerged from a dark corner of one pavilion and vanished into the darkness of another pavilion on the other side.

She came to the doorway of the Japanese-style dormitory and placed her bamboo staff by the side of the door. She still had her clogs in her hands; her two bare feet were caked with mud and wet from the dew.

The dormitory was completely dark. Was he asleep? Had he gone out?

Could he really have gone out with that other teacher? she asked herself.

She tapped on the glass door, her heart beating wildly.

No one answered. Would he be angry at her for coming so late at night?

She circled the house, walked to the bathroom on the side, washed her feet clean, put on her clogs, and walked back to the door again.

Knock, knock, knock.

There was still no answer.

She pushed the door lightly and looked in through the crack. There was no light inside.

Should she go in? She had come here before, before Mother-in-law had ordered their separation. It had felt completely different then.

She knocked on the door very loudly. There was still no answer.

She pushed the door half open and let herself in. There was no one inside. She walked into the bedroom. The bed was not made, nor was there a mosquito net hanging over it.

"He really isn't in?"

She walked to the corridor by the backyard. She saw a shadow sitting there quietly, like a monk in meditation.

This was completely unexpected. The figure sat half immersed in moonlight, half in shadows. Before him was a small table, and on the table was a bottle of red wine, a little wine cup, a plate of duck meat, a pile of peanuts, two pies, and a grapefruit. Hadn't she brought him the duck meat, pies, and grapefruit that morning?

"It's you," he said, turning around.

"Yes," she answered softly.

"What are you doing here?" There wasn't a hint of anger in his tone.

She said nothing.

"Does Auntie know you've come?"

"No."

She should know, she thought to herself.

"You came by yourself?"

"Yes."

"You have a lot of guts."

Her ears suddenly felt hot.

"Come here." She recognized his expression from that morning. His penetrating gaze took in her head, breasts, waist, hips, thighs, ankles, and toes.

She sat down. She set her collar right. She suddenly remembered she was wearing a coarse cloth shirt.

"Come closer."

She could not refuse.

"Have a drink." He poured wine into the cup.

"I can't."

"I know you can drink. During your month of maternity rest, you drank wine as if it were tea. In a week's time, you drank almost a barrel of wine."

She drank up and handed him the wine cup. She lowered her head.

"You can drink."

"It's your birthday."

"You walked such a long distance in the middle of night just because it's my birthday?"

"Yes."

"You've worked up quite a sweat." He took her hand. Her hands were shaking. On the night of their wedding, when he had taken her hands for the first time, they had been shaking, too, even more violently.

"Let me—let me peel it" she said, reaching for the grapefruit.

"Silly." He took her into his arms. "I'm going to peel your grapefruit."

"No, no."

"No? Then why did you come?" There still wasn't any hint of scorn in his voice.

But his words unleashed the tears that she could no longer hold back.

She stood up slowly.

"Where are you going?"

"I'm going back because you think I should."

"Silly girl."

"I'm afraid Auntie will . . ."

"I'll stand up for you. I'll take care of things."

"Really?"

"Of course. Come here."

"I, I . . ."

"You're trembling."

"I'm scared."

"You're a silly girl." He held her tightly.

"No, no . . ."

Spring Rain

It was Sunday, cold, and pouring rain outside. I was going for my usual mountain hike.

I took a minibus up the mountain. I liked the drivers on this route; they made small talk and joked around, and sometimes they pulled over to say hello to people they knew. On regular buses, this kind of thing no longer happened.

There were seventeen or eighteen people on the bus. Except for a few hikers, most were returning home from shopping.

The rain came down in torrents, pelting the front and sides of the bus. The windows were all fogged up, except for a few spots that had been wiped clear, through which you could look out.

The bus was headed toward Chengchi University. From the window you could see people waiting for buses, some in rain-coats, some holding umbrellas, both men and women. A man in his fifties boarded the bus last. A child in a cloth infant carrier was strapped to his chest. The child's head was completely hidden inside the carrier; all you could see was a little cap and two tiny legs swinging out from below. Cream-colored knit socks covered the baby's feet.

The man looked familiar. I recognized him immediately from the large black mole on his forehead: he was An-min, from the grocery store near where I used to live.

I was sitting in the back. At first, I wanted to call to him, but the bus was crowded, and someone in the front gave up a seat for him as soon as he got on.

We had moved out of that neighborhood almost twenty years ago. I still recognized him, though his hair was thinner and had started to turn gray.

His family name was Su, but we never called him anything but An-min. Children usually called him Uncle An-min, and a few people called him "boss"; but if you called him "boss," he wouldn't look at you directly when he answered.

At the time we moved, there were still some rice paddies and stands of bamboo bisected by an irrigation ditch, even though it was right in the city. Sometimes, at night, you could even hear a chorus of frogs.

An-min's store sat beside the irrigation ditch right below a clump of bamboo. There were lots of mosquitoes there, and at night you could see them swarming with their other winged friends around the streetlamps. I've heard that now those fields have all been filled in and covered over with tall apartment buildings.

The reason we never called him by his surname was that he had married into his wife's family with the understanding that any children they had would bear their mother's name, not his. His wife's family name was Lin—her full name was Lin Su-chen—and we always called her A-chen. She was the only daughter of the owner of the grocery store, whom people called Uncle A-tu.

Uncle A-tu had started out as a farmer. Aside from the grocery store, the family had a small garden plot where they grew vegetables; all in all, they owned about three or three-and-a-half thousand square feet of land. The productivity of their land was limited, and although there were some ups and downs in the real estate market at the time, prices never skyrocketed. So the family depended mostly on the income from the grocery store for their day-to-day expenses.

I remembered A-chen, too. She wasn't even thirty back then and had a very slender, flat figure. Her face was rather pale, with a sharp chin, and large, somewhat sunken eyes. She was given to fits of blinking rapidly, probably a nervous tic. Her hair was cut short in a career woman's perm. She wasn't a woman to stop traffic by any means, but she had a warm and friendly manner, a swift hand, and a good head for totaling up bills quickly and accurately. She would often lower prices for her customers, and people in the neighborhood thought highly of her. The Lins did a good business.

Since A-chen was both an only child and female, Uncle A-tu insisted that whoever was seriously interested in her would have to take on their family name. So it took quite a while to marry her off.

A-chen's and An-min's marriage was arranged by an orphanage. Word had it that A-chen's maternal uncle had had a lot to do with this. He believed that most men would be unwilling to give their children the mother's family name but an abandoned orphan might be less concerned about such a thing. He also thought an orphanage might be a good place to find an honest, reliable, hardworking man. And he himself just happened to have a good friend who ran an orphanage and knew all the orphans personally, putting him in an excellent position to select a suitable mate for A-chen. An-min was the director's first choice.

An-min had been abandoned as an infant. Nobody knew who his parents were. Parents sometimes left their names, or a letter, or some personal object, in case they ever decided to return and claim their children. An-min showed up without any of these, meaning that his parents never intended to come back for him. The director of the orphanage named him An-min; Su was the director's own surname. In fact, all unidentified orphans were given the family name Su.

An-min grew up in the orphanage, leaving it when he was fifteen to go to work as a delivery boy at the grocery store. He was an honest, upright young man and actually rather an ideal choice for a son-in-law to take on the Lin family name.

After marrying into the Lin family, An-min worked very hard. We often saw him in cutoff pants and flip-flops, riding a secondhand bicycle with a metal frame in back to hold large packages. Day and night, he shuttled from destination to destination with his deliveries. We lived on the fourth floor of our building; often we saw him dash up the stairs panting, hardly stopping to catch his breath or wipe the sweat off his forehead with the back of his hand.

A-chen and An-min didn't talk much in front of other people and acted more like employer and employee than man and wife. But I would sometimes see them going out together for a late-night snack after work, so they must have had a reasonably good relationship. We also knew that Uncle A-tu was very satisfied with An-min and that he trusted him. The only thing that left them all unsatisfied was that several years of marriage had produced no children.

Everybody assumed that the problem was A-chen, since she looked so weak and sickly. We didn't know if A-chen ever went to see a doctor about it.

I remember going to their store once for a pack of cigarettes. A-chen wasn't in; An-min was kneeling in the bamboo stand. He picked up a discarded rice bowl and used it to scoop half a bowl of water from the ditch that flowed by his doorway. Then he put the bowl down again. Back then, the water in the ditch was quite clear. Bright green seaweed waved back and forth in it. Sometimes you could even spot small fish darting around.

He froze when he saw me, like a small child caught doing something wrong. I was puzzled and a little uneasy. What in the world was he doing? Some kind of magic? I guessed that whatever it was, it had something to do with childbearing. Maybe it was some kind of fertility rite. I knew that A-chen frequented temples far and wide to pray for a child.

"Look here," he said, "the water in this ditch comes from a place very far from here and flows on to some other faraway place. As long as the water keeps flowing, the ditch won't ever dry up. But water scooped into a bowl doesn't flow. No source feeds it, so it dries up quickly, in less than a week."

"Oh," I replied.

I didn't really know what he was talking about at the time, but I was sure his words meant something. It had never occurred to me that such an ordinary person might have such an impenetrable side.

"You mean . . ."

"Mm."

He didn't give me a direct answer, and I didn't feel I should pursue the matter.

Less than a year after this happened, and about a year before we moved, something unfortunate occurred. An-min became involved with a barbershop woman named A-chü.

Some neighbors said it was a lousy thing to do. "He got himself a wife and a family, and he still wasn't satisfied."

Others said, "Feed a rat, and it'll gnaw a hole in the grain bag."

Others said he was "repaying a loaf with a stone."

Others were surprised that someone so straight could turn out to be such a playboy.

Others quoted Confucius, citing "having no descendants" as one of the three cardinal violations of a child's responsibilities to his parents.

"A-chü says she is willing to bear a child for us. She says that

143

as soon as the child is born, we can register it as our own," An-min explained.

I remembered An-min scooping up ditch water with the rice bowl and thought I had found the solution to that puzzle: An-min was an orphan who didn't know who his own parents were. And now A-chen was not giving him a son. He knew nothing about the source of his own life, and it didn't look as though he would have any descendants either. Once his own life ended, his entire line would be broken; just like the water in the bowl, it would dry up and leave nothing behind.

"What are you saying?" A-chen asked.

We had lived in that neighborhood for more than seven years, and never once had we seen A-chen lose her temper. And even this time, from all appearances, she didn't seem particularly angry. But we could almost feel that something momentous was about to happen.

"A-chen, I made a mistake. Please forgive me. It's all my fault. I'll never do such a thing again . . ." An-min pleaded.

"There will be no 'again,' " A-chen replied dryly.

"A-chen . . ."

"Get out of here, and never come back," she ordered. "You can take all your belongings with you."

Uncle A-tu tried to intervene on An-min's behalf. We all knew how highly Uncle A-tu thought of An-min. But A-chen wouldn't give an inch.

An-min disappeared for two days; on the third day, he was back. The strange thing was that A-chen didn't drive him away again. He continued to make his deliveries by bicycle, just as before. By the looks of things, everything was back to normal. But after that, we never again saw the two of them go out together for a late-night snack.

About three months later, A-chü, the barbershop woman, left. She showed no signs of being pregnant. The rumor spread that, in fact, it was An-min, and not A-chen, who couldn't have children.

Maybe it was these events that brought about a fundamental change in A-chen.

About a month after A-chü left, A-chen told An-min that she was taking a trip south. She didn't say why she was going or exactly where in the south she was headed. And An-min didn't ask.

A few months later, A-chen's belly began to swell. She was a very thin woman, so the change was immediately apparent. At first, everyone thought An-min was the father. But soon rumors spread that A-chen had brought this gift back from the south. No one knew for certain.

Of course, lots of people didn't believe that A-chen would ever do such a thing. Others thought it highly probable that she had, indeed, done such a thing. An-min had taken the first wrong step; how could anyone blame A-chen? Some said that since An-min was a man, it was OK for him but not for A-chen. Others pointed out that it was the Lin family who was in charge; whether the child was An-min's or not didn't matter. Some said A-chen did it for revenge. Others thought that A-chen wanted to show An-min it was his fault, and not hers, that they had no children.

If An-min had any reaction, he kept it to himself. Of course, he had no right to take a position anyway. Some said An-min implied that the baby was his. But their report was somewhat vague, and I, personally, doubted the accuracy of it.

A-chen eventually miscarried. I heard it was a boy. Everyone thought she lost the baby because she was so frail. After the miscarriage, she seemed even weaker than before. Once I saw her sitting inside the grocery store with a tremulous look on her face. She didn't seem to recognize me.

Three weeks later, we moved. We didn't know what happened after that.

"Here we are!" someone shouted from inside the bus.

The bus stopped at Changhu. The minibuses followed two different routes: one went to Maokung, one went only as far as Changhu.

An-min was still in his seat when someone came over to tell him that this was the last stop. The rain was coming down in sheets. He opened a black umbrella and looked around. He seemed to be unsure about which way to go.

"An-min," I called out to him as I headed in his direction.

"Oh," he replied as he turned around. He didn't seem to recognize me right away.

It was cold, and his breath came out in thick white clouds.

"Where are you going?" I asked.

I looked at his face. Maybe it was because he was still a delivery man that his skin was so brown, but it had a tinge of yellow in it, and his eyes looked puffy. Was it age? Or was it because of the rain? Or was he just tired?

"I wanted to go to Maokung. I seem to have taken the wrong bus," he said.

"This bus only goes this far," I explained. "I'm going by Maokung myself. We can go together."

"Is it very far from here?" he asked.

"It's about twenty or thirty minutes by foot," I replied. "But it's pouring." We cut across a short tree-lined road to the courtyard of the Shang-ti-kung Temple. We stopped to rest under an open shelter. An-min laid down his umbrella, walked toward the front of the temple, brought his palms together, and bowed several times. He looked down as he paid his respects, as though he were afraid.

I watched him from the side. He was wearing a light green jacket, the kind American soldiers wear, with a hood hanging down in back. He had on navy blue dress trousers, which were wet halfway up each leg by now. The worn shoes on his feet were also soaked. Small air bubbles squeezed out of the seams as he walked.

In the center of the courtyard was an oblong altar with a padded kneeler in front of it. On either side of the altar were long wooden tables flanked by wooden benches where worshipers could rest. The red paint on the wooden tables and benches was beginning to chip and show signs of wear. The temple was dimly lit; all you could really see were two flickering red candles.

A woman of about sixty greeted us with a smile. "Have a seat! Like some tea?" she offered.

"Do you have any hot water?" An-min asked.

"We certainly do," she said obligingly.

"I'm going to mix up some formula," An-min said. He opened up the carrier to reveal the baby he was toting and then pulled out some powdered formula and a bottle from a bag. He used the hot water to mix up a little less than half a bottle of formula.

It was a boy, probably under a year old. He was fair skinned and plump. His cheeks were full and red, as though painted with rouge, from the warmth of the carrier. His bright black eyes were wide open. He didn't squirm a bit inside his little pouch. I thought he was asleep.

"A-jen," An-min called to him. An-min chucked the baby's cheek. The child first smiled and then laughed out loud.

An-min carried the baby over to a ditch to let him pee, then brought him back. He shook the bottle a few times before popping the nipple into the baby's mouth. An-min's movements were rapid and precise. The infant's mouth worked vigorously, and in no time flat he had emptied the entire contents of his bottle. An-min wiped the baby's mouth, and he smiled again.

An-min gently felt the child's socks to see if they had gotten wet.

"Your grandson?"

"No, I guess you could say he's my son."

"A-chen's?" I asked, suddenly puzzled.

"No, A-chen passed away. She died quite a long time ago."

"Oh."

Then An-min had remarried? I wondered, but I didn't ask.

Based on what An-min said and my own deductions, I figured that A-chen must have died less than a year after we moved.

"She wasn't in good health and had been dealt a harsh blow." I was referring to her miscarriage.

"She really regretted that," An-min replied pensively.

Was An-min talking about A-chen's trip south? This remark seemed to confirm the rumors. But even so, An-min shouldn't have said such a thing. He was really in no position to make that kind of a statement. Maybe he thought that everybody knew anyway, including me.

"She said something to me on her deathbed: 'A child doesn't have to be your own seed to be your son.' Even though she didn't make it clear exactly what she meant, I knew she was saying that though I was an orphan and never knew my parents, someone had raised me to adulthood. Mr. Su, the director of the orphanage, was my father and my mother. He made no distinction between his biological and his adopted children. I adopted this child."

"From the orphanage?"

"Yes. He's an orphan. He won't ever know where he was born or who his birth parents are. He is just like me: neither of us has a birthday or an ancestral home. A-chen said on her deathbed that you didn't have to bear a child yourself for him to be your son. She was just too weak at the time to explain herself any more clearly than that. But I know what she meant. We had put too much stock in the idea of having a child born of our own flesh and blood. Human life is neither a bowl of water nor water running through a ditch. After A-chen died, I went to the orphanage and adopted a child. That child is now twenty years old; he's just graduated from vocational school and is about to go into the army. After he's out, he can come back home and stay with me if he wants to, or he can go out and seek his fortune, if that's what he prefers. Even though I say this so nonchalantly, I know that if he really does decide to strike out on his own, I'll be very lonely. So I've adopted another child: this one. With my current means, I should be able to afford a couple more. A couple's childbearing years are limited, but there is no limit on adoption. I wonder why I didn't think of this sooner. Next time, I don't think I'll wait so long; maybe I can adopt a new one every five years or so. I know A-chen would approve."

I was shocked at his words. Twenty years ago, near our old house, he had picked up a broken rice bowl and scooped some water from the ditch to express his thoughts. He still remembered this. I never imagined that so ordinary a person could think in these ways. Life was not water flowing through a ditch, that I could understand. Some other, larger metaphor was more appropriate. Maybe life was a great river that belonged to all humanity. Maybe that's what he meant.

I looked at him again. What a transformation. What lay behind this change in him? It must have been a very powerful force. Did it come from A-chen? Or from himself? Or from a shared awakening?

He tucked the child back into the carrier. The carrier was too small for him, and his legs dangled free.

"So you're going to Maokung?"

He told me that A-chen's grave was in Maokung. She had originally been buried in the public cemetery in Ankang, but urban development projects had forced the move to Maokung. He was on his way to see A-chen with his child, to pay his respects.

"Why today?" I asked.

"Today is the anniversary of her death," he answered.

"Oh."

"We often neglect important things when our loved ones are still with us," he said as he opened his umbrella.

"Use this one," I said, offering him the oversized umbrella I take in case of rain whenever I go on mountain hikes.

We exchanged umbrellas.

The storm was unusually fierce. It was still raining hard and showed no signs of relenting. And it was windy. The wind was not all that strong, but it was chilly and penetrating. "Chilly springs bring heavy rains," a Taiwanese saying goes. It was as though the rain were being dumped in buckets from the sky.

Once it's spring, you never know if it's the cold weather that brings the rain or vice versa. In spring, cold and rain seem inseparable.

There were only a very few brave souls out for a mountain hike.

We walked along the service road in the direction of Maokung. After exchanging umbrellas with An-min, I discovered that the one he had brought was fairly useless. The mountain wind seemed to keep changing directions; sometimes it came from the front; sometimes from behind. My pants were soon soaked halfway up my legs.

The rain also managed to hit my shoulders. When it came in from the right, I shifted the umbrella to the right; when it came in from the left, I shifted it to the left. Soon both shoulders were soaking wet.

The service road slanted to the left, with rice paddies, vegetable gardens, and, mostly, tea farms, on both sides. Quite a few of the tea bushes were already in bloom, their branches lined with tender new buds. If this kind of weather kept up, I thought, the leaves would mature too quickly.

Gazing up to the right I saw staircases of terraced fields. As soon as the rain flooded one step, water poured down onto the next one, creating a mountainside of miniature waterfalls varying in height. The water produced sloshing and splashing sounds. Flooded streams roared in response.

A freshet of rainwater whipped down a mountain path. This was both a hiking trail and a flood channel. The water carried with it large amounts of mud and gravel, which it deposited on the service road. Then it continued coursing down the road, divided now into two rivulets, one clear and one turbid. The rain pelted the road surface, splashing back up in a thick spray.

Rainwater flowed down the road in wavy, patterned sheets. Raindrops transformed into bubbles as they hit the stormy current and then vaporized with a *pop*.

Fresh green leaves poked out from the plants along the side of the road and on the mountain slope. The rain beat them down mercilessly. But all of them—the acacia trees, the shell ginger, the pleated typhoon grass, the various ferns, even the lowliest floss flowers and showa grass—hung on tight, waiting for the clouds finally to draw back and reveal a clear sky.

New shoots of bamboo had sprung up, though the leaves were not yet fully developed. Reaching skyward, one bamboo shoot had already surpassed the parent plant in height. The ground below was blanketed with yellow leaves.

Some deciduous trees had already begun to bud. The leaves and heads of last year's broom grass were slowly withering and dying; the new leaves were taking over, adding strokes of bright green to the red-violet awns. Yes, those were new awns, weren't they? But broom grass was a late summer and fall plant; why was it joining in this spring rally of new growth?

The leaves of the broom grass stood quietly, firm and erect, despite the blustery weather, while the leaves of the typhoon grass waved wildly in the wind.

I also saw a clump of taro leaves by the roadside. The taro leaves were not as large as those of the giant elephant ears. But the giant elephant ear leaves were flatter; they weren't battered down by the rain.

Rain pooled at the center of the taro leaves. Once full, the leaves tilted to the side to dump out their contents. Then they straightened on their stems to repeat the process all over again.

An-min walked in front of me. His gaze was fixed on a distant point, and he seemed to be rushing toward his destination.

He had a sure step. His shoes squeaked with a *pata pata* sound as he walked along the puddled road. Little bubbles kept forcing themselves out of his shoes. What we were walking along was more like a river than a road. The baby was still safely stowed in the carrier with only his legs dangling out, swinging to the rhythm of An-min's stride.

We saw farmhouses on either side of the mountain road, along with quite a few grave sites. Several of the farmhouses were surrounded by flowers and hedges, especially azaleas. We also passed peach, apricot, and cherry trees in full blossom.

"Should we stop for a rest?"

We had arrived at a platform with four or five tables in front of a tea farmer's home, where you could sit to taste tea.

"No. No need to."

We sloshed on ahead.

"An-min, you look pale . . ."

I was worried about his health. In his condition, I wondered how he could possibly continue to adopt children, but I didn't know how to broach the subject with him.

"So you think I look a little pale? Well, I'm vegetarian . . . strict."

This did not satisfy me. It wasn't just that his face looked pale, it also looked swollen.

Soon we soon came to a white sign with red characters on an electric pole, warning cemetery visitors who planned to burn incense and other ritual objects to be careful not to start any brush fires. Maokung was straight ahead. I knew there were a number of grave sites in this area, mostly scattered individual plots.

"Where is A-chen's grave?" I asked.

"Up there," An-min answered, pointing up a slope to our right.

Terraced fields, high and low, covered the slope. Rainwater poured down level by level, in some places like beaded curtains, in others like squirt guns fired off at set intervals. Water, water, everywhere you looked.

"How are you planning on getting up there?" I asked.

"There's a path going up. Don't worry," he said. He started to hand my oversized umbrella back to me.

"I think I know a path. I'll take you there," I told him.

I had hiked in this area before and more or less knew my way around.

We walked on another fifty feet or so, till we saw a pavilion about halfway up the mountain. I remembered a road next to it that led to the cemetery.

We continued on up to the pavilion, which was quite small. The wind blew rain into it from all sides. Like the other pavilions in the area, this one had a small, square table in the center framed by four benches made of poured concrete and painted to look like split logs.

The entire pavilion was wet, including the table and benches. I saw some objects piled on a bench leaning against the table. I didn't see them clearly at first. But when I looked at them from another angle, I saw they were two people, a man and a woman, huddled close together under a yellow plastic sheet that they had pulled over their heads and backs. Rain spilled down from above, and the plastic was completely drenched. Their heads rested against the table close together. I looked at their faces; they both were wearing rain-speckled glasses, so I couldn't see their eyes clearly. Below their eyes I saw two mouths or, more precisely, two sets of snowy white teeth. So they were laughing! I couldn't tell if these two young people had come here to get out of the rain or to get drenched.

I turned to look at An-min and saw that he had noticed the two under the pavilion. His expression seemed stony. Maybe this was all too far behind him. Then I saw him turn toward the mountain slope. From the pavilion, the slope still looked like a sheet of tall and short waterfalls. An-min turned to me, said nothing, and tried again to hand back the oversized umbrella.

"Keep it," I said.

"But you're soaked to the bone."

"Oh, I'll be OK. You need to keep the baby dry." I pointed to the dangling legs. The baby had lost one of his socks, I noticed, and a little bare white foot was sticking out.

As soon as An-min heard the word *baby*, he stopped resisting.

He left the pavilion. I watched him as he mounted the flooding mountain path, step by step, right . . . left . . . right . . . left . . . up the mountainside. Suddenly he swayed to one side, almost dropping the umbrella.

Just as I was about to run over to him, he regained his balance and righted himself on the path. With his one free arm and both feet, he negotiated the steep slope, half climbing, half crawling.

The rain began pelting down harder and harder. A sudden extended cloud burst reduced visibility almost to zero: you could hardly see ten yards in front of you. By the time the rain finally began to let up a bit, An-min had disappeared without a trace.

The young couple still huddled under the pavilion. I set off in a different direction. The mountains and valleys were shrouded in a dense rainy mist.

TEN

The Three-Legged Horse

The bus ride from Taipei to the village where Lai Kuo-lin lived took three hours. He had been a classmate of mine at the technical college. Recently, at our class reunion, we had seen each other for the first time in more than twenty years. We had all been asked to introduce ourselves, and that was how I'd learned that he had returned to his village, where he now operated a wood-carving factory.

His factory was quite large, easily occupying some 200 p'ing. The front served as his display shop. The main purpose of my visit was to look for wood carvings of horses for my collection. I began this hobby many, many years ago, and I now owned more than two thousand pieces, some carved from wood, others from stone. This was the Year of the Horse, and I wanted to use this opportunity to add a few more pieces to my collection.

Lao Kuo-lin had already shown me quite a number of carvings. Perhaps because they were mass-produced, the articles appeared too standardized and regular. As we were looking over the goods, a strange-looking horse in the corner suddenly caught my attention. The horse's eyes were downcast. The animal appeared to be grazing but only from one particular angle. The dark, gloomy expression on its face made the animal look as though it were suffering from pain, or was it a sense of remorse? I couldn't tell. In all my long years of pursuing this hobby, I'd never seen such an expression on a carved horse. No, I don't think I'd ever seen it on a painted horse either.

I picked up the horse for a closer look and saw that it had one crippled leg. A feeling of surprise and pity suddenly came over me. The lines on the horse's body made it more vivid and powerful than the other carvings. The facial expression, especially, was something the other works could not match. This horse was not painted. The wood looked and felt rough here and there. From the way it had been lying in a corner, I gathered it wasn't considered very important. After seeing how I handled the artwork and how reluctantly I put it down, Lao Kuo-lin explained:

"That horse was done by a strange man. He likes to carve disabled horses. Whenever we go to his place to pick up his work, he usually gives us a few disabled ones just to complete the number. But he doesn't let us sell them. He says that he'll replace them with good ones next time. So they serve as IOUs in our transactions."

"Do you have more of his work here? I mean ordinary horses," I asked.

"Yes, here's one," Lai Kuo-lin replied as he fished out one and handed it to me. "What do you think?"

"Very strange. It's not much different from the rest, is it? Perhaps it's because you use a pattern. But its eyes are quite special. Other horses' eyes look sideways. His horse looks straight ahead. And its mane, tail, and leg hair are not identical. Still, it doesn't compare to the crippled one. See, this one is a living horse; it has feelings. It is no easy job to give carved animals such expression," I said at length.

"We retouch the horses he carves. We think he's too lazy. He doesn't even sand them. We've even deducted from his pay for this," Lai Kuo-lin said.

"Does he carve a lot?" I asked curiously.

"I can't tell. He stacks everything he does together. We can't tell what's finished and what he's still working on. I have noticed, though, that he's doing less and less of what we like. We used to pick up his work once a week. Now, it's every two or three weeks or maybe even a month. He's given up doing respectable carvings. He just sits inside working on the most bizarre-looking objects," Lai Kuo-lin replied.

"He really won't sell? I mean those crippled horses?" I asked.

"I don't know. Who knows what he's thinking?"

"Would you take me to see him?"

"What for?"

"I want to see what special things he has."

"Special things?"

"I mean crippled horses and such."

Lai Kuo-lin took me there on his motorcycle. After a half-hour drive up a winding mountain road, we reached the sloping summit of a hill. Looking down, we saw a clearing. There was a small village, twenty houses or less. A few of the houses huddled together, while others were situated some distance away.

"That's the village of Shenp'u," Lai Kuo-lin said before starting the motorcycle again to go down the slope.

The man's home was a simple structure of mud bricks. The bricks were so eroded by the elements that the straw inside them was visible and coming loose; it jutted out like inchworms. The house sat in a corner of the courtyard. The central hall gave an impression of relative tidiness.

The door was ajar, so Lai Kuo-lin decided to give it a little push. Once inside, I immediately noticed the sweet smell of fresh wood. Having been outdoors in bright sunshine for a long time,

I could not see a thing at first. We stood there for some moments. As our eyes adjusted to the darkness, we could make out an elderly man sitting below a small bamboo-latticed window. The man was about sixty years old. His short hair was more gray than black, and his mustache was two or three inches long.

The old man opened his mouth. "Is that you, Kuo-lin?"

"Yes, Uncle Chi-hsiang. I brought you a visitor," Kuo-lin answered.

"A visitor? From where?" the old man glanced quickly at me.

"Taipei."

"Taipei City?"

"Yes," Kuo-lin responded.

By this time, my eyes had gotten used to the darkness of the room. Right below the small window was a worktable, probably a foot high, on which lay a wooden mallet and all sorts of carving tools. The old man sat on a low stool, his legs stretched out in front of him and slightly bent. Between his legs was a block of wood, its shape still too rough to be recognizable. The floor was littered with wood chips. Some finished work was piled high in one corner.

"Is your friend from Taipei?" the old man asked again before I had had enough time to get a good look at the wood carvings.

"Yes. He was my classmate when I was studying in Taipei," Kuo-lin answered.

"Do you know a place called Old Town in the suburbs of Taipei?"

"I am from Old Town. I lived there for thirty years before I moved to Taipei City some ten years ago."

"In which part of the town did you live?"

"Right across from the police station."

"Police station? Was that the old site of the County Penitentiary?"

"Yes, it was."

"Judging from your age and where you lived, you must've known me," the old man said as he turned toward me slowly.

"I . . . know you?"

"Don't you remember me?" he said, pointing to the bridge of his own nose. A band of white skin stretched from between his eyebrows to his nose. It looked like some kind of skin disease.

"Are you . . .?"

"So you've finally recognized me! I'm 'White-nosed Raccoon'! Who's your father?"

I told him my father's name. I added that my father used to run a shop where he sold woodcraft.

"I remember him. I hit him once."

"I know. My father told me."

"Is he still around?"

"No, he's passed away."

"Did he ever tell you anything else about me?"

I hesitated.

"Go on, I won't mind."

"My father said that three-leggeds are more detestable than four-leggeds."

He was silent for a moment. Then he picked up a small picture frame from his worktable. "Do you know her?"

"No."

"She's my wife."

"If I'm not mistaken, her older and younger sisters were teachers."

"Yes. That's right."

"How about this person?" I asked, pointing to a smaller picture tucked into the frame's lower left-hand corner. The picture was yellowed with age.

"That was the first photograph ever taken of me, from the first time I went to Taipei. I sent a copy to my mother."

In the picture, he was bald. I looked at the bridge of his nose. There was no sign of the white band.

As if he guessed what was going through my mind, he explained, "It was retouched by the photographer. He charged an extra five cents for that."

"So you mean it was there from a very young age?"

"Yeah. From the time I was quite small . . ."

I

"Black-footed Elk, White-nosed Raccoon . . ."

Headed by Ah Kou and all clutching their wooden tops, five boys were making their way toward the village burial grounds, half walking and half running. Ah Hsiang, a head shorter than Ah Ho, the smallest of the five, was following closely behind.

"Black-footed Elk and White-nosed Raccoon, go back! Don't come with us!" Ah Chin, at the end of the pack, shouted as he spun out his wooden top.

"But I have a . . ." Ah Hsiang began. It was a cold day. Steam escaped his mouth as he spoke.

"What do you have? A penis?" Ah Cheng said.

"I have a top, too."

"What top? Did you make it yourself? It's smaller than your balls!" Ah Chin jeered.

"My uncle promised to buy me one this big," Ah Hsiang said, making his hands into a circle the size of rice bowl.

"It's too early to brag about it," Ah Chin replied.

"My uncle lives in Taipei."

"So what?"

"Go back, or I'll pull your pants down!"

Ah Hsiang was holding his top in one hand while the other held closed his fly. A cloth rope was wound around his waist. Ah Hsiang had a small build, making it impossible for him to fold and tighten the fly of his pants the way grown-up men do.

"Go back!" Ah Chin turned around and gave Ah Hsiang a

push. Ah Hsiang took one step backward. Ah Chin was the youngest son of Uncle Ah Fu. He was the very first person to call him "White-nosed Raccoon."

Once, on one of his trips to the mountains, Uncle Ah Fu had caught a raccoon. He put the animal in a cage, thinking he'd sell it. The animal's fur was yellow with a tinge of black. A thin stripe of white hair ran from the bridge to the tip of its round, reddish nose. One of its legs had been mangled by the trap, and the raccoon limped badly in its cage.

"You're a white-nosed raccoon, too," Ah Chin said suddenly as he pointed his finger at him.

From that day on, the name had stuck. Nobody seemed to remember what his real name was.

He looked on anxiously as the five turned a bend toward the other side of the bamboo fence.

He raised his hand and unleashed the top. It skidded sideways across the ground.

"Shit! What a lousy top," Ah Hsiang let out a curse.

He picked up the top and wound the rope around it. Then he walked back the way he'd come. Seeing a kettle of tea by the roadside, he squatted on the ground and helped himself to two cupfuls.

Then he returned to Ah Fu's vegetable farm. Surrounded by hills and mountains, this patch of farmland used to be planted with sweet potatoes, cassava, and peanuts because the soil was so bad. Uncle Ah Fu, who often visited the outlying towns and villages, listened to the advice he got there and planted leafy vegetables on his small plot instead.

Ah Hsiang felt a certain heaviness in his bladder, but it wasn't really full. He stood beside the vegetable plot and waited. The curly white cabbage must have been growing for a month now, he thought. He noticed that the inner leaves had started to turn yellow. If not for Ah Chin, nobody would call him Raccoon, he told himself.

He felt a draft of cold air. It made a whistling sound as it hit the bamboo fence. He hunched over, which made him become more aware of the pressure in his bladder. A shower of urine, steaming in the cold air, spattered on the fourth cabbage. It moistened the leaves and dripped into the vegetable's core. He applied more pressure, aiming the stream at another head of cabbage. The liquid formed bubbles on the soil's surface before seeping into the lower layers. He felt very relieved. If anyone had seen him, he would say he was adding fertilizer, he thought.

Suddenly, he heard a loud cry. Somebody rushed out from behind the bamboo fence.

Ah Hsiang jumped in surprise. Even before realizing who it was, he felt his urine shrinking back up inside him.

It was Ah Kou, Ah Chin, and the rest. He couldn't believe his eyes. How could they possibly have looped around and hid themselves behind the bamboo fence?

"I knew it was you, you White-nosed Raccoon!"

"I didn't do anything."

"You pissed on the vegetables!"

"I was fertilizing them for you. What's wrong with that?"

"Don't you know that warm urine can choke vegetables? Look at those three cabbages."

"I didn't have anything to do with that."

"Who else could it be?"

"Really, it wasn't me, I tell you."

"Would the white-nosed raccoon admit eating an apple if he were guilty? Let's catch the raccoon and skin it alive. Pull down his pants!" Ah Chin grabbed hold of Ah Hsiang as he said this.

"Stop it! Stop it!" Ah Hsiang struggled to break free of Ah Chin's grip, his arms thrashing and his feet kicking wildly.

Ah Jin grabbed the hand that was holding the wooden top while Ah Ho and Ah Cheng held his legs. Only Ah Kou stood off to one side, laughing all the while.

Ah Chin pulled down Ah Hsiang's pants. Immediately, the rope broke loose like a bamboo shoot shedding its outer skin. His fly flapped open, and Ah Hsiang's pants slid down his legs.

"Ha, ha, ha!" Ah Chin laughed triumphantly as he pulled off Ah Hsiang's pants and threw them into the air. They fluttered in the wind and fell to the ground.

"Ha, ha, ha!" everybody roared with laughter.

Ah Hsiang kept on thrashing violently. The air felt cold as it blew against his bare buttocks and legs. Heedless of the consequences, he picked up the top and stabbed it hard into Ah Chin's back.

"Ouch!" Ah Chin turned around and swung his fist, aiming directly at Ah Hsiang's face.

Ah Hsiang felt his upper teeth colliding with the lower ones. He bit his own tongue, tasted salt, and immediately knew he was bleeding.

II

It was a bright sunny day. Against a backdrop of blue sky, the rolling mountains seemed lost in the distance. A pomegranate tree stood motionless in the windless expanse, its foliage thick and green in the bright sun.

Ah Hsiang had been walking for two hours now. The unpaved mountain path, not more than a couple yards wide, meandered down the mountain toward a brook. This was the only way out of town. On a rainy day, this path would be all muddy and marked with the hoofprints of water buffalo. The next day, baked by the sun, the mud would be cracked and difficult to walk on.

Ah Hsiang walked and ran, his feet bare. A bundle holding his books and lunch box was strapped across his right shoulder and tied at the left side of his waist.

He continued along a section of the mountain path and then began to cross the brook, stepping on stones that lay just below the surface of the water. When the water level was low, the stones, set at intervals of half a step, usually rose above the water. After a downpour, the water level increased so that the brook was waist deep in some spots. During the rainy season, the water level could rise suddenly. Once, someone tried to brave the current and was swept away by it.

Someone was coming toward Ah Hsiang. It was Uncle Ah Fu. In rural areas, people who lived as much as three hours away were still considered neighbors and addressed as aunt or uncle.

"Uncle Ah Fu," he greeted the man, unable to hide his embarrassment. He was afraid of meeting someone he knew along the way. But here he was, right in the middle of the brook, where it was impossible for him to hide.

"Are you going to town, Ah Hsiang?"

Uncle Ah Fu did not ask why he wasn't in school. Rural folks did not pay much attention to the days of the week; nor did they care if students missed their classes. Ah Hsiang sunk one foot into the water to give Uncle Ah Fu the right of way. The water felt cold and relaxing. Instinctively, he immersed the other foot. The stone he was standing on felt slippery. It must be the moss, he said to himself. He steadied his footing and dipped both his hands into the water, enjoying its exhilarating effect.

What if Uncle Ah Fu met his father and told him about their encounter? How would he explain to his father? Ah Hsiang climbed back onto the stepping-stones and looked after Uncle Ah Fu. Deep inside, he felt a greater sense of fear of the new Japanese teacher. Mr. Inoue was a fair-skinned, chubby man, a stark contrast to the dark and emaciated residents of the village. On the second day of school, Mr. Inoue had told his students to move all the desks and chairs to the back of the classroom. Then he told everyone to kneel down on the floor. With a bamboo stick, he hit each one on the head. When he came to

Ah Hsiang, Mr. Inoue noticed the bridge of his nose and hit him twice.

"Uneducated beasts and savages! *Bakaro!*" he cursed as he swung his stick. Nobody knew the reason for this show of violence. The following day, a tenth of the students did not come to class.

"What's the use of going to school?" somebody said.

"I will never go back and kneel before him. I only do that for my ancestors."

Ah Hsiang received a greater ration of beatings than his classmates. He was hit at least once every week or two. Each time, his head swelled and boils seemed to develop. He could not think of any possible reason for these beatings, except perhaps that white band on his nose.

He didn't feel like attending school anymore, but he kept remembering his maternal uncle. It was this uncle who had convinced his father to allow him to attend school in Neip'u, an hour's walk from his own village.

"Be diligent in your studies and then come to Taipei when you finish," he would encourage Ah Hsiang.

Ah Hsiang knew he would get a beating again today. He wasn't supposed to be late, but he'd seen a strange-looking bird perched in a tree on his way to school. It looked like a waterfowl, but it had a wattle above its beak. The wattle looked like a duck's, only much smaller. Ah Hsiang didn't know the name of this bird. He chased it for some time before deciding he'd better hurry on to school. Yet he was still late.

The image of Mr. Inoue brandishing his bamboo stick filled his mind. He could almost hear the sharp sound of the stick. How many times had he knelt down on the floor, hoping that the inevitable would be over quickly? Deep inside, he was really afraid. When they came, the blows hurt so much that he grimaced in pain, and though his eyes were squeezed shut, tears still escaped from them.

Ah Hsiang lingered for some time near the school or, as it should have been called, the indoctrination center. He thought of his uncle in Taipei and wished he could take the train to the city. Back then, he had never even been to a train station. From others he had learned that trains traveled on railroad tracks. These could only be seen in the village of Waichuang.

He had passed the village of Chungp'u. By this time, the sun was high in the sky, and its rays seemed to pierce his bare skin. Ah Hsiang walked toward a shade tree and loosened his bundle to get at his lunch box. Rice would have been sufficient, but all he found were three slices of salted fish. Sometimes his parents would buy salted fish in the market. In an instant, he'd eaten everything. He noticed that the sun was almost directly overhead. It took more than an hour to walk the distance from his house to the school in Neip'u. He had walked for almost that long from Neip'u to Chungp'u. He figured it would take him another hour or so to reach Waichuang.

His heart beat faster again, just as it did when he thought of Mr. Inoue's stick. Right now, however, he had forgotten everything about his Japanese teacher.

He didn't have any idea what a train—or, for that matter, a railroad track—looked like. Although his uncle made a sketch for him in a rice paddy once, he was left with only a very vague impression.

Once he'd asked his parents to take him along, but they'd said he was still too small to go.

Ah Hsiang climbed over a hillock. Then he realized that it was a canyon. He was standing on the crest of the hill when he saw the winding railroad tracks below. Was it really the railroad track? He'd always thought it could only be seen from Waichuang. Ah Hsiang knew now that he could not be far from Waichuang.

The tracks stretched in opposite directions. He couldn't tell which led toward Taipei. He stood there motionless. Only his eyes shifted back and forth. In one direction, he saw the mouth of a cave some distance away.

He decided to climb down the slope. He discovered that the tracks were laid on wooden ties. Coal and rust stained the wooden surfaces. Then he stooped down and took a closer look at the track. It was silvery smooth and shining. In fact, it glistened in the bright sunshine. He held out his hand to touch the metal gingerly, the way he did once when he'd secretly stroked the face of the earth god's image in the village temple.

Choo . . . choo . . . choo came the sound of the locomotive from the direction of the cave.

Awakened by the sound, he stood up and drew back to the mountainside. It took an instant for the train to brush past his face. He didn't see a thing. After it passed, he realized that people inside had been watching and smiling at him.

Ah Hsiang took to his heels in pursuit. The train was speeding along in front of him. He kept on running.

III

As soon as he had finished elementary school, Ah Hsiang went to Taipei, where he worked in an eatery that belonged to his uncle. He started with the meanest of tasks: sweeping the floor, clearing tables, washing dishes. Then he learned how to wait tables and greet patrons. Later, he also learned how to ride a bicycle and deliver orders. Ah Hsiang was a fast learner. He was especially good at finding his way around. Although he was new to the city, Ah Hsiang proved more useful than older boys who had been there longer.

Pleased with Ah Hsiang's performance, his uncle sometimes sent him to the market or the bank. It didn't take long for him to became his uncle's most efficient assistant.

Late one night, about eleven o'clock, he delivered noodles to a cloth merchant in Jungting. Four or five salesclerks were there playing cards.

"The noodles are here. Are they still hot?" one of them asked.

"Hey, Raccoon, how come there's not much soup? Did you drink it on the sly?" someone else asked.

Ah Hsiang had delivered the noodle soup on his bike. He couldn't avoid spilling some of it along the way. Besides, noodles absorb water if left soaking for long.

"Yeah. He really looks like a white-nosed raccoon. I heard you come from the mountains, sonny. I bet there are a lot of raccoons up there," a third jeered.

"Don't mind him. Shuffle the cards."

"Who was the raccoon, your father or your mother?"

"Stop kidding around," the other said.

Afraid of spilling any more soup, Ah Hsiang set the bowls of noodles on the table in silence. It took all his effort; his hands were shaking. Then he replaced the lid of the serving box. By the time he was back on his bicycle, tears were rolling down his cheeks. Resting one foot on the ground, he wiped them away with the back of his hand. Why does everyone call me Raccoon? he protested. He'd left his village because everyone called him that. Here in the city, he'd come to know very few people. But as soon as they became familiar, they called him by that name, too.

These guys didn't even know him and still they called him that. They even insulted his parents. Ah Hsiang did not return to the eatery immediately. Instead, he went to the police station beside the park to report the gambling.

Ah Hsiang had often delivered noodles to the policemen and was quite familiar with them. They asked him to lead the way. As a result, the gamblers were arrested. Although Ah Hsiang had only pointed out the location to the police, the gamblers knew who had reported them. When he delivered their orders to the prison, they blamed Ah Hsiang and scolded him over and over.

This, too, Ah Hsiang reported to the police, who warned them that they wouldn't be released if they kept behaving that way.

This experience convinced Ah Hsiang that he was right in believing there were only two kinds of people in the world: the bully and the bullied. Mr. Inoue belonged to the first type. He belonged to the second. But now he had seen how the salesclerks had switched from one type to the other. Likewise, Ah Hsiang felt himself turning into the bully.

After their release, the salesclerks came to see Ah Hsiang and his uncle at the eatery and swore they would get revenge. But he was not intimidated. The police praised Ah Hsiang as a good citizen, a good Japanese citizen, in fact. They encouraged his continued contact with them.

One night, during one of his deliveries, Ah Hsiang was attacked by several men in an alley. They pushed him and his bicycle down and beat him severely. By the time he got free, the serving box and noodle bowls were ruined. Even the bicycle tires were not spared. He reported all this to the police, but his attackers had long since vanished.

His uncle was extremely displeased when he returned to the eatery.

"I've told you time and again that we must stick to our business and avoid meddling in other things, but you don't listen. Now, it's best for you to go back home. I'll send for you again in a little while."

Ah Hsiang did not go back home. Instead, he ran to the police and told them about his predicament. Realizing that Ah Hsiang was an intelligent boy, the policemen asked him to stay on as a janitor. Ah Hsiang's knowledge of the Taiwanese dialect would be helpful. Besides, his experience delivering noodles made him quite familiar with the area and its residents. Sometimes he joined the policemen in carrying out their duties. At other times it was his job to gather information for them. Although Ah Hsiang was called a janitor, to some extent, he acted as a police informer.

What now made a deep impression on Ah Hsiang was the prison cell, with its wooden bars. He noticed that whoever was placed behind those bars usually lost his cockiness. They made everyone very submissive. Even intellectuals and rich traders would come around to begging him for just a bowl of water.

Sometimes, the policemen would take the inmates to the bathroom at the back of the precinct. Using hoses, they would douse the inmates with water, just like rats in a trap. They were left dripping wet, their knees wobbling with cold. Sometimes, one policeman would shove a hose into an inmate's mouth and pump water down his throat while another held his nose. This treatment made the inmates scream. When their bellies were bloated enough, the inmates were forced to lie down on the floor, and a policeman would step on their stomachs to make them vomit.

Ah Hsiang was only a janitor and a boy. But because he was on the other side of the bars, inmates looked at him with pleading eyes. Nobody inside a prison cell ever called him "White-nosed Raccoon."

Naturally, Ah Hsiang wanted to remain on this side of the prison bars forever, but he wouldn't be a janitor all his life, or even an informer. He wanted this prison cell to contain the whole of society. One day, he would become a policeman, he told himself. Only then could he command fear and respect from everyone.

He confessed his ambitions to the policemen, who gave him tips on which books to read, how to read them, and how to take the tests. The first time, he failed. The second time, not only did he pass; he came through with flying colors.

IV

Tseng Chi-hsiang and Wu Yu-lan were sitting side by side on the stone staircase. There were more than twenty steps, each one about two feet wide and eight inches high. The stairs led up to a wide path to the Tz'uyou Temple and down to the banks of Tashui River. The staircase actually formed part of the river dike and doubled as a quay.

A few stars were clearly visible in the black sky. From all directions, searchlights appeared and then faded. A few of the light beams intersected momentarily in the night sky.

These precautions had only recently become necessary. Japan had declared war against the United States.

"No, my father insists that we cannot adopt the Japanese wedding rites," Wu Yu-lan said, her head facing down, her eyes looking intently at the flowing Tashui River. Reflections from the searchlights gleamed and disappeared on the surface of the water.

"Your father is such a stubborn man."

"You can't call him that. He says we have our own wedding rites."

"But you're an educated person. Why are you behaving like your father, who isn't educated?"

"My father went to school, too, but he read different books from the ones we did. He used to say that sending my sister and me to school was the most useless thing he ever did. He complains that we say strange things and he can't understand us."

"My supervisor advised me to follow the Japanese rites. Actually, it was more like an order."

"My brother-in-law also said we should get married according to our own rites. He's been to the mainland to study."

"Don't bring him into this. He's a suspicious character. He needs my protection, and some day he'll need me to save him. Having someone like him for a relative is a real disadvantage. They'll lose their confidence in me because of him, if they don't stop trusting me altogether. It's because you have relatives like him that I've decided to follow the Japanese rites."

"But my father won't give us his permission if we don't go by Chinese rites."

"If he doesn't give his permission, then . . ." Tseng Chi-hsiang jumped to his feet before finishing his sentence.

Wu Yu-lan also stood up.

"What do you think?"

". . ."

"Your decision is crucial. It's never been done in Taiwan, and because it's the first time, it will be special. Don't you know that the government is about to launch a campaign toward Japanization? In the future, it won't only be weddings that have to be done the Japanese way. We'll be asked to worship their gods and adopt Japanese names. In my case, for example, my surname Tseng would be changed into Katsute. Your surname, Wu, is also a Japanese surname, although it's not very common, and it's pronounced differently. Adopting Japanese names is necessary for thorough Japanization. Japan has already occupied much of Southeast Asia. Some day, we'll go there and become leaders ourselves."

"My brother-in-law said that Japan will . . ."

"Stop. I know what you were going to say. It's a crime to say that. I'll have to make arrests. I cannot arrest you, but in the case of your relatives, I'd have no choice. It is my duty to protect my country. Anybody who spreads rumors is a threat to the country. I'm sure Japan will win the war. My supervisor was right. He said we must serve as models and start new trends. We'll live to see many people following us."

". . ."

"What do you think?"

"I'll keep any promise I've made to you."

Two months before, the two of them had played tennis behind the dormitory. The tennis court was a public facility, but because of the nature of the game, only Japanese citizens, policemen, teachers, and students, both boys and girls, could use it.

After the game, the two went to his dormitory to rest a bit

and look at his new tennis racket. She'd been there before, but the other times, they'd been with friends.

Ah Hsiang had learned how to play tennis while attending the training center. He'd also learned judo and fencing. Both judo and fencing were for self-defense. They were also a means of getting promoted. He had now earned his black belt. Playing tennis was an important part of his social life. He'd watched this sport when he was still working as a janitor in Taipei.

Her tennis skills were nothing extraordinary. What he liked was how she looked on the court. He'd been thinking of her constantly since the first time they had played. He remembered she'd worn a short white blouse with matching shorts, socks, and canvas shoes. Her hair was tied with a white handkerchief. He could picture her clearly, her tennis racket in one hand, bending slightly forward. He could still hear her sweet and melodious voice. He knew from the way she moved that she came from a good family and had received a good education.

She was much better educated than he was. Although she didn't go one of the famous schools, the school she attended was a private and exclusive one for girls. His elementary education was nothing in comparison.

Today, she was again all in white from head to toe. The only difference was her somewhat disheveled hair. She took off her white hair band and pulled her hair back with her hand. She was sitting quite close to him. But there was only one way of closing this gap. And now might be his only opportunity.

Suddenly he lunged at her.

"Talk it over with me if you want me. If you touch me again, I'll die of shame right here in front of you," she said darkly.

"Forgive me," he said, kneeling down, his hands stretched forward and his forehead almost touching the tatami mat, "I love you. Please be mine."

". . ."

"Yu-lan . . ."

"Are your parents also in favor of Japanese rites?"

"My parents are rural folk. They won't have any opinion at all. Even if they objected, I could convince them. And even if I couldn't, it wouldn't stop me." His voice was firm and confident.

Slowly, he looked away from Wu Yu-lan and straight across to the other side of the river. Then he looked overhead. Searchlight beams were still criss-crossing the night sky. Tashui River flowed toward the city of Taipei. From where he sat, he could just make out the shape of the building that housed the governor-general's office.

Splash! The sound came from the far end of the river. Somebody was throwing stones into the water.

The splashing sounds became louder as the stones landed closer to where they sat. One stone narrowly missed the lowest step of the stone staircase.

"Who is that?" Tseng Chi-hsiang called out in a loud voice.

"Don't mind them."

"They're doing it on purpose."

"Even if that's so, tonight, we won't mind them."

From the top of the dike, someone blew a whistle.

"A man and a woman together." It was a child's voice.

A whistle sounded again.

Splash.

"A man and a woman together."

"White nose!"

"Bastard!" Tseng Chi-hsiang stood up angrily.

"Please! Chi-hsiang, don't!"

"Okay. But . . ."

"I'll do it."

"How about your parents?"

"I'll convince them."

V

"Japan has lost the war."

"Japan has lost the war."

In the beginning, people spoke secretly in subdued tones, their voices sounding incredulous. Everybody had known that Japan could not hold out for long. Earlier, Japanese newspapers had reported the fall of Okinawa. The Americans had dropped atomic bombs in the cities of Hiroshima and Nagasaki, making Japanese surrender imminent. But nobody had expected the defeat to come so soon.

Today, everyone felt a bit strange. This morning, the sky was clear and bright, but it was unusually silent. No alarms were heard. The normal sound of airplanes was missing.

Inside the penitentiary, everyone was nervous and seemed lost in thought.

Someone thought of putting a radio in the penitentiary lobby. Around noon, everyone was crowded around it, kneeling down as they listened to the voice of the Japanese emperor. The reception was very poor. The emperor spoke with a trembling voice, almost unintelligible through the static. He was obviously crying.

At first, everyone knelt there silently. Then someone started to sob. Fists were tightly clenched, and heads were bowed lower and lower. Someone pounded the floor with his fist.

Just like everybody else, Tseng Chi-hsiang knelt down listening. Today's events made him feel bitter and sad. His mind was a blank. Paradoxically, he felt as though this had nothing to do with him and that Japan's defeat affected him personally.

When the broadcast ended, everyone in the room bowed before the radio and remained kneeling for sometime.

"Japan has lost the war."

These same words took on a different weight now. Tseng Chi-hsiang saw the penitentiary chief stand up, followed by the street chief, section chief, director, and the investigation chief. A few of them appeared disheartened. Some, however, looked quite resolved.

"Japan has lost the war!" By the time he was in the streets, people had begun to speak louder and more boldly.

"Japan has lost the war?" His wife asked when he showed up at the door. She helped him take off his coat.

"Yes."

"What's going to happen now?"

"I don't know." In all his life, he had never felt so unsure.

"Will the Americans kill everybody?"

"Do you think so?"

"Of course not."

"Why do you ask?"

"The Japanese were good at propaganda. I still remember what they said about the female students who committed suicide by jumping off the cliff in Okinawa. I mean those *himeyuri*."

"What makes you think of that?"

"If you . . ."

"What about me?"

"I won't be afraid to do whatever you command."

"We're different. We're not Japanese."

"I know. But you're a policeman working for the Japanese."

"If worse comes to worst, I'll throw these uniforms away."

"Can you do that?"

"Without a country, will the Japanese still care?"

"But . . ."

"The penitentiary has ordered locals to maintain peace and order."

"Yu-lan . . . Yu-lan . . ." Someone called at the door.

"It's you, sister. Come in."

"Your brother-in-law says that Chi-hsiang must leave this place immediately."

"Why?"

"People are still calm right now. The announcement came so suddenly that they don't know how to react yet. But tomorrow or next week, things could get dangerous. People might get killed."

"What about my son and me?"

"You can leave the boy with me for the time being."

Tseng Chi-hsiang did not believe that people would go to such extremes. He insisted it was his duty to maintain peace and order in Old Town.

The very next day, things started to happen.

First came the news of the investigation chief's suicide. On the day the emperor's message was broadcast, several Japanese officials in remote areas committed suicide. It was like an epidemic. The newspapers reported suicides for days on end. Although the chief was a low-level official, his suicide was big news in Old Town.

Old Town was a peaceful little town whose residents were law-abiding and disciplined. However, within a few days, it was engulfed by the atmosphere of revenge so pervasive in other areas.

Some said that the first incident involved the son of a dentist who was practicing without a license. During the war, another dentist just starting up his practice had testified against the unlicensed dentist, who was subsequently arrested and jailed. As soon as the war ended, the dentist's son, who had learned judo in high school, went to his father's accuser to get even. In front of everybody, he flung the dentist on the pavement. Later, the son also confronted the policeman from Ryukyu who had carried out his father's arrest.

All of a sudden, these events awakened the people from their initial stupor. Everyone went looking for his enemies and tried to get even.

A few policemen were dragged to the temple square and forced to kneel down before the gods as a punishment for their sins. A butcher who had undergone the water-engorgement torture for illegal butchering during the war held two policemen at knifepoint and paraded them from Haishant'ou to Ts'aotianwei. The butcher seemed quite pleased during the whole process.

Most Taiwanese policemen had only office or civil responsibilities. For this reason, they rarely confronted the public and so were spared from reprisals. One exception, though, was a policeman named Lai who was dragged to the Tz'uyou Temple square.

"Beat him to death!" someone shouted.

"Kill the dog!" another added.

"Spare me. Spare me!" The man knelt down on the pavement, kowtowing again and again. His wife also knelt beside him.

"Kill him!" someone shouted angrily again.

"Dog! Three-legged dog! You better die!" a man shouted as he kicked the policeman.

"Running dog! I'll kill you!" Another man hit him with a wooden pole.

"Ow! Ow!"

This policeman was only their second most hated enemy, and still the mob broke one of his legs.

Then someone in the crowd shouted, "Let's get White-nosed Raccoon."

But nobody knew where Tseng Chi-hsiang had fled.

When the mob knocked at his door, Tseng Chi-hsiang had quickly climbed to the rooftop. On that same night, he fled the town. He didn't even have time to bring his wife and son along with him.

Yet the people didn't give up. After destroying all his furniture, they took Yu-lan into custody.

"I don't have any idea where he is now. I am willing to do anything you want. Even if you kill me, I won't resist."

They made a decision that she had to hire a theatrical group to perform at the temple square for three consecutive nights.

During those three nights, she had to arrange for an unlimited supply of cigarettes for everyone in the town.

At that time, local drama, which had long been suppressed by the Japanese, was slowly making a comeback. The sound of firecrackers had replaced gunshots. Everywhere the sounds of cymbals and drums could be heard once again. People resumed their visits to temples and shrines, thanking their gods for bringing peace to the land.

A makeshift stage was set up in front of the Tz'uyou Temple, in a spot adjacent to the river dike. On the front awning of the stage were emblazoned large red characters that read "Compliments of the People's Sinner: Tseng Chi-hsiang." Between the stage and the temple, several baskets filled with cigarettes could be seen. This passageway was illumined by powerful electric lights. Each of the baskets carried a red banner on which were written the same characters that were on the stage. Tseng Chi-hsiang's wife, Yu-lan, was kneeling in the temple as a punishment for her husband's sins.

"Come. Smoke a cigarette from White-nosed Raccoon," people invited each other as the crowd milled around the temple square in a festive mood. "Let's watch the opera courtesy of White-nosed Raccoon."

The townspeople were not sorry he had fled the town. As days passed, they soon forgot the whole affair.

VI

"How old were you at that time?" the old man asked.

"Around twelve," I said, after making some mental calculations.

"Do you still remember it?"

"It was a big event."

"It's been almost thirty-three years, hasn't it?"

"Yes. Thirty-three years now."

"Old Town . . . Old Town . . ."

"Did you ever return?"

"Return? How could I?" He lifted his head slightly to look at me and then lowered his gaze again. From where I stood, I could clearly see his nose. The passing of time had aged his face, but it could not hide that white mark across the bridge.

"Old Town . . . it was my nightmare." Again he heaved a deep sigh, his eyes staring blankly at the wall. But by his expression, you could imagine he was seeing through the wall, looking at some distant point outside.

"I do not know what a nightmare is. Perhaps, my experience in Old Town was my nightmare. I have tried again and again to forget that place but have never succeeded. It's been so long now since I left Old Town, but when I close my eyes, I still see the faces of those good-hearted, though sometimes stupid people. I remember your father. He had a small build, and his feet pointed out. He was a good-hearted carpenter, respected by the townsfolk. They called him uncle. Did you say he's already gone?"

"Yes, he's gone."

"I asked him to make an office table, and he didn't agree to it at once. For that, I slapped him. He was older than I was, but I still slapped him. At that time, I thought that I was carrying the whole country on my shoulder. I still remember the expression in his eyes. They were filled with contempt and hatred. But I still thought that power was stronger than hatred.

"I also remember that woman everybody called Chai Pafeng. She must have been one of your neighbors. She didn't get in line during meat rationing. I made her kneel down in front of everybody with a pail of water on her head. Since it was a rationing, everybody had the chance to buy. But some still refused to get in line. It was a small incident. I could have pretended not to notice if I'd wanted to. But I'd heard the Japanese remarking on this before. They called the Taiwanese stupid and ignorant for caring more about their own little vested interests than for order. When I was small, my Japanese teachers looked down on me the same way. And then I learned to look at my own people that way, too.

"I also remember Ah Chao, the butcher. Someone accused him of injecting water into the pork he sold. He denied the allegation, so I forced a lot of water down his throat. Now I can still hear him screaming and pleading.

"It was a nightmare, a never-ending nightmare. I had a good memory and excellent judgment. These were the tools I used to build myself up. I lorded it over Old Town the way a king would. I considered myself a tiger or a lion. Deep inside, I was a cat or a dog at best. I learned how to capitalize on the power of the Japanese."

"I thought I was the king, but people of the town considered me a plague. I knew they all avoided me. Although there were those who tried to curry favor with me the way I did with the Japanese. Yu-lan used to try to keep me in line. Old Town was a small place, and hers was one of its oldest families. About a third of the townspeople were either relatives or family friends. But how could I give up my power? Anybody who enjoys power naturally immerses himself in it, even to the extent of abandoning himself.

"Yet one day the Japanese were defeated. Frankly, the Japanese themselves had an inkling of what was to come, but nobody ever thought that it would come so soon. Because it happened so suddenly, before I could even react, Yu-lan's brother-in-law, the lawyer, tried to persuade me to flee the town.

"I didn't listen to him. I was convinced that I could still control the townsfolk, until the day when I suddenly realized that the tame deer had turned into a fierce tiger. In haste, I fled alone and returned to my boyhood home. This was the only place I could hide. I never thought that my father would refuse to take me in. He said that I was no longer his son. I knew it was the wedding rite that infuriated him. I never expected such courage and conviction from a man who had lived in the country all his life. Fortunately, my mother pleaded with him. He agreed to let me stay temporarily in this small warehouse, which was then used for storing farm implements. My father had some farmland, but he refused to let me plant on it. Actually, I didn't know how to plant. My mother secretly brought me food.

"In silence, I waited to rejoin Yu-lan. I had hoped that things would settle down, and I could go look for her. Less than two months had passed before she died after catching a simple cold. I couldn't believe it when the news came.

"I remember being told that our home had been sealed off. Everyone said she'd died of a contagious disease, and so they avoided her house.

"I suddenly felt that I was the most solitary person on earth. Nothing in the world could take her place. I could still vividly recall her poise as we played tennis. Soon after the war, she told me that if I committed suicide, she would not hesitate to follow me. I could almost see her there on her knees as people milled around her at the temple square.

"I was told that she faced the enraged mob calmly and bravely. For my sake, a woman shouldered the burden of a public enemy's guilt. When they cursed her, she pleaded for forgiveness, but not for herself. When someone spit on her, she didn't wipe it away. What kind of a man was I to allow my wife to suffer such great humiliation?

"Didn't she have any words of complaint? I couldn't even see her again for one last time before she died. Even if she wanted to pour out her anger, there was no one for her to turn to. How could she have died in peace?

"I was fortunate to have had such a wife. Are my sins so unforgivable that I had to win her only to lose her? When everybody, including my own family, despised me, only she, in her quiet way, bore up. Before I could even show her my gratitude and remorse, she just left this world in silence.

"My heart died with her. Actually, I should have died as soon as the Japanese surrendered. That's when many Japanese committed suicide. I wasn't as brave. I said I wasn't Japanese. I am a people's sinner. I should have died to win forgiveness for my sins. But I didn't and instead fled to the safety of the mountains. See how shameless I am? I escaped to this place so that she could ask forgiveness from the people. In my heart, I was still hoping that when things settled down, I could return and become a policeman again.

"Her death totally changed the way I thought. From that day on, Tseng Chi-hsiang no longer existed in this world. Actually, on that fateful day when the Japanese surrendered, his existence should have ended. His people, his relatives and friends, his own parents had all deserted him. But he shame-lessly clung on.

"Ah . . . Yu-lan," he picked up the photograph carefully for a closer look. "You really can't remember her?" His hands were trembling as he spoke. His eyes were blank and dry.

"I knew her. But I was small then; it's difficult for me to recognize her now."

"You're not the only one who couldn't recognize her. If someone your age can't recognize her, then maybe no one from the town would. A while ago, you said that Old Town has changed so much, you barely know the people on the streets when you go back. I knew she would quickly be forgotten."

"Why didn't you do a carving of her?"

"I did try, but I couldn't. Although she was my wife and once very close to me, I couldn't carve an image of her. She's too far away from me now. Once I touched her body, but it didn't be-long to me. Her heart used to belong to me, but I couldn't grasp it. Her face, what was the expression on her face before she died? I'm still waiting to be told that.

"I knew she had only one wish. That was to die beside me and be buried beside me. I learned that her parents died one after the other. I've heard that Old Town has changed, but I've never returned, not even once. I dare not go. At first I was afraid that those people still hated me. Then I was afraid that my sins would contaminate her home. I couldn't face her relatives. I wanted to bring her remains here, but I was afraid she would find this place too unfamiliar, never having come here in her lifetime.

"Her son has grown up into a man. I say 'her son' because I am not fit to be called his father. He's left Old Town now for Taipei. I thought that when things had settled down, I would bring them here to be with me. I never thought she would leave us so soon. Her son was brought up by her older sister. He's come here and asked me to live with him. But I couldn't bear to face him. Seeing him was more painful than anything else. He took after his mother. I wish that, like everybody else, he would despise me.

"I thought that I should tell him the story of Yu-lan and myself, but I didn't know how to begin. When I was alone, I could talk to Yu-lan. But if she really appeared before me, I'm afraid I wouldn't be able to utter a word. Maybe that's one of the reasons I couldn't carve an image of her."

"You were condemning yourself when you carved those horses?" I asked him.

"In my time, the Taiwanese called the Japanese 'dogs,' 'four-legged dogs.' Those who worked for the Japanese were called 'three-legged dogs.' "

"But you only carve horses. Why not other animals?"

"Because they only wanted horses. I kept on carving horses, and all of a sudden one day I saw myself in them. So I included myself in my carvings."

I picked the horses up. Although their positions varied, they had one thing in common: their postures and expressions emanated pain and remorse.

"What do you plan to do with them?"

"I don't know," he hesitated, "perhaps one day, I'll burn them all."

"Burn them?"

"Because nothing connects them to other people," he said in a feeble voice.

"Would you sell one to me?" I asked boldly. Actually, I was thinking that if I could afford them, I'd take them all.

"Sell you one?" Again he hesitated. Slowly, he turned his face toward me. "Okay, choose one. During these past thirty-three years, I have not met anybody from Old Town except you. Though it's something I've wanted, it's something I've always been afraid of."

"But I've left Old Town, too."

"At least you still remember there was a policeman in Old Town by the name of White-nosed Raccoon."

I chose one horse. Three of its legs were kneeling on the ground, and the only standing leg supported the weight of its body. The horse's head was slightly bent, its mouth wide open, and its nostrils flared out, as if panting or neighing. Its mane was matted and wild. I took a closer look. One of its hind legs was broken and dragging uselessly.

"That one is a gift," he said hesitantly.

"Why?"

"I was afraid you would choose that one. Usually, things you're afraid of come true sooner than you would expect. One night, I dreamt of Yu-lan. I hadn't dreamt of her for a long time. I was afraid I'd forgotten her. In the dream, I saw her kneeling before me with tears in her eyes. I was also crying. I'd thought till then that there wouldn't be any more tears. But that night, my pillows were wet. The next morning, I decided to stop all my work and concentrate on carving a horse. The result was that horse in your hand. If you look at horses, always look at their eyes. See those eyes for yourself."

185

I looked first at the wooden horse and then turned to look at him. It was then I noticed that his dry and lifeless eyes had suddenly turned moist.

Quickly I looked away. Very carefully, I put the wooden horse back where I had found it. Lai Kuo-lin and I stepped out of the house in silence.

ELEVEN

Hair

I ran into Chin-chih when I returned to Hsiaputsai for my eldest brother's funeral two years ago. The last time I had seen him was toward the end of the war, some forty years before.

When my brother died, he was eighty-one years old by Chinese reckoning, and Chin-chih was at least seventy. Chin-chih looked the same as ever, with his dark, ruddy complexion. He didn't have many wrinkles for someone his age; his cheeks were quite smooth. But his hair was thinner and grayer than before. His gait was still punctuated with that same limp. I always used to see him in short pants, but that day he was wearing long trousers.

"Remember me?" he asked.

"You're Chin-chih."

"You got it right this time."

When I was young, Chin-chih had been a mysterious character. I heard his name more often than I actually saw him. He was a fisherman, and he spent more time outdoors than in.

Back then, whenever I returned to Hsiaputsai, I called him

"Brother" Chin-chih, as my nieces and nephews did. My eldest brother was twenty-six years older than me, and even my eldest niece was two years my senior. At that time, Chin-chih was already an adult, and I was used to hearing my nieces and nephews calling him "Brother Chin-chih," so I wrongly adopted the same form of address for him.

Despite his age, he was, in fact, a generation behind me. But because I was only a kid, and also because I was raised by my maternal uncle and didn't know him all that well, he, on his part, called me by my name rather than "Uncle" as he should have, according to convention.

Chin-chih's family were rice farmers. Perhaps it was because of his bad leg that he turned to the rivers and ponds for his livelihood. Whenever I used to run into him, he'd be carrying a large fish basket on his back, either going or coming from fishing or on his way to market to sell his catch.

Those were the days before pollution, when the rivers and ponds were full of fish. If he had just come from fishing or was on his way to market, he often had white eels, jumbo catfish, or even larger carps, all weighing in at almost two pounds. You don't see eels or catfish that size anymore.

People said that Chin-chih was the best fisherman in all of Hsiaputsai. Every time I ran into him, I would ask him to take me fishing sometime, and he would always agree, but it never actually happened.

Once I ran into him on road along the Hou-bi Canal and asked him again if he'd take me fishing.

"OK," he said and then rolled up his pants and waded into the canal.

The Hou-bi Canal ran behind our house and was used for irrigation and washing. At its narrowest, it was only a few feet wide, but the broadest part was probably more than ten yards. This was the part used for washing clothes and where the water buffalo soaked.

I watched as he walked slowly up to the edge of the canal where a lot of seaweed grew and then bent down and reached his arm into the water.

"Ha, ha! Got one!" he cried.

Something very long wriggled wildly in his hand. It wasn't any kind of eel that I'd ever seen before. Could it be a snake?

"What is that?"

"Look." He climbed back up the bank, clutching the water snake in his hand.

"A snake!" It startled me. "That's not a fish!"

"They're harder to catch than fish. Like to try it?"

This incident left a deep impression on me.

This all happened during my summer vacation. But Hsiaputsai's biggest event was to occur that winter.

I was thirteen years old that year—twelve, according to Western calculations—and it was the last winter before the end of the war. As always, I went back to the country during my winter vacation. My uncle had been raising me since I was very small, but I genuinely liked the country. Every winter and summer vacation, I would spend some time there.

My father was still alive and lived in the country, too, but my eldest brother was the head of the household. My father had left home when he was very young to work in a mine up north. My brother rented and farmed the family land.

Toward the end of the war launched by the Japanese in the Pacific, there were serious shortages of all kinds of goods. In the country, though, you grew your own crops and raised your own ducks and chickens, and each family could keep a certain amount of rice, sweet potatoes, or poultry for its own use. There were restrictions on hogs; you could raise them but weren't allowed to slaughter them for your own consumption. You would be given a small amount of pork and lard, however, when you had them slaughtered. Of course, some people slaughtered them on the sly. There were no such restrictions on poultry, and each family was free to do what it wanted: you could eat the meat yourself, or sell it, or use it to barter for things like cloth, sugar, salt, or salted fish.

During that winter visit to the country, the big fat capon my brother was raising suddenly disappeared. My brother's farm was between plantings at the time, so the ducks and chickens were allowed to run free in the fields or bamboo groves and eat whatever grain or insects they could find.

You don't see capons in Taiwan anymore, but there were still some around when I was growing up. Sometimes a middle-aged man would come riding on a rickety old bike over the narrow village road, blowing now and again on his little whistle. He could castrate both roosters and hogs. People believed that castrated stock would not go into heat, would have gentler dispositions, wouldn't fight, and would put all their energy into eating, so they'd grow plump faster and produce tender, juicy meat.

The farmers would go out and catch the roosters weighing under a pound and a half. The castrater would pin each rooster down right on the edge of a courtyard, make a small incision near the animal's back end, and insert a metal hook to hold the slit open. He would then slip a loop of what looked like horse hair over the tiny testicles, yank them off, and set the young rooster free. It was that easy. For hogs, you had to apply cooking ashes to the wound. This was supposed to discourage infection.

Hsiaputsai, the village where my brother and his family lived, was about an hour's drive from the city. It was a quiet, peaceful village. It wasn't one of those places where all the residents shared the same family name, but everybody pretty much knew everybody else. Most people called each other by some familial term, like "Uncle" or "Brother," according to age and generation. No thefts ever occurred in this kind of village. And my brother was one of the pillars of the community; it was almost unimaginable that someone would steal a capon from him. What was worse, a young laying hen had been stolen a little while earlier from his next-door neighbor. Soon money and valuables started disappearing from other nearby homes.

The whole town was buzzing with talk at the disappearance of the capon. When the neighbor had lost his mother hen, some people thought at first that a stray dog might have dragged it away. Now everybody was suspicious.

There was a tradition in the village regarding capons. They were raised for Chinese New Year; for the ninth day of the first lunar month, the birthday of the god of heaven; and for the fifteenth day of the first lunar month, the Lantern Festival. The two most important holidays were Chinese New Year and the god of heaven's birthday; capons, not ordinary chickens, were required for the sacrifices offered to the god of heaven. I remember how, when I was young, four or five long tail feathers had to be left on the capons for these occasions.

The Japanese forbade the Taiwanese to worship their own idols back then. But most people did it secretly anyway, especially rural folk.

Since things were getting stolen, there had to be a thief. Hsiaputsai was a farming village, far removed from the city, with only one oxcart road that connected it to the outside world. Very seldom did you see a stranger come or go, so everybody assumed that the thief was living there among them.

This was a serious matter to the residents of Hsiaputsai, because never before had anything like this happened in their quiet, peaceful farming village. And now it was happening again and again. And how did they know that it wouldn't continue?

My brother, it seemed, was determined to take the matter into his own hands. My brother was twenty-six years older than me; he was thirty-nine that year. The first person he suspected was Li-ching. Li-ching was Chin-chih's wife.

"It *must* be her." Almost the entire village suspected Li-ching.

Chin-chih had brought Li-ching back from Houchuwei, not far from the village. Because Chin-chih fished for a living, his work took him to many different places. Sometimes he'd be gone for a week at a time. It was said that Li-ching had been evacuated to Houchuwei from the streets of some city. Toward the end of the war, as Japan's position went from bad to worse, the Japanese evacuated city people to the countryside to reduce war casualties. In fact, because of the frequent air raids then, many people moved to rural areas voluntarily.

So it was in the nearby community of Houchuwei that Chin-chih met Li-ching and eventually brought her home with him. Because this was wartime, no one bothered with elaborate rituals like engagements and weddings. If you brought someone home with you, that's all it took: you were man and wife.

Actually, with the shortage of men at the time, a woman was considered lucky to be able to find a marriage partner at all.

In our family, for example, my second brother was sent to the Philippines, my third brother to New Guinea, and my fourth brother went to "serve faithfully" patching up the airport, which was in constant need of repairs. There were almost no strong young men at home in those times. Chin-chih had apparently escaped the draft because of his bad leg.

My brother called for Li-ching, who promptly denied having anything to do with the thefts. But my brother was not willing to let her off the hook so easily. His reasoning was simple: nothing had ever been stolen before Li-ching had come to Hsiaputsai, and since her arrival, wherever she went, thefts followed in her wake.

"Are you willing to take an oath?"

"Yes."

"Well, let's hear it."

"If I have stolen anything, you can cut my head off."

"Oaths are not to be taken lightly," my brother said.

"I honestly did not steal anything."

"All right." My brother produced a dustpan with a handful of moist chicken feathers in it.

"I dug this out of the ash pit of your kitchen stove. Now what do you have to say? Chin-chih, you come here, too, and have a look."

Smack went Chin-chih's palm across Li-ching's face.

Li-ching nearly lost her balance.

"Li-ching, they were right: it *was* you!"

Li-ching hung her head and said nothing.

"All right, where's the chicken then?" Chin-chih asked in a shrill voice. Apparently, he really didn't know anything about the matter.

"It's under the bed."

Everybody went along to see. Li-ching uncovered a small ceramic pot from under the sweet potatoes beneath the bed. It was half full of chicken meat.

"Why?!" Chin-chih bellowed.

"I didn't have enough milk . . . for the baby . . ." Li-ching sobbed, tears streaming down her face.

Li-ching had borne a child two months before and had had only one chicken all month. It was wartime. But, Chin-chih said, he had left a number of white eels for her, and they were even more nutritious than chicken.

"Uncle A-pao . . ." Although my brother was the eldest in our immediate family, our father was the youngest son of our grandfather, and Chin-chih's father and his brothers were all older than my brother. So Chin-chih referred to my brother using a title that means "younger uncle."

"Uncle A-pao, I want you to handle this."

"You handle it yourself."

In fact, Chin-chih had beaten Li-ching for stealing before. But Li-ching found it hard to change her ways, and her fingers were still as sticky as ever.

One afternoon, three days after my brother found the chicken feathers, Chin-chih showed up suddenly and asked my brother to come along to his house. He said it was time to deal with Li-ching's theft. I tagged along behind.

"Li-ching is going to be put to death."

The women quickly gathered, speaking to each other in low voices. They followed us at a distance. Whenever my brother looked back, they stopped for a moment.

My brother put on his three-inch-high clogs made of palm wood. Usually farmers in the village, both men and women, went barefoot, and my brother did, too. About the only time he wore wooden clogs was during Chinese New Year when he went to play cards at a neighbor's house. The time clogs this high proved most practical was when you had to walk over a muddy road on a rainy day. My brother was not very tall, so the clogs added noticeably to his height.

My brother had a dark complexion, which made his eyes and teeth appear especially bright. Some people said he resembled Judge Pao, a Chinese magistrate of the Song dynasty known for his dark face as well as his severe and just handling of criminals. What they meant was that he looked a little scary.

Chin-chih's house was set back-to-back against my brother's. Chin-chih and his family occupied the large, main part of the building; my brother lived in a smaller extension of it. Each household had its own rice paddy and was run separately, though the land was adjoining.

Chin-chih was the third male among his siblings. His eldest brother Tien-sung and second brother Chang-keng were both waiting in the main hall for him to return. They seemed to be older than my brother. As soon as they saw him, both stood up to offer him a seat in the center.

My brother sat on a bench. Even with his clogs on, his feet did not reach to the floor, so he removed the clogs and pulled up his legs to sit cross-legged instead.

In the center of the main room was a high wooden table for

religious objects. By the left wall sat a pale square table. The paint was completely gone from years of use, or maybe country people left their furniture unpainted to save money; I don't know. In any case, by then it was old, faded, and dirty, its corners worn smooth.

A miniature kerosene lamp hung on the wall above the square table. Soot blackened the wall above the lamp.

One side of the table was pushed up against the wall, and benches had been placed around the other three sides. The wall was made of earthen bricks; rice straw poked out of it everywhere you looked.

My brother sat on the bench nearest the center of the room. The benches were of the same pale wood as the table. The room had an uneven mud floor, still showing traces of the chicken droppings that had just been swept away.

The high mantlelike table occupied a central place at the very back of the main hall facing the entrance. It was nearing the end of the war, and the Japanese were strongly promoting recognition of their emperor as divine and of all the people under Japanese rule as his subjects. Displaying traditional Chinese religious figures or objects was not permitted; they were to be replaced by models of Japanese Shinto shrines, so that the people could worship the *Ameterasu Omikami*, or sun goddess.

Back then, most people kept their religious figures and incense burners in vegetable baskets stored in their attics, to be brought out secretly only on religious holidays. Chin-chih had brought out his vegetable basket, which contained a shrine to Fu Teh, the local guardian deity of earth. Although Fu Teh was a minor god, he was the most important deity to farmers. Most farmers were very poor then. Not only did few people have a figurine of the deity in their homes, even outdoor shrines built under trees often had none. Or if they did, it was usually a very primitive one, perhaps a crudely carved piece of wood dabbed with brightly colored paint but without jewels or other ornaments.

Chin-chih pushed aside the figure of the Japanese sun goddess and carefully set the guardian deity in its proper place.

I hid under the square table alone. I don't know why I hid there. Maybe it was because of the charged atmosphere, or maybe because the room was filled with adults. I didn't see any other children around and couldn't find a place for myself. Even though I was a kid, I belonged to the senior generation. As long as my brother didn't say anything, nobody should have shooed me away. But at the time, I wasn't so sure about this.

I looked out now and then from under the table at my brother's wooden clogs, wishing I could borrow one to use as a stool. But I didn't dare make a move. Some women were standing at a distance outside the door.

I saw Chin-chih take out a large wooden chopping block and place it in the center of the room. I felt the atmosphere grow even tenser.

The chopping block was over a foot in diameter and was usually used by country people to butcher pork. It had a depression worn in the center from its many years of use. On the chopping block lay a meat cleaver, just sharpened and sparkling.

Chin-chih also produced a rectangular tray. This kind of tray was originally used to carry large bowls of soup, but during the atonement ceremonies of the seventh lunar month, it was also used to hold the three sacrificial animals. Sometimes the tray held a whole hog's head.

"Uncle A-pao . . ." Tien-sung and Chang-keng moved a bit closer to my brother. "What are we going to do?"

"Let's see what Chin-chih does first."

"Uncle A-pao, I've decided I'd like to handle Li-ching's case myself," Chin-chih said. He went to fetch Li-ching.

Li-ching was wearing an old faded blue-and-white-plaid blouse with matching pants.

Li-ching couldn't help from hesitating a moment when she

saw how many people were in the room. And they were all her elders. She tried first to retreat before reluctantly entering.

"Come on; you chose your punishment yourself."

"You really plan to kill me, Chin-chih?" Li-ching must have noticed the chopping block and cleaver by then.

"You're afraid? If you're afraid, then why did you ever do such a thing?" Chin-chih said, yanking at her roughly.

"I . . . I had to nurse the baby. I didn't have enough milk. The baby . . ." Li-ching mumbled, her voice trembling slightly.

"You didn't have enough milk, so you went out and stole?"

"Really, I didn't have enough milk. The baby would have starved to death . . ."

"On your knees!" Chin-chih ordered Li-ching to kneel in front of the shrine of the guardian deity. In those days, because of the war, the Japanese discouraged women from perming their hair. Li-ching plaited her hair into two braids in back, secured with barrettes.

"The guardian deity now presides over us. For almost sixty years we, the Li family, have lived in Hsiaputsai. Not one single family member has ever been involved in theft. But now this unworthy woman, Li-ching, has done just such a thing, bringing shame to the entire Li family. I, Chin-chih, of the younger generation, will now handle this matter personally." Chin-chih lit three sticks of incense, bowed three times, and then knelt down and kowtowed another three times.

"You bow three times, too."

Chin-chih led Li-ching over to the family ancestral shrine at the left end of the altar table. The shrine was over a foot high and was the most brightly painted object on the altar . . . no, in the whole room. It was protected by a glass case and on it were written the names of the family forefathers in small, close characters.

"Kneel down!"

After homage was paid before the family shrine, Chin-chih brought Li-ching over to my brother.

"Uncle A-pao, I won't do it again. I'm truly sorry. I promise I won't do it again." Li-ching entreated. She knelt pleading in front of my brother, her face stained with tears.

My brother remained silent.

"I don't know how many times we've been told this already," Chin-chih said.

"Uncle A-pao . . ." Tien-sung and Chang-keng drew closer to my brother.

"Look at him."

Chin-chih pulled Li-ching over and ordered her to prostrate herself on the floor and then to place her head on the chopping block, with her face turned to one side.

"Chin-chih, I'm afraid . . . don't kill me, don't kill me, please!"

People said that Li-ching was the prettiest woman in Hsia-putsai, though I couldn't personally vouch for that. But she had that kind of very fair skin you just never saw in the country. She looked even paler with her head turned sideways on the chopping block. She couldn't stop twitching.

"Uncle A-pao . . ." Tien-sung and Chang-keng took hold of my brother's hand. Both of them were older and taller than my brother. My brother closed his eyes for a moment, as though thinking, but still did not utter a word.

"I . . . I don't want to die." One of Li-ching's cheeks was flattened against the chopping block, and she murmured nonstop. Her voice was high pitched, and her skin was the color of paper. Her lips had turned purple and quivered ceaselessly. Her forehead was dotted with beads of sweat.

"I don't want to die! Who will take care of the baby if I die?"

Chin-chih paid no attention to her. He held her braids tightly in one hand and raised the cleaver high with the other.

My brother seemed to give a start. I thought maybe he meant to stop Chin-chih. Chin-chih's arm descended swiftly.

We heard a resounding *clang*. The cleaver had struck.

"Ay yo!" Li-ching screamed.

Chin-chih held in his hand two severed hanks of hair, with the barrettes still clipped on.

"Whew," both Tien-sung and Chang-keng let out sighs of relief. The expressions on all the faces in the room seemed to relax.

Li-ching did not die, but she fainted. Chin-chih slapped her face lightly to bring her to and then started grilling her as one would a disobedient child.

"Are you going to try and pull something like this again?" he demanded. He put the lopped-off hair on the soup tray. With her braids gone, Li-ching's hair hung straight as a stick, like a school girl's.

"No!"

"Are you sure?"

"Yes. I won't ever do it again!"

"Uncle A-pao . . ." Chin-chih still crouched in front of the chopping block.

"All right, all right."

"Uncle A-pao . . ."

"That'll do."

Chin-chih slapped Li-ching's cheeks again lightly until she calmed down. He tried to help her up, but she just sat there. There was a puddle on the floor. At first I thought it was blood, but then I heard the others say that Li-ching had been so terrified, she'd wet her pants.

I looked at my brother. He slid down a bit to put his feet into his clogs and then got up from the bench. I followed behind. My brother didn't say a word all the way home. He just trudged ahead, his head hanging down a bit. His step was considerably more relaxed than when we'd come.

Tien-sung and Chang-keng came over sometime after eight that evening to tell my brother that Chin-chih wanted to move away.

"Where to?"

"They'll move back to Houchuwei for the time being."

"Must they?"

"Chin-chih insists."

"Well then, I guess it's for the better."

As soon as I heard that my brother didn't oppose the idea, I went to wait on the road behind our house. It was the only road leading out of the village.

Since it was winter, it turned dark early. The moon wasn't out yet.

I waited all alone on the road. Wind blew through the bamboo grove. The jet black bamboo responded with a soft *yee-ya, yee-ya* as it creaked forward and back. The wind was frigid.

I remembered the time Chin-chih had caught a water snake with his bare hands. And that he was the only adult who ever said he would take me fishing.

I waited alone near the canal for almost twenty minutes. Chin-chih brought Li-ching out with him. There was nobody there to see them off. Was that because of the cold or the dark?

I could see that Li-ching was wearing the same style of pants but not the same pair as that afternoon. She carried her new baby on her back and had a bundle tied to her arm. Chin-chih carried his loads on a shoulder pole, his fishing gear hanging from one end and a slightly larger cloth bundle at the other. Was that everything they had?

Like most country people back then, they weren't wearing shoes.

Chin-chih still walked with a limp, but he had a firm, sure step. I remember that he had wide, thick feet, probably from all the walking he did.

Li-ching followed behind and was also limping. I noticed myself that the road was very uneven, embedded with sharp stones or pieces of dried earth that pierced my feet as I walked.

Whenever Li-ching couldn't quite keep up, Chin-chih would stop and wait for her. Sometimes he rested his hand on her shoulder, and now and then he would ask her if she was able to keep going. As I looked at him, I could hardly imagine that this was the same man I had been watching at noon.

The two of them had been walking for some time, and I was still shadowing them. I didn't understand at the time why I was following them. Chin-chih was a very special person to me. Maybe I knew somehow that I wouldn't be seeing them again for a long, long time.

And, in fact, I never did see the two of them together again.

"Go back! There are dogs around the houses up ahead."

"Are they mean?"

"Mm-hmm. *Very* mean."

I stopped and was afraid to keep following. I watched them as they disappeared. Li-ching's gait was not very different from Chin-chih's hobble. Noticing this gave me a strange feeling.

It was dark. The barely discernible oxcart road led into the black.

Just at that moment, a searchlight shot into the sky. Then there were two, and then three of them. They swept east and west, high and low, traversing the sky in fits and starts. Sometimes a light would fall on clouds and produce a round or oblong patch of white. Sometimes the searchlights shone brightly, sometimes they disappeared; sometimes they separated, and sometimes they fused together or crossed each other. I had never seen them light up an enemy plane. I had heard the adults say that they scrambled for cover whenever an enemy plane appeared. I wondered if it was really true.

I let my thoughts wander, continuing to follow Chin-chih and wife with my eyes until I couldn't have spotted them even with those searchlights.

I had no idea then that I would meet up with Chin-chih

again, some forty years later, at my brother's funeral and think back to all these events.

"You're here alone?"

"Yes, just me. Didn't you hear that Li-ching died? She's been gone for over forty years now."

"Oh."

Actually, I had known about Li-ching's death. I was thinking of their child, the one that Li-ching left behind. He must be over forty by now. But I didn't think it was worth the trouble of clarifying myself.

Not long after Chin-chih and Li-ching moved to Houchuwei, before the war was over, Li-ching went into a field one night to steal a cabbage and was discovered by the farmer.

Actually it was the farmer's dog who heard her first. The dog barked a few times and then tore out toward the cabbage patch.

Generally, when a farmer's dog discovered something un-usual it would stay near the farmhouse and bark. If it chased after the thing, it could be that someone had commanded it to do so or that it was specially trained.

Li-ching got up and ran along the irrigation ditch, which was about thirty feet wide. There happened to be water in the ditch, in preparation for the spring planting.

Li-ching knew how to dog-paddle. But with the dog after her, she knew she couldn't escape, so she slipped into the irrigation ditch and inched slowly away along the edge.

"*Woof, woof*!" The dog had caught up with her.

"Where did that blasted thief run off to?" Soon there were several pursuers.

"This is already the third time. We can't let him get away this time."

"If I catch him, I'll kill him."

The dog barked and whined.

The dog was right over Li-ching's head when its barking turned into whining. Maybe it was sniffing around. Li-ching remained still as a corpse and pressed her face against the wall of the ditch.

Irrigation ditches were usually drained in the winter for maintenance and repair. Any seaweed was also removed from the ditch walls in the process.

Both the men and the dog were now right above her. She ducked her head down and clung fast to the side of the ditch.

She was not worried about how deep the ditch was. But the water was freezing cold, and that was hard to endure.

"That's strange."

"Think she might be in the ditch?"

There were at least two people there. If they didn't leave soon, Li-ching would freeze to death.

"I found her! Here she is!" someone shouted.

"Right here! It's a woman!"

"Help!"

The farmer let down his carrying pole into the ditch for her to grab onto. Her whole body was quaking, and she held on to the pole only with the greatest difficulty.

"Kill her."

"Break her legs."

She saw the whining dog's glistening green eyes.

The two men waved the pole. Both seemed to be young, not more than twenty.

"Don't hit me!" She knelt down. Actually, it was because the cold water had turned her legs to jelly.

"Wait a minute," an older voice spoke up. "Isn't it Chin-chih's woman?"

Rather than beating her, the farmer took her home.

Li-ching sneezed the whole way back. She came down with a terrible cold, which eventually turned into an acute case of pneumonia, not a disease easily cured back in those days. In less than two weeks, she was dead.

Chin-chih left the area soon after Li-ching's death. This time he moved even farther away. Though it had been more than forty years since Li-ching's death, Chin-chih had never remarried.

"That woman . . . that woman . . ." Chin-chih murmured to himself.

I noticed that his eyes were red.

TWELVE

The Coconut Palms on Campus

I

The department chairman just told me I've been appointed lecturer. It's very unusual for a promotion to be approved after only three years, so no wonder he wanted to tell me personally. I am delighted, but I'm also a bit worried about what Hsiu-chuan and the others will say. Last time, I overheard her saying, "We should feel sorry for her; she spends all her time studying her heart out."

That was unfair of her, but she's not the only one to treat me unfairly. I don't understand why everyone has to link my academic success with my physical defect.

They haven't done as well in school as I have, and now, with my promotion, I've moved one more step ahead of them. Naturally, this means they need to find a way to console themselves or, rather, a way in which they are still superior to me. In fact, it is actually my defect, rather than their superiority, in which they take comfort. But they are just deluding themselves by all this, and that's exactly what I find so aggravating. Why do people have to fool themselves all the time?

I'm looking out the window; it's beautiful outside, and there are lots of people on campus. Some are upperclassmen, and some, I suppose, are new students. Soon I'll stand at the lectern, and maybe one or two of these young men and women, the chosen elite from the entire province, will be my students. I feel a sense of triumph, but it's overshadowed by an even stronger feeling.

The campus is neat, with paths and lawns between buildings. The avenue leading in from the main entrance consists of five lanes. The avenue has safety islands on both sides, neatly planted with azaleas. Between each pair of azaleas is planted, appropriately, a coconut palm. Over the past few years, I have come to know and understand them very well.

Books are piled everywhere in my room; some are the school's, some were loaned to me by professors, but most of them are my own. I have spent nearly my whole salary on them. I used to want nothing more than to bury myself in books. At least when I was lost in them, I could forget the outside world with all its hassles.

But lately I've come to feel that even in the world of books, I am often conscious of some uncertainty. Even while my eyes are focused on the page, my mind continually wanders. More than once, this has led me to wonder if knowledge only makes me more profoundly aware of the agony of human life.

Every time I consider this, I worry and become anxious. I seem to feel as if I'm falling apart. I'm afraid of falling apart, yet at the same time I don't seem to be able to help myself. What's worse, it's not the books' fault at all, and that just makes me feel more pathetic. Some days, I decide to leave all these books behind, maybe even tear them up, one by one, and then light a fire and burn them all to ashes.

But I never do it. Even though I don't have much faith in

books or derive much encouragement from them, at least they give me a bit of support. I'm afraid that if I really burned my books, I would lose my last foothold and fall apart completely.

II

Chang Ying-ming was tall, at least six feet. He had just recently returned from studying in the United States, and I'd heard that his spoken English was as good as any American's. This alone would have been enough to make any woman longing to study in the United States admire him. Professor Chao pulled me aside, saying, "How many Chinese are able to earn their living speaking English in the USA? This guy is a big fish. Don't let him get away!" Professor Chao wasn't serious, but in fact I was very grateful to him for looking out for me.

At first, Chang spoke to me in English. I don't know if this was out of habit or because he wanted to show off, or if he was testing me. I go out of my way to avoid speaking English, not because I'm afraid of being outshone, but because I am not used to it. Besides, I don't feel it's necessary. I guess he got the message, because he immediately switched to Chinese.

Despite this, I saw no evidence that he was disappointed in me; on the contrary, he seemed to grow more and more animated as we talked. He was very knowledgeable about many things; perhaps this is what characterizes someone who is well traveled and experienced. General knowledge like that is great, but I have more respect for the specialist who knows everything about one subject.

I am not being too particular; people are entitled to their ideals. I know people will say I should be grateful when others aren't picky about me. But, no matter what anyone thinks, I will always stick to my ideals.

Fortunately, Chang Ying-ming did not only know a lot about many things, he had also studied Greek drama in depth. In this one respect, he knew enough to be my teacher.

Then he spotted my right hand, the one small enough to be a child's, the five fingers that cannot be curled at will. It looks like the plucked head of a duck on display at a noodle stand. His eyes fixed on it, staring strangely. I could sense his gaze but dared not look him in the eye. It was as if my awkward hand was not a part of my body, as if it had been forgotten and left on the table.

I felt uneasy, like a culprit awaiting a verdict, anxious to know my fate but afraid that what the judge was about to utter would condemn me to hell.

I still recall the first time this happened. I had a friend named Wang. This was long ago, before I had graduated. At first, he seemed to have plenty to talk about with me. Naturally, I was aware of my defect, but I believed that he would not mind it, given the kind of person he was, especially since we both seemed to be enjoying our conversation so much up to that point.

I would never have guessed that when he spotted my right hand, he would go silent immediately, as if he had completely forgotten how to talk, as if he had completely forgotten his very existence! His utterly flabbergasted expression made me panic; stunned and dumbfounded, it was all I could do to watch his contorted face. I couldn't believe a person's expression could change that quickly.

I sensed the gravity of this change, and, despite myself, my eyes started to burn. But I held back the tears, not letting them fall. I didn't want him to see me cry.

It wasn't his fault, I knew. We all have the right to choose our friends. But the difference in his attitude before and after he saw my hand was like day and night, and that abrupt change, or the reason behind it, was what caused me so much pain. And I became even more acutely aware of my defect.

When my classmates learned of it, my hand became their scapegoat. On more than one occasion, they would refer to my "deformed hand." And not just my classmates, even my younger sister does this. Romance writers always delight in giving their favorite characters some minute feature that distinguishes them from others, yet I have only one wish: to be in no way different.

That night, I couldn't sleep. I just lay in bed crying. I couldn't understand. In a split second, had I become a completely different person? I was always gaining more knowledge, yet I was beginning to doubt whether it was of any use.

After that, I began to understand that this defect would have a decisive influence on my future. Two opposing forces began to do battle in my heart: should I hide my defect or expose it entirely?

Exaggerating one's imperfections or glossing over them are both manifestations of an inferiority complex. But as soon as they saw the slightest opening, these two options resumed combat. The space that books used to occupy was gradually being overrun by these thoughts. I could never again regain the self-confidence I'd once had.

The uncertainty I felt made me keep my distance from men. I barricaded myself in my study, yet I could not completely avoid the outside world. My broken heart was slow to heal, and I was left with scars that would never recover completely.

I learned more every day, yet I always felt something lacking in my heart. If knowledge only makes one miserable, I would rather be an idiot.

Naturally, I hoped I would get some encouragement from my family, that they would offer me some warmth. But what I received from them was exactly the opposite.

On graduation, my professors asked me over and over to stay on at my alma mater and teach, particularly Professor Chao, who took pains to secure me a study, my only safe haven.

After more than two years, I had come to feel somewhat at ease again, so I was totally unprepared when I ran into that fellow, Lin.

As soon as I saw him, my resolve to live the life of a recluse began to waver. He was very good-looking, like the portrait of the poet Lord Byron. However, his personality rather clashed with his appearance. Although he had had quite a bit of schooling, he was fond of pretending he knew more than he did.

I don't know if it was because I was lonely or because I had started to give up on myself. In any case, I couldn't help falling for him, even though I knew perfectly well he wasn't my kind of man.

I detested myself for my weakness, because I knew that without a doubt this boat was bound for hell. Yet I grabbed on to it for all I was worth.

Once again, those two forces clashed in my heart. Should I expose my physical defect or hide it? If I wanted to experience a moment of satisfaction, I should choose the latter. I could at least fool him for a while. I realized, however, that he would eventually find out.

But it was another force that constantly impelled me. I could fool others, but I could not fool myself. Fooling others in the short run amounted to fooling oneself in the long run. I had to have confidence in myself. This thought began to gain the upper hand, supplanting the former one. I seemed to see myself in a new light, and this bolstered my courage.

When he saw my hand, he was surprised at first, but his expression changed quickly to one of annoyance. I marveled at how different this time was from the first time: I was able to look him in the eye.

I didn't understand why he had acted the way he did. Perhaps he felt tricked and humiliated. So I slowly pulled my hand back.

Suddenly, he reached out and grabbed my hand. He was too brusque and too rude, and I immediately blushed. I don't know if it was because this was the first time a man had ever done that or because his action was so crude and sudden.

My hand struggled in his, but he held on to it firmly, turning it back and forth to examine it.

"Please don't do that." My voice was extremely unnatural, as if it had not come from my own throat. I said this with all the courage I could muster. I guess I sounded very unpleasant.

He looked at me, and then his tense expression suddenly relaxed, and the trace of a grin appeared at the corners of his mouth. But it was a sneer, full of disdain and rejection. At the same time, he threw down my hand.

I don't know if he used force or not when he dropped my hand like that, but he might as well have pushed me off a tall cliff into a gaping abyss, a thousand fathoms deep. I felt dizzy and faint.

From the outset I had felt he was not the right person for me, yet I kept giving in. In recent years, I'd been trying constantly to make myself stronger and tougher, but now I was just the opposite. This only made it doubly painful.

The shock he gave me was far worse than the first time, and the heartbreak that followed also more intense.

It is hard to describe the pain I feel in my heart when I must expose my flaw to others. It takes all my physical strength. And what adds to the pain is that I must go against my own will, even to the point of losing all sense of dignity.

This has put me on guard against men. I have even lost my respect and regard for Lord Byron. I have sunk to the point of being ruled by feelings. What does Byron have to do with this fellow? Yet whenever I read Byron's poetry, I think of him, think of his eyes filled with disdain. Still, I chose to get involved, so who can I blame but myself?

After this second disastrous attempt, I lost all confidence in myself as well as in men. I closed myself in my study and avoided all contact with them.

My getting to know Chang Ying-ming was Professor Chao's idea. Given what I'd learned from my two earlier experiences, I was very wary, but Professor Chao was someone I respected. I simply could not refuse him.

I was very nervous, for those two forces were going at it again in my mind. Again I thought of Professor Chao's joke, and I blushed. If Chang was a "big fish," then what was I? Professor Chao meant no harm by his remark. He knows me very well. However, his words sat uneasily with me.

When Chang spotted my hand, he immediately grew silent, just like the other two had done before. The room suddenly felt stuffy. His gaze was suffocating me.

However, I mustered my courage and held out my hand. I had only one thought in my mind: that I had to be honest with myself. Maybe all men on this earth are the same, maybe not, but whatever the case, I have to have confidence in myself.

Although I had been through two bad experiences, I still plucked up enough courage to pick up a tea cup with my right hand—that disfigured duck head—in the same way a duck would turn its neck to scratch under its wing.

His gaze remained fixed on my hand, making me feel tense and embarrassed. Suddenly my hand began to tremble. I did my best to steady it, but it only trembled more. All my energy was concentrated on my hand and that tea cup. I could feel my blood pumping in my veins: for this I had to expend all my effort, even my life. I had only one conviction: I don't play any games.

Nevertheless, the more I concentrated my energy, the more my hand refused to be controlled. Small ripples began to appear on the tea's surface, then more pronounced ones, and then finally they splashed over the rim of the cup.

I wanted to cry. I didn't understand why I'd wanted to make a fool of myself before a strange man, but still I held back my tears.

"Can I help?"

"No, no."

He was very calm, and I was quite upset. I knew that I had lost another battle. The expression on his face was full of sympathy. Although his sympathy made me indignant, at the same time I felt quite uneasy as I tried to make out from his expression whether or not he would accept my defect.

III

Going home is an ordeal. There are so many people without homes, a home of their own is all they want, but not me. I don't know anything about convent life, but I would be glad to live at school. My mother has never consented to it. "How can a girl live away from home?" I could give her a thousand reasons if she would listen to them.

I can't stand her cold expression. It is not just cold; at times, it seems full of hatred and scorn. If she really had a reason for hating me, I wouldn't blame her, but I don't believe that she has any reason.

My younger sister's attitude is even more insufferable. The way she looks at me out of the corner of her eye and flares her nostrils makes her disdain and her determination to pick a fight evident. I can put up with my mother, but it is a real challenge to put up with my sister.

I know that the way my mother treats me has something to do with my father. He's been dead for several years, and my impressions of him have faded. Yet every time I see my mother glare at his portrait, I wonder if she regards me with the same frightful look. I don't understand it. If Mother detests him so much, why does she keep his portrait on the table? In order to keep her hatred alive to the bitter end? I really don't understand.

My father's death must have been a great shock to my mother. Who can endure her own husband dying in the arms of another woman? But what does this have to do with me? I certainly don't feel like it's an honor. If anyone is a victim in this, it's me. And, anyway, I was just a little child at the time.

And yet my mother's attitude toward my younger sister is completely different. Aren't we both her own children? Does she detest me because I most resemble my father? Or is it because he was involved with that woman while she was pregnant with me?

But my mother doesn't talk about it; she just remains cold. This is not just something I sense, even her close friends are keenly aware of it. Whenever they mention that, between my sister and me, they would gladly choose me as their daughter, my mother always smiles coldly, but she neither agrees nor argues with them.

Certainly they are hinting that my younger sister has been completely spoiled by my mother. Nevertheless, my mother goes on spoiling her. This is why my sister's performance in school got progressively worse. She attended a first-class junior high school, but a third-class high school. She took the college entrance exams three times in a row and didn't get accepted anywhere. The only reason she kept taking the test was because of my mother. And my mother urged her to because I was already attending university. I know that the final time she didn't even show up for the exam.

I reported this to my mother. "I'm only telling you this for her sake." However, my mother showed no sign of gratitude or approval. "Women don't have to go to university!" Her remark humiliated me. I resolved from then on never again to get involved in my sister's affairs.

However, my sister would not leave me alone.

"What's so special about attending university? I'm just not interested. Don't you realize that if my hand were like yours, I would study as hard as you do?"

I couldn't believe that my own sister said that!

"Don't you know that you can't open other people's mail?"

"I didn't open it. It was already opened."

"What? You're lying. You aren't even fit to be a teaching assistant!"

To my younger sister, remaining at school as a teaching assistant has no future in it. If I had been good enough, I should have gone abroad to study long ago. As far as she's concerned, there's not much difference between being a lecturer and being a teaching assistant.

I've decided not to tell my mother about my promotion. They hardly know the difference, so telling them about it would only add another sore point between us.

Then I suddenly thought of Harvey. I knew he couldn't understand what I was saying, but at least he'd cock his head and look at me as I spoke.

He whined all during the night last night, so I hardly slept. In the morning, my sister complained about it, but not for as long as she has in the past.

I thought he might have been hungry, so that morning I'd prepared a bowl of rice before I left for school and put it in front of his doghouse. I suddenly felt uneasy: he'd never been like this before.

In the afternoon, I hurried home. I pushed the door open and squatted before his doghouse, calling "Harvey, Harvey!" He didn't move. Usually as soon as he heard me pushing open the door, he would pull at his chain to come out and greet me, wagging his fluffy tail, his red tongue darting in and out of his black mouth as he jumped on me.

I looked inside. Harvey was stretched out, lying quietly on the bed of straw. His beautiful long fur looked wet and tangled. I reached in. His body already felt still and cold.

Harvey was dead, but for a long time I simply could not comprehend this. What was going on? Death seemed to have nothing to do with Harvey. Could he really be dead?

The bowl of rice I had set out for him in the morning was still sitting there. So it wasn't that he'd been hungry. I remembered his forlorn, low whimpering. He'd been sick and struggling in pain. That must have been the case.

When I thought it through, the reality began to hit me.

"He's dead!" I suddenly cried out, but immediately I put my hand over my mouth and clenched my teeth, as if to catch those awful words I had just uttered and swallow them back down.

IV

I don't know when he actually died. I will never forget him. I had to tell someone. Something like being promoted to lecturer I could stand not telling anyone, but this was something I could not keep in my heart.

But who should I tell? Anyone would do, as long as they would listen to me.

I decided never to get another dog. I don't know enough about dogs. Maybe I had done Harvey in. One thing is certain: I don't understand dog language.

As I was thinking, I found myself at the entrance of the Bright Moon. My heart suddenly started to tremble. I remembered that I'd had a date with Chang Ying-ming here. Did I come here to tell him? What a silly idea!

He told me that he would write to me. But since he'd not given me another thought, why should I think of him? I recalled his face again, full of sympathy. That was what hurt the most and made me most indignant. I didn't want sympathy. What I wanted was understanding and respect. Why couldn't he treat me as a person? I wasn't afraid of being ordinary, as long as he could regard me as an ordinary person.

I had every good reason to reject him. But not only could I not reject him, my heart actually yearned for him. At the moment, it seemed like an irresistible force was slowly and steadily pulling me, slowly drawing me to the steps of the Bright Moon.

The Bright Moon's decor was simple and unpretentious. One could even say that it had none at all. A friend came here from Kaohsiung the other day just to drink a cup of coffee at the Bright Moon. The coffee there is considered the best in town.

Chang Ying-ming said, too, that their coffee was as good as any you could get anywhere outside the country. He's been overseas, so he must have been right about that.

I looked around the place. The spot where Chang Ying-ming and I had sat was vacant. It was only then that I realized how my heart was pounding. My ears also felt a bit hot.

I sat down and quickly glanced in all directions, but no one was looking at me. That day, Chang Ying-ming had sat opposite me just like this.

"Harvey is dead," I said to the empty seat. My heart felt a bit easier.

"Don't take it so hard. This sort of thing is bound to happen, given that dogs only live one-fifth as long as people."

"I won't ever raise a dog again."

"Stop thinking about the dog."

"Really, I won't ever get another dog. It was tough raising him, having him see you off every day and greeting you when you got home. If he saw that you were going out, he would whine and act hurt. When you came back in, he would be so happy, he'd rush right up to you, regardless of what you were wearing. I really won't ever raise another dog."

I spoke to the empty chair, just as if I could see him and hear his voice. Surely he had said that he would write to me. Did I hear him wrong? He had said it with such sincerity.

Perhaps he had only said that at the moment to smooth things over. There had been such an uncomfortable silence then it had been frightening, enough to make you suffocate.

I still remember that his face was full of sympathy. If it was like the past, I would surely hate him for this. But I felt no inclination to blame him. Did that mean I had lost my good judgment?

This time, I am defeated. Is this how it ends? If it always ends like this, then why should I try at all? All this has done is add to my heavy sense of defeat.

Well, if that's what he's like, why think about him? But I think about him constantly, and now he's there before me, and I'm talking to him. I don't know why. Why am I telling him this? But, in fact, my heart feels more relaxed than it did before.

I don't need sympathy. This is my own business. If he wants to be sympathetic to others, that's his business. Those two things have nothing to do with each other.

If I don't need sympathy, then why did I come here? Isn't this the same as fooling myself? But I don't want to fool myself.

At night, I used to kneel down to pray before going to bed. I didn't pray for anything except the strength I needed. But now things are different; I've read so many books, and it seems they were all written to deny the existence of God.

I no longer pray. Every time my heart feels troubled, I urge myself to think of those who are less fortunate than I am. Sometimes I feel like such a hypocrite, but then I think, no, I really am not the most unfortunate person in the world.

I know that I am weak, but I don't give up. I'm aware of Chang Ying-ming's face full of sympathy as it suddenly appears before my eyes. I don't need sympathy, but winning it from him is no sin.

But then why doesn't he write? What I need now is neither prayer nor pity. Before Harvey died, whenever I had something on my mind, I would hug him and tell him everything. Now he's dead. So I can't tell Harvey, but I can tell someone else. If there is no one to tell, I can tell myself. It was him I wanted to tell only because I happened to think of him.

I have often thought of him since that day we met, only not as vividly as today. I'm thinking of him because he has not left me without hope.

You can see how I go back and forth on this. However, of all the people I've met, he is the only one who has left me with even a sliver of hope. It seems that what he said might have just been to smooth over an awkward moment, but I cherish his words because what I did prompted them.

Just then, the door opened. At first, I thought it was Chang Ying-ming; I almost called out his name. But after a closer look, I saw that he wasn't anything at all like Chang, except for being tall.

As soon as he came in, he looked at me. Then he sat down at the round table next to me. He was much younger than Chang Ying-ming, perhaps still in college.

He sat there uneasily, his eyes darting around. He looked me over once. I deliberately stretched out my ducklike hand and stirred my coffee. It was then that I realized I hadn't even drunk a drop of it.

"Are you waiting for someone, miss?" Suddenly he scooted over. This was the seat that Chang Ying-ming had sat in.

"No."

"May I talk with you?" His eyes were riveted on my hand.

"Hmm . . ."

"Where do you work?" He figured that he would start with the preliminaries.

"Our family dog just died."

Originally, I hadn't meant to tell him this, but I also did not want to talk about myself too much. So I thought I'd divert the conversation. I didn't expect my tears to begin to fall as soon as I mentioned Harvey.

I felt both hurt and angry. It was as if I'd revealed my weakness to the enemy.

"Are you lonely?"

At first, I wanted to deny it, but I said nothing. I didn't want to leave with him.

"Aren't you going to drink your coffee?" He had already noticed my full cup of coffee, but I still didn't reply. It seemed like I had already said too much. He didn't understand and kept trying to think of things to talk about. If I had not just spoken to him, I would certainly have told him to shut up.

He seemed to get my meaning and suddenly fell silent. For a minute or two, neither of us said anything; it was a scary silence. I waited for him to speak again, but he seemed determined to keep his mouth shut. I went from waiting, to expecting, and finally to hoping. His eyes shone with unusual brightness, staring at my deformed right hand.

My heart began to race again. I wanted to break the silence but could not. I was wishing he was Chang Ying-ming. But Chang hadn't written me.

Suddenly, he reached out and grabbed my hand. In his hand it was like a toy. I felt pathetic. First he pried my hand open, and then he squeezed it gently in his. His hand was warm.

No one had ever done this before. All my blood rushed to my head; my heart seemed about to escape my chest. I didn't know if I was lucky or wretched. Maybe I was both.

I wanted to struggle, but his hand was so big, my entire palm fit into his. I knew struggling would be useless. I wished he were Chang Ying-ming, but what difference did it make, after all? Chang or no Chang, he was the first man able to face my defect.

Slowly I raised my head and looked at him. Our eyes met for a full minute; neither of us flinched. Then I realized how my heart was pounding, the blood flooding from my head through my veins to my palm and then to my fingertips. Where his hand touched mine, his pulse was also throbbing, his blood sluicing through his veins to his heart.

This was a wondrous feeling, and this was a wondrous moment. My palm, which I had always thought had no feeling, had now become a bridge. At its two ends, our two hearts were beating together.

However, it lasted only a moment. Suddenly I realized again that he was a stranger; I had never seen him before, and it wasn't likely I would ever see him again.

My blood suddenly raced to my head, not because he was pressing my hand but because I had let him do so.

"Please let go of my hand."

"Can't we go somewhere?"

"No."

"Why?"

"Because I must get beyond loneliness."

He let go of my hand. I was very grateful to him; I knew that he was sincere. I also knew that he was very lonely, but I didn't want loneliness to be the reason for our being together.

"Can't we see each other again?"

I made no reply.

V

It was night, and only a few people remained on campus. Some were hurrying along, some seemed to be counting their steps, walking slowly. A slight breeze was blowing. It was already cool.

He was a stranger, a complete stranger. Nevertheless, his image was engraved in my heart. Why hadn't I accepted him? Because he was a stranger? But wasn't Chang Ying-ming also a stranger? Apart from learning his name and a few details about his background from Professor Chao, wasn't he a complete stranger just like this person? Of course, that made a difference, but it was like the difference between the sun and the moon. Even if the moon is four hundred times closer than the sun, aren't they equally far away from us humans?

I walked slowly on the cement paths between the lawns. A couple walked toward me. At first, they were walking close together, but as they approached, they split apart and brushed by me, as if I were a knife slicing through them. I knew that behind me, they would immediately rejoin each other.

They appeared very suddenly. I didn't know where they had come from or where they were going. I could look back, but I didn't dare.

Didn't I dare to look happiness in the face? Why did I reject it? I thought again of the scene just now when I'd left the Bright Moon.

"Really, sit a while longer. We can talk. If you don't want to talk, we can sit quietly."

"No."

I pushed away my cup of coffee. It seemed that I had come to the Bright Moon just to stir a cup of coffee slowly until it was cold and then leave without drinking a drop.

He suddenly stood up, as if to block me, his eyes bright and imploring.

"Please don't do this."

My voice was quite low yet very firm. I repeated the same explanation, that loneliness should not be the reason for two people to get together. This time, he didn't argue. I noticed a change in his eyes. That sullen look of bitterness and resentment made me want to cry.

He was being so humble, but this in no way made him seem less of a person. He was pleading with me simply because I wouldn't plead with him. Far from stripping him of his dignity, this seemed an expression of noble sentiment. If he could implore me with such meekness and humility, why did I persist in rejecting him?

Still, I said no. I believe I understand him. Our predicaments are certainly similar. We are both people who have been defeated. By rights we should band together and lick each other's wounds. There was no reason for us, too, to hurt each other. I understood how grateful he would have been if I had consented. Right now he needed comforting, and so did I.

A couple snuggled together on the grass, whispering. I quickly averted my gaze. His image suddenly appeared again before my eyes; his downcast look was etched in my heart. What a wretch I was! Not even a million eloquent reasons could make up for my arrogance.

Didn't I realize he was asking nothing from me? Didn't he say that he just wanted to talk? I could have sat there quietly and continued to stir my cold coffee while he sipped his. At least then I'd have a reason to give myself if I didn't sleep again tonight.

If I had wanted to, I could have told him all about Harvey's death; I could have told him about my job. He would have given me his full and rapt attention. I also could have told him of my promotion to lecturer. This is something I've been wanting and haven't had the chance to do. He would certainly have been astonished. Also, I could have told him about all the trouble my awkward hand has caused me. He would have stroked it and sighed. I could have let him or told him not to. If I had said yes, he would have been delighted; if I had said no, he would have been disappointed. But either way, he would have listened to me.

Then I would have asked him to talk. I would have listened very carefully. I'd have nodded and occasionally raised my head and examined the expression on his face. I would have asked him to tell me about his past, and, like an innocent child chasing a frog, I would followed his train of thought. Then, when he was finished, I would have picked up the conversation and talked some more. When I got tired of talking, it would have been his turn again. And when we had both finally talked ourselves out, we could have sat quietly, like two friends who don't share a language. We would have sat there in silence, just reading each other's smiles, each other's worried brows. And when even this seemed superfluous, we would have shut our eyes and sat in the stillness of each other's existence.

So why then did I say no to him? Because Chang Ying-ming promised to write to me? Because of my position as lecturer? Because Harvey was dead? Or because he was completely unknown to me, a stranger?

On the grass, beneath the trees, couples lingered, talking

quietly. Why? Could they even tell me? Did they need a reason? As long as one initiates it, and the other doesn't object, can't two people be together? Right, as long as I didn't object, couldn't Chang and I be like these couples? At least for a while?

Does this mean that when I said no, I was really saying no to "for a while?" But, "for a while" is a part of "always"; "always" is only an extension of "for a while." He had given me a chance, had opened the door leading from "for a while" to "always." Of course, I didn't know if that "always" was real or false, but I didn't even have the courage to try the door.

Although he did not promise anything, he did not bar any promises, either. Could these friends on the grass make any promises to each other?

I could still feel his firm hold on my hand. The heat of his body still makes my heart race and my face turn red. He seems to have been the first man capable of facing my defect. His behavior was almost cold; he seemed as detached as an anatomist dissecting a human body. But it's true that both sympathy and contempt weigh on me more heavily; I find them intolerable.

Honestly, he is the very first person to show such self-possession and understanding toward me. Perhaps because of his own troubles or his own personality, he really is able to understand the feelings of others. But I had rejected him, and I myself was at a loss as to why.

I ran across another couple talking quietly on the grass. Who knows how many couples there are. I averted my gaze; ahead lay only darkness. Why did I come here? Slowly I looked up. Just then, against the gloomy backdrop of the sky, I faintly made out the dark silhouette of a coconut palm. No, not just one tree, but an entire row of trees. These trees had been standing there from the time I first came to this school, but only at this moment did I become aware of their existence.

It was as if I had suddenly recovered a long-lost friend. At once my heart was overcome with gratitude. Until tonight, these strange-looking coconut trees had been far away from me, but now they were so close. I had always imagined them as true but distant friends; in fact, they had been right there in front of me all along.

I felt ashamed as I never had before. I had paid them no attention because I had always been looking down, because I was unwilling to direct my gaze upward.

However, this feeling of shame was replaced by an even stronger emotion. Although it was dark, as long as I fixed my gaze and looked, I could see clearly row after row of coconut trees. I rushed over to them. It was as if some energy long pent up in my body was suddenly released. I grabbed one with all my strength. I forgot everything else, enchanted by a marvelous mental state I had never known before.

Then I gradually came out of it. I suddenly became aware of my own breathing and heard the blood rushing in my veins, as if both my breathing and circulation had, for a moment, stopped. My hand still rested on the tree trunk; it was as if my pulse was coming out of that tree.

The trunk was rough. The upper part showed ring after ring of gray scars. Each ringlike scar stood for a leaf. When that leaf left the trunk, it left a round circle on its mother's body. The falling of a leaf did not signify its death but rather the tree's growth.

Almost every day I must cross this campus, and every day I see these rows of trees neatly planted on both sides of the avenue. I have seen them in bright sunshine and soft moonlight. Strong winds have tossed them, and hard rains have pounded and soaked them. They have been through a great deal, and they know how to persevere. At times, they have even drawn strength from their enemies.

I gazed at their perfectly straight trunks. They never bend, but they are not proud, either. They just grow in one direction, quietly, inch by inch, stubbornly and slowly.

On this pitch-dark night I couldn't see their pluck in the sunlight, nor their resilience in the moonlight, yet it was clear that they were intent on only one thing: quietly growing.

At that moment, I recovered a long-lost me. I understood: loneliness could not become the reason for two people to be close. It is a powerful reason, but not a complete one.